TENDER WITH A TWIST

RAINBOW COVE BOOK TWO

ANNABETH ALBERT

To Quinn Ward, whose cover art on the book's first cover brought Curtis beautifully to life, and whose friendship enriches my life & to Edie Danford who pushed me hard in edits to do right by Curtis and Logan. My stories are immeasurably greater for your input. Your friendship also means the world to me. I'm so lucky to have both of you in my life

Cover Credit: Cate Ashwood Designs

❀ Created with Vellum

ONE

Logan

The crazy woodcarver was shirtless. Again. It was a sleepy Thursday in January on the Oregon Coast which meant most sane people were in flannel and jackets and bundled for the sharp bite of the wind. I was wearing fleece-lined bike pants and a long-sleeved cycling jacket myself as I celebrated the first good ride of the year, and I was still chilly when I stopped my ride near the jewelry store on 101—the main highway running through Rainbow Cove. I told myself that I'd stopped for some water from my bottle, but I knew it was a weak excuse. Really, I'd been transfixed by the sight of Curtis Hunt carving up a giant tree trunk with his chainsaw.

For all that rumors flew about his eccentricity, the man was an unparalleled artist, and watching him do his thing was a true pleasure. Sweat dripped from his head and back despite the cool temperature, and he worked like a man possessed, moving this way and that around the piece, dancing almost as his chainsaw flitted about with the sort of grace I'd expect from the jeweler, not this buff lumberjack with heavy machinery.

He wore sawdust splattered jeans, heavy boots, safety googles and ear protectors, but his red flannel shirt lay discarded on a nearby sculpture of a falcon, showing off his shimmering muscles and tats that even from a distance were impressive. For all that the guy had probably fifteen years on me, he was in amazing shape. Hell, if I had ink and muscles like that, I wouldn't keep my shirt on, either. All the muscles made something warm unfurl in my gut, but I dismissed the low thrum of arousal as a never-happening-in-this-lifetime thing. Chances were very high that he'd laugh at any of my fantasies, especially the ones involving him, some rope, and his usual intense stare replaced with something closer to supplication.

But, a guy could still look. And want. So I took my time drinking my water, watching as the outline of a bird slowly emerged from the raw tree trunk.

In a town as tiny as Rainbow Cove, the rumor mill worked overtime, and I knew all the rumors about Curtis. Knew he'd lost his longtime lover a year or two ago and that the two of them had been mythic fixtures in the area. Curtis had apparently gotten more eccentric since the other guy had passed, moving into the old gas station he used as a gallery for his carvings, growing his own food, and going notoriously cranky about change.

And change was what had driven me to Rainbow Cove. Change was what my restaurant represented — hope that the area economy could find a new foothold in tourism. So it wasn't surprising that Curtis didn't seem to like my friends and me any. Probably wouldn't appreciate me looking at him like he was a lumbersexual Tumblr all queued up for my viewing pleasure. But damn, those muscles…

I gave myself last look before I pedaled away, heading away from the center of town, taking the turnoff that would lead me to the narrow residential road that skirted the beach to the south. I was alone on the road, glorious, vast gray skies and sprawling blue ocean my only companions. This was what I'd come to Rainbow Cove for, the space to be alone, the quietness that I'd only ever found before in a dojo. Portland was crowded, and not just with people. My parents' expectations always loomed large, as did past mistakes and hurts, and the general hustle of the area made it hard to catch my breath, hard to think and breathe and simply be. The traffic. The noise. The demands. All of it had gotten to be too much for me, and when my friend Mason had proposed the idea of the bar and grille here on the coast, I'd leapt at the chance to start fresh, especially since I'd loved the coast from some of my earliest memories of family weekends away.

Eventually, my ride returned me to the tavern where Mason was signing off on a meat delivery from a local farm.

"Chef!" The driver greeted me with a wave as I locked up the bike. "We've got some new fillets in. Think you might want some for a special this week?"

My mind immediately flitted away the shirtless woodcarver and back to my real passion—cooking. I loved being the chef here, the guy who made the decisions and the specials. I'd had years of sous chef positions in Portland, growing ever more eager for my own menu, one where I could play with sauces and presentation and choose my own local ingredients.

"I'm picturing a peppercorn crusted fillet with red wine reduction." I inspected packages Mason was loading into the freezer and fridge. We'd do most of our business with the endless stacks of burger patties, but I loved changing things up with my daily specials, too.

"Don't know if anyone will pay fillet prices." Mason shook his head. The slow winter season was starting to wear on my friend, who also served as our business manager. "You can try it as a special, but let's not over-order."

I reluctantly took a small order of fillets, ceding to Mason's wishes, and rounded out my weekly specials plan with cheaper options like shepherd's pie.

"How was your ride?" Mason asked after the delivery guy was on his way.

"Fine." I didn't feel the need to report on my perving of the woodcarver. It had been a little personal indulgence. Not to mention the fact that Mason's police chief boyfriend, Nash Flint, was close friends with Curtis, which meant I'd be in for double the teasing if I let on that I'd let my eyes wander in that direction.

"You're not too lonely, are you?" Mason pressed. "It's your first winter on the coast, and I know that can be hard."

"Not lonely," I said, truthfully. I was so happy to be free of all the voices of Portland—my well-meaning parents, my ex, my aikido master, my many opinionated friends, the executive chefs and restaurant managers who hadn't seen fit to promote me. The silence of the off season meant that for the first time in my life I was finally free to figure out my own direction, and I intended to seize that. I wasn't telling Mason, but that was my New Year's resolution—be the person I'd been reluctant to embrace in Portland. It was high time I took a chance on myself.

———

Curtis

I brushed a stray piece of sawdust off my knee right before Bill said hello to my call. I'd been carving too close to dinner again.

"Ready the restraints. I'm coming for dinner Friday." I forced my voice into happy mode for Bill. I was sitting in the parking lot of the Rainbow Tavern on a Saturday that felt more like a Monday, and I needed to set up a date before I had to go inside to eat a dinner I was dreading.

"Curtis! Nice to hear from you, but *this* Friday? Did we have plans?" Bill sounded more distracted than usual. He was an old friend, and I'd watched him evolve from a long-haired biker into a refined, if often over-scheduled, college professor.

"It's the third Friday of the month. We seem to have fallen into a routine…" A routine that I desperately, desperately needed.

"Ah. Well, I guess I needed to talk to you about that. Tom and I have big news. The adoption agency came through. We're picking them up on Thursday. Siblings—

a boy and a girl. Two and four. We're just over the moon."

This was where I needed to say congrats. Bill and Tom had been waiting for a foster-adopt situation to materialize for the better part of a year. I needed to not be petty or disappointed. A happy guy—a genuinely happy one—would say the right things after hearing their news. But what popped out was, "So no kink this Friday?"

Bill sighed like he hadn't expected more from me. "No kink for a while. Tom and I talked. We're going to focus on the family for the next few months, take a break from the scene. We'll reevaluate then whether we want to get back into it."

"Take a break? You? You won Mr. Leather the year you finished your dissertation. I've never known you to take time away."

"Things have changed." Bill's voice was gentler now. "I'm not a spring chicken anymore. The scene gets tiring after a time, don't you think?"

Yes, yes, I did think. That was exactly why I loved my arrangement with Bill—no strings, no feelings, no wasting time at a bar or meet-up, no ridiculous swiping this way or that on whatever the latest app was.

"You seemed to like it plenty a few weeks ago."

"I'm sorry. I should have called you right after Tom and I talked. To be honest, I didn't think you'd care." Bill was drumming something against his desk, pen maybe, and the click-click-click drove me as nuts as his patronizing tone.

"I don't. It's great for you guys." I forced the words out. I didn't want him to think I was emotional or something—not about the end of what had basically been a mutually convenient business arrangement. "Troy would be thrilled, too. You let me know if you need anything for the kids. You register somewhere?"

"We're all set, but we're asking friends to send favorite children's books if they want. And, Curtis, we miss him, too. A lot. But maybe it's time you think about finding someone. Someone for *you.*"

I didn't have a favorite children's book, and I didn't need someone. I'd had someone. Troy. He'd been more than enough for this lifetime. And as much as I appreciated Bill's longtime friendship, I'd had enough of his condescending tone. "You guys take care. I'm meeting up with Nash, so I better go."

"Nash Flint? Troy's old high school friend? Heard he came out a few months back."

"Yup. Got himself a man and everything." Because it wasn't enough to have Bill and Tom among the flock of ridiculously happy friends in my life. I had Nash who had gone from stoic police chief to besotted boyfriend of Mason, the bar owner, and their little family now, too. And I was happy for them all. I was. They deserved to find family and love and all that jazz that had consistently avoided me other than my years with Troy. But, I had to admit, it did make it more than a little challenging to be around them, what with jealousy stinging me like a cat o' nine tails flogger.

As I ended the call with Bill, I saw Nash's jeep pull into the lot.

"You know I'm only eating with you out of pity." I made myself smile widely as I crossed the gravel lot to him. "That man of yours abandoned you."

"Ha." Nash snorted. "He's on an aquarium field trip with his niece Lilac's scout troop. He'll be back in the morning. But, yes, thank you for saving me from the horrors of my own cooking."

"Three hours one way with twenty-odd little girls? Lordy, deliver me from such a thing." I mock shuddered as I followed him into the tavern. "Did y'all have a nice holiday, though? Bet you spoiled her rotten."

See? I did know the right things to say at the right time, hard as it was sometimes to make the words cooperate. And sure enough, Nash smiled broadly.

"We did. We shouldn't have. But we did." And he rattled on about doll houses this and American Girl that for a good five minutes after we found our regular table by the window. Nash's man Mason co-owned this place with two friends.

"Do you want drinks?" The server didn't look that much older than Mason's niece, some fresh-faced local girl the guys had hired to help. I supposed it was highly likely that Nash, Troy, and I had gone to school with her parents, because that's the age we were getting to be now, somewhere between forty and death.

I got a beer to help me with the nodding and listening to Nash's happiness business, and Nash got a tea because he might get called out again for police stuff before the night was through.

It was a slow Saturday night, so the server was back with our drinks quickly. Nash and I both got our usuals to eat, him a regular burger with a salad, and me a veggie burger with some sweet-potato fries.

"What's this?" I fingered the paper advertising tent

on the side of the table between the ketchup and salt. "Leather Night?"

"Something the guys are trying out. More people have been showing up to their pride nights, so they had the idea of adding in some theme nights, maybe attract different people. You should tell those friends of yours in Eugene."

I growled at the mention of Bill, the pang of his rejection still fresh. "They're busy. Having kids and all. Leaving that scene behind."

"Ah. Well, that's too bad." Nash and me, we were never ones to discuss our private bedroom activities, but he knew me well enough to have some sympathy shining in his eyes. "Still, though, you and Troy had some… contacts, right? I know Mason would appreciate you spreading the word."

"I'm not the kink welcome wagon."

"You know, you could be more supportive of the guys' efforts to make Rainbow Cove a gay tourism destination. It would mean more business for you, too," Nash chided before taking a sip of his tea.

"Need I remind you that *you* weren't on board for their plan not that awfully long ago. And of course I want more business. We all do this time of year." The chilly, rainy, dank days of early January were never good for any of us dependent on the tourist trade. "I'll put some feelers out. Happy?"

"Ecstatic." Nash looked like he wanted to say more, but right then our server returned. Without our food.

"I'm *super* sorry, but the chef says he thinks he's out of veggie-burger patties. His special today is a veggie Reuben and on the menu—"

"Sweetie. They're frozen little hockey pucks. I'm pretty sure he's got one somewhere in the deep freeze. This is what I always order. Always." I made a little scoot-scoot gesture with my hand because I was simply over not getting what I wanted tonight.

"Bobby, hon, could you ask Logan to double-check?" Nash's tone was far nicer than mine. "We'd appreciate it."

After she retreated, he turned a glare on me. "You're gonna scare away the good help. Mason just got Bobby all trained. Chill. We'll find you something suitably grassy to eat."

"I like what I like." I wasn't in the mood to argue my dietary preferences.

"Yeah, well, I'm paying, so you can find some calm. And maybe tell me what's got you in such a funk lately? Usually you're the charming one and I'm the cranky one, but lately we've switched."

"Hate this time of year." I fiddled with a sugar packet. I wasn't going to tell him that him all happy and partnered up was a big part of it, something I hadn't expected. "Nothing other than that. Short days. Short temper. You know how it goes."

"I know the anniversary—"

"Don't mention it." I waved away his concern like I didn't know exactly the second when Troy had died, didn't know that the anniversary was this coming week. "I'm not that morbid. I don't calendar watch."

"I miss him, too. Miss *you*. You always get so down in the winter, but it's worse now." Concern marred Nash's handsome face.

"Mason's got you all emotional now. Talking feelings

and shit." I shook my head. A domesticated Nash Flint was indeed a sight to behold. "How about you tell me more about the holidays? What did Mason cook?"

Nash sighed like the change of subject pained him, but he took the bait, telling me about rib roasts and eggnog cookies. I liked a world where Nash got his happy ending, where there was a little family like his, like the one Bill and Tom were forming, where there were holiday meals and presents and overflowing good-will. I just didn't get to live in that world. I'd only ever been a tourist there with Troy anyway. No, I'd sip my beer and wait for my damn burger and be glad the world at least smiled on my friends.

Logan

"The customer says you must have a veggie burger in the freezer." Bobby's timid voice sounded from behind me. I swore that the woman was going to make me burn myself one of these days, the way she liked to sneak up on me.

"I don't. I'm sorry. Did you offer him a veggie Reuben or the black-bean soup?"

"He wasn't interested. He was *mean*." Her voice trembled. She looked far younger than she was, but I knew she was twenty-one and had had a hard time finding a local job before Mason took her under his wing. "Police Chief Flint asked, too, said you should double-check."

Oh, I knew exactly who we were dealing with now. Curtis. The same crazy-ass chainsaw wood-carver artist I'd been ogling the other day when I shouldn't have.

Temperamental as fuck. And despite my considerable efforts to expand our vegetarian offerings, the man only ordered one thing.

"Tell them there are none. We're sorry. I'll comp the veggie Reuben if he'll give it a try."

"Don't make me tell them." The quaver in her voice was matched with some serious shine to her eyes. If we had tears, we were all going to be in trouble, and Mason wouldn't forgive me if we lost another server.

"Is Adam back yet?" With Mason chaperoning a field trip, we were short-staffed. Adam, Mason's best friend and fellow partner with us in the tavern, usually manned our bar and worked the dining room, but he was running a fast errand for his mother.

"Not yet." Bobby's face paled.

"Horatio, can you watch the grill? We've got fries due up." It was just me and one kitchen helper on duty.

"Sure thing, boss." Like Bobby, this was one of Horatio's first jobs, and while he was happy for the experience, he was also green as the Oregon moss that covered everything this time of year. I wasn't sure I trusted him not to burn the place down, but I didn't have a lot of options.

I'd just finished plating two salads for the only other customers in the place, so I handed them to Bobby. "You take these out. I'll deal with Curtis and Flint."

I ran a hand through my hair, though making it look presentable was probably hopeless. Working a kitchen was sweaty, messy business. Off duty, I took certain pains with my appearance, and it irked me a little that Curtis was going to see me all rumpled. Not that it should bother me. It wasn't like Curtis knew I'd been watching him the other day. Or like I had any reason to care about his opinion of me.

Heart beating faster than I'd like, I approached their table. Flint wore his out-of-uniform usual of a polo shirt and jeans, while Curtis worked his typical refugee-from-a-biker-gang vibe in an old Harley T-shirt that showed off his arm tats. Paint-stained jeans, wild brown hair, and a beard added more oomph to his rough image.

Flint had a smile for me—ever since he started living with Mason, he'd been way friendlier than he used to be—but Curtis merely scowled. Par for the course with him. The few times we'd spoken, he'd always been dismissive, like I was younger than Bobby and Horatio and even less worthy of his time. And, for whatever reason, tonight I wasn't going to take it.

"We're out of veggie burgers. They come from a local supplier in Eugene, and they had fluke snow this week and didn't make it out. Now I'd like—"

"Do you have the fries? Just bring me some of them. I'll eat those while Nash has *his* dinner." Something about the way Curtis sneered got to me, made me want to pin him to the wall with far more than a glare.

"Look. Every day I make sure one of our specials is vegetarian. There are also a bunch of options on the regular menu. I can do a vegan pizza for you, even. Vegan grilled cheese if it was a sandwich you were after. Pick something and I'll comp it." I used a tone that I didn't trot out very often, a don't-argue-with-me sternness. I was an easygoing guy, but Curtis Hunt pressed all my buttons.

Curtis and Flint both blinked at me. I doubted Flint had ever heard me get upset before, but too bad.

"Suppose I could try a grilled cheese," Curtis said at last. "Can you add some of the sautéed onions you usually put on the burger, or you out of those, too?"

"Absolutely I can add them. Maybe toss in some grilled peppers and a little—"

"Just the onions." Curtis shook his head like I was all kinds of dumb.

"You'll like your sandwich." I kept the stern tone going. "And you'll be nice to Bobby about it. You got a problem, you can ask for me."

"Oh, I will." Curtis's tone was somewhere between dry and mildly amused.

"He'll like it," Flint added.

"Good."

I was about to turn to return to the kitchen, but Flint spoke again. "While you're here, why don't you tell Curtis what all you guys have planned for Leather Night?"

Oh, of course Flint thought Curtis might be interested in *that*. Curtis was probably one of those guys who believed that some scowling and rude remarks made him a Dom. He'd pull on some dusty motorcycle pants from his closet and undoubtedly assume he'd be laid before the night was done.

And, sadly, he might not be wrong. He had the sort of dangerous vibe that always seemed to pull hookups in the leather bars in Portland and, despite the limitations of his wardrobe, he wasn't a bad-looking guy—arm muscles for days, lean frame, eyes so pale blue they were almost haunting in their intensity, and full lips that even the beard couldn't hide.

"We're starting after the usual dinner rush. Nine

through midnight there will be specials on drinks and appetizers. We've got a DJ coming over from Eugene, and we've advertised in Eugene, Roseburg, Portland, Coos Bay, and some online leather communities. We're hoping for a decent turnout."

"I hope you get it," Flint said encouragingly. "I know business has been slow."

"It's not just a publicity stunt—we're trying to reach all facets of the LGBTQ community."

"Gotta get those tourist dollars." Curtis's patronizing tone had me back to envisioning him pinned to a bed, held down until he was begging. Maybe cuffed to it, that smirk wiped off his face and replaced with pleas for more. It would never happen, but, man, the guy really needed to be taken down about seven pegs.

"I'm going to make your food." As I headed to the kitchen, I gave him a final scathing look, one that probably wouldn't even register. If he'd decided I was an annoying kid, then an annoying kid I'd remain. I knew his type all too well. Didn't matter how stern I got, I was always going to be a baby-faced weakling to guys like Curtis.

And God help me, the bar was going to be filled with that type next week. Unfortunately, I had only myself to blame—I'd been the one to suggest doing a leather night. I still thought it was a good idea, even if it was likely to bring up every bad memory I had of trying the Portland leather scene. But I'd be stuck in the kitchen, far from the action, in any event. Which was what I wanted, right? I whacked the ingredients for Curtis's order together far more forcefully than I needed to.

"What did that sandwich do to you?" Adam came into the kitchen, finally back.

"Nothing." I couldn't keep the frustration out of my tone.

"Sorry that took longer than expected. But I got the part for Mom's furnace and installed it. Luckily they weren't without heat too long."

"Yeah, that would suck. Does she have many visitors right now?" Adam's mother ran a popular B&B on the edge of town.

"A few." Adam shrugged. "Business is down for everyone. She says hi. Says she misses you and that you should come around for dinner sometime."

"I'll text her, see what's a good time." When I'd first come to town, I'd rented a room above Adam's mother's garage, but I'd recently taken over Mason's lease when he moved in with Nash. I'd wanted more privacy and a kitchen of my own, but I did get nostalgic for Adam's chatty mother's generous hospitality.

"Did I miss anything good?"

"Flint is in with Curtis. And we're out of veggie burgers. I'm going to need you to take this order out in a second. They scared Bobby."

"Oh, man. Out of the veggie burgers. Curtis must be in a snit." Adam laughed.

"He is. And Flint was trying to sell him on Leather Night, but it's obvious he thinks it's a stupid idea."

"He's just in a permanent bad mood. Don't let him get you down. And him and Troy were really into that scene, from what I heard. Too bad Troy died in that accident—he would have made the perfect bouncer for the event. You've never seen a guy so big and scary—I'm talking Hagrid huge."

"Seriously?" I'd heard about Curtis's dead lover before, but I'd always pictured some mild and meek man, happily playing second fiddle to the force of Curtis's large personality.

"Oh, yeah." Adam watched as I plated Flint's burger and Curtis's sandwich. "He knew how to keep Curtis in line, too. Curtis wasn't always this cranky. And he got a lot more…eccentric after Troy died. Moved into that old gas station he uses as a studio. Did you know they had a place by the beach and it sits empty now? He won't use it but won't sell, either."

"Not surprised." I'd heard enough Curtis stories to not be shocked at anything he did. "Here you go. Get their food out."

"He's probably gonna complain, but don't take it personally." Adam smiled at me before scooping up the plates.

"I won't." I needed to remember that. Taking anything about Curtis personally would only be a recipe for a disaster, as would letting myself become curious about his relationship with Troy. If Troy had been some big dude keeping Curtis in line, where did that leave my assumptions about what Curtis was into?

Nowhere. That's where. I could *not* go getting hung up on him. I needed to focus on helping the business through this slow patch, creating specials that drew in more traffic, surviving Leather Night, and making it through this long, dreary coastal winter. Even caring about whether Curtis liked the sandwich was more than I should have done.

But that didn't stop me from looking through the order window, glimpsing him biting into the sandwich. I knew it was the perfect ratio of almond cheese, sourdough bread, and sautéed onions, but still, the pleasure on his face was gratifying. And if I wondered what else could cause his eyes to darken like that, well, I seriously needed to get a grip. He wasn't my type and I had a business to save.

TWO

Curtis

I wasn't going to Leather Night. Not even tempted. And the fact that the kid chef had made a decent sandwich didn't change that one bit. He'd proved to have some unexpected backbone, but it was a bit like watching a toy poodle bark down a Rottweiler. Funny, but ill-advised. With that baby face, he really should watch who he turned that temper on. Not everyone was as forgiving as me and Nash.

And what was I doing thinking of him several days later while I was splitting wood for Janice? I'd brought her dog, Chopper, outside with me, and he was running back and forth trying to make friends with two squirrels who were having nothing to do with him. A big mutt who had to be going on ten now, he still reminded me so much of the puppy he'd been when Troy had rescued him almost a decade prior.

"Give it up, boy." I tossed a stray stick for him. "You

don't need any stuck-up squirrels anyway. Guys like us, we're best on our own."

I pulled my flannel off, stripping down to my white undershirt while waiting for him to return with the stick. Despite the lower temperatures, splitting wood was sweaty work, especially in the sort of quantities Janice needed for her wood stove. I'd done two cords for her back in October, but this had been an unusually cool winter, and she already needed to restock her woodpile.

Chopper took his sweet time bringing the stick back, and I looked up from my work, making sure he hadn't gone too close to the road. Janice's property was a corner lot, and I was working in the side yard, stacking the split wood in the rack she kept on the side of the house, near the kitchen door. The side yard wasn't fenced, something I wished she'd let me fix, but she'd thus far resisted my efforts. The street was deserted this time of morning, everyone either at work or school or sleeping off the night before.

But wait. A guy on a bicycle lurked on the edge of the property, giving Chopper a pet on the head. "Chop. You get over here *now*."

He really did know better than to make friends with random strangers. I strode over. Janice lived alone, and even with Chopper around, I worried about her.

But as I got closer, I realized I did recognize the guy. It was the kid chef, looking all preppy in a silver helmet, close-fitting black and silver shirt, and the sort of biking tights that belonged in a pro bike race you might see on TV. Even then, I didn't really get the point of them. Wasn't like the snazzy tights were any barrier to road rash if he wiped out.

"Can I help you?" I asked.

"Oh, sorry. Didn't realize… The dog looked like he was going to run in the road, so I stopped to see where he belongs."

"Here."

"I figured that out, thanks." Just like the other night at the tavern, he wasn't cowed by my short tone, which was a surprise. With his build and face, I would have expected him to jump out of the way of my temper, but that wasn't the case. "I didn't know you did firewood. Is that a side thing for you?"

His gaze swept over me, lingering a bit too long on my biceps. Well, two could play at that game. I gave him an appraising stare of my own. His get-up didn't hide any of his long, lean body. I'd seen him biking around town before but never really stopped to take in his muscular thighs or flat abs. Too young. Too thin. But I could still make him uncomfortable, so I let my eyes zoom in on his full mouth.

"See something you like, kid?"

He didn't blush, but he did flinch. "Nope. And the name's Logan."

"All right, *Logan.*"

"I was *trying* to ask you about your business. You sell firewood? There's a wood stove at my rental, but I haven't tried to light it yet."

"Don't. Not until you have someone check the chimney. Mason's old man has a wood stove, I'm pretty sure. Have Mason find you someone to check it over if he can't do it himself. Last thing we need is you burning the place down."

I didn't volunteer to be the one doing the checking,

but I was serious. Messing around with wood heat was serious business, and I might not care much for the kid, but I still didn't want him burnt like the charcoal sticks my mom had passed off as French fries.

"And the wood? You sell that?"

Why he was so fired up to give me business I couldn't say, but I didn't much like it. Made the hairs on my arms prickle. Felt dangerously close to pity.

"Nope. Do favors for a few friends here and there. Every now and then a buddy will call me in for a big job." I made it clear from my tone that he was neither a friend nor a big job worth my time.

"Oh." The way his face fell made me feel like when I stepped on Chopper's leg by accident.

"Listen, you get that stove looked at, and I'll tell my buddy you're in the market for wood, see what his price is running right now." I had no idea why I was volunteering to call Johnny on the kid's behalf when the grocery store, as well as several other places in town, all had firewood. Usually at a jacked-up cost, though. Johnny would give the kid a fair deal.

"Thanks. I appreciate it." He kicked at the dirt near the front tire of his bike. "I…uh…did you like the sandwich? The other night?"

It had be the best damn thing I'd eaten in a month, but I wasn't telling him that. "It was okay. Fries were a little past done, though."

"I'm still working with Horatio on that. I'll talk to him." He nodded seriously, like I was one of those food critics doing a write-up on his joint. "I'm tinkering with the sandwich a little—slow-cooking the onions, adding thyme and garlic, using mozzarella or the vegan equivalent, putting it on a sourdough bun and calling it a French onion sub."

That did sound tasty, but I merely said, "Sounds all right."

"You should come by, try it. I'll probably have it on the menu by Leather Night."

"We'll see." I only said that instead of an outright no because I knew Nash wanted me to give the tavern more business and would probably drag me there at some point soon. Still wasn't going to Leather Night.

"Well, think about it." He sounded as firm as he'd been when he'd told me to order the sandwich the other night. Surprising, really, that he could go that deep and commanding. Almost cute, like a bear cub discovering he had claws. And, despite myself, I nodded.

He took off on the bike with a final wave, and I watched him disappear down the road far longer than I should have.

"Who was that?" Leaning on her cane, Janice made her way down the walk.

"Just a kid. The chef at the tavern. You know, that venture of Nash's new man?"

"I know." She wasn't one to keep up on town gossip. Or get out. This stroll down her walk was as far she'd go all week. Tossing the ball for Chopper out back was a big expedition for her.

"Hey, you want a burger from there sometime? Nash says their beef is good. I could drop it by."

"I get my beef from Swanigan's. Half a steer. Same order for thirty-odd years now." She nodded sharply. "I've got a roast in the slow cooker now, but I don't suppose you'll have some."

"No, ma'am." If ever there was someone in this life I'd eat meat for, Janice was it, and still I had to keep back a shudder at the thought of roast. "But did I smell cookies?"

"You did, charmer." She lightly boxed my shoulder. Years ago, she'd learned to bake a basic vegan oatmeal cookie with raisins. I didn't much care for raisins, but I looked forward to them nonetheless. She was as close as I got to family, and her taking a minute to bake them for me made my chest all warm and tight. Also, she was the last person left to find me charming, and I wasn't about to burst that opinion. So I followed her back into the small white cottage where she had it cloyingly warm as usual. This level of warm made me more than a little claustrophobic.

"I saw on the TV about a new creamer made of coconuts. Added it to my order this week." She pulled a small box from the fridge. The little grocery store in Rainbow Cove didn't do delivery as a regular thing, but they made an exception for Janice and a few others. "You want some for the coffee?"

"Sure." I usually drank my coffee sweet without the creamer, but I wasn't gonna let her purchase go to waste. I filled my mug from the coffee pot on her counter and added a healthy glob of the creamer. "I'll have the wood done pretty soon. Should be out of your hair by noon or so unless you've got something else that needs doing."

"The light bulb in the bathroom keeps flickering, but I don't want to keep you…"

"Not a problem. I'll take a look after I finish with the wood. You let me know if you think of anything else."

I headed back outside, coffee in my thermal mug and

Chopper at my heels. As I passed through the kitchen hallway, I tried hard not to look at the pictures on either side. There were pictures all over this damn house, in the bathroom, even. Stairs heading to the attic. No space was off limits to her collection, but there was one here in the hallway that I always tried not to see and yet stopped at every time.

Like so many of Janice's pictures, it was one she'd taken, back in the years when she got out of the house, bringing that camera of hers everywhere. This picture had a wooden frame shaped like the exterior of a log cabin, and the photo was of Troy and me, standing in front of the "sold" sign by our place. She'd been so proud of Troy, how he'd combed foreclosure listings for months, found just the right bargain, and put in the work after the sale to make it into home. I'd helped, of course, but Troy had been the driving engine of that project.

And Lord, but it hurt, seeing the big guy's smile in that picture. He was looking at me, not the camera, and his gaze was everything I'd carry with me until the grave. Tenderness. Affection. Warmth. Pride. Just a hint of control, because yeah, that was him, too. It was this huge domestic moment, and he still was a total badass with a shit-eating grin that was all for me. Every damn time I passed that picture, my skin lost another layer, a new level of raw exposed to the elements. I knew from experience that eventually with enough hours of work, I'd toughen my skin, get a callus built up for the next time grief stripped me bare.

Logan

"Taste this." I carefully cut a sandwich into bite-sized chunks so we could all taste my latest creation. I'd slow-cooked the onions with vegan butter, thyme, and a little balsamic vinegar. The guys each took a piece and dutifully chewed.

"Needs steak. Medium rare. Sliced thin." Adam took a second piece even as he complained. "Seriously. What's with all the veggie stuff?"

"It's popular." I tried not to sound too defensive. "Especially this time of year. Everyone always tries to be healthy in January, keep their New Year's resolutions."

"What's yours?" Mason asked, probably trying to keep Adam and me from bickering about the merits of vegetarian menu items.

I'd made my resolution last week about embracing my true self, but I sure as hell wasn't sharing something so corny with these two. So instead I shrugged and gave what I hoped was a wicked grin. "Eat more veggies."

"Well, congrats. It's working. How about next year you resolve to add venison and elk to the menu?" Adam laughed and grabbed a third piece before I could move the plate away.

"Maybe. You just want an excuse to go hunting."

"Guilty." Adam grinned. In addition to thinking himself God's gift to flannel, he was a major outdoors person. I didn't get giving up a perfectly good day off to go somewhere cold and dank and wait for the remote possibility of Bambi wandering by. Give me a nice long, paved bike route any day.

"I'm going to do a variation on this one with fire-roasted peppers next week." Then, because this was how my brain worked, I rapped my knuckles on my head. "Oh. Fire. Just remembered—Mase, do you know someone who could come look at the wood stove in the rental? I'd rather not bug Flora about it, but the baseboard heaters just aren't cutting it. I want to try the wood stove but don't want to burn the place down if the flux—"

"Flue. It's not the DeLorean." Mason laughed at his own *Back to the Future* joke. "And yeah, my uncle services his and my dad's every year. I can probably lean on him to swing by and take a look."

"Cool." I'd been careful to not mention my weird roadside conversation with Curtis, not wanting to open myself up to more teasing. I got enough of that as it was. And sure enough, Adam had another crack coming.

"Are we all set for Leather Night? I'm seriously worried about Logan, though. Maybe we need a leash or code word in case some big biker dude tries to escape with him."

"*Logan* can handle himself. And I'll be busy in the kitchen, not looking for a hookup."

"I'm just saying, Angel Face. I worry about you. You're probably a Dom's wet dream. Not that I get that. How do you look at someone and think, 'I'd like to leave bruises on that?' Who does that?"

Me. All the time. "Kinky people. Of which you are not one." I rolled my eyes. "And you're just mad that you're not likely to score a bake-cookies-and-drink-milk vanilla hookup at this thing."

"No hookups. From either of you." Mason glared at us. "We don't hit on customers. Remember?"

"Yes, boss." Adam rolled his eyes on his way to the

stockroom. Mason left to go make the specials board, and then I was alone with my prep until Horatio came in shortly before the lunch crowd. At least I hoped there was a crowd. Even a moderate one would be a vast improvement over the last few weeks. Unlike some chef friends, I loved prep work. Getting everything diced, chopped, grated, and arranged in separate containers soothed the restless thrum in my chest.

Lunch was slow but steady until around 1:30 when Mason popped his head in. "My boyfriend is in. With Curtis. And apparently they want to talk to you."

"Me? What did I do?"

"I don't know, but I'll take over here for you while you go see." Mason made a shooing motion with his hand.

"Afternoon," I said as I approached the duo. They had their usual table, Flint in his uniform, Curtis in a flannel shirt that had seen better decades. And damn if my eyes didn't go to Curtis first. Forget uniform porn— that did nothing for me. Apparently my traitorous body had developed a thing for bearded and broody. "Mason said you wanted me?"

"Yeah. Mase said you're cold at the rental?" Flint looked at me critically. He always reminded me of my old geometry teacher in high school, like he could see all my shortcomings and found me lacking. "You should have spoken up sooner."

"It's okay." I shrugged. "He told me his uncle—"

"Is not who I'd use." Flint shook his head. His dislike of Mason's family was legendary. "Arnie Fletcher does chimney sweep work for heaters and fireplaces and stoves. He'll be around tomorrow. And Curtis made a call about the wood."

Something told me that Mason had leaned hard on Nash, who had, in turn, put a boot in Curtis's ass, but Curtis nodded. He held out a scrap of paper where he'd written a name, phone number, and a hefty sum. His handwriting was blocky, like he had to try hard to stay neat.

"That's for a cord, split and ready for the stove. Cash. Probably be enough to see you through the rest of the winter since you're not home that much, and you've got other heat, too. But you just wanna take the stove for a test drive, you might want to get a quarter cord. That's about a pickup load."

It was the most sentences Curtis had strung together around me, and I liked his voice when he wasn't being a sarcastic ass. He spoke slow, like he'd thought about each word, and his natural speaking voice had a melodic quality that wasn't noticeable when he was cranky.

"Sounds like what I should do. I'll get the quarter cord."

"You got a truck? Johnny doesn't deliver for less than a cord." And cranky was back, just like that.

"Only the bike and my Miata. I could probably borrow Adam's—"

"Or Curtis could stop being a pain in the rear and take you to get the quarter cord." Nash gave Curtis a pointed look.

Releasing a great sigh, Curtis leaned back in his chair. "Monday. Afternoon? You guys usually slow around then, right?"

"Right." I honestly wasn't sure I wanted to be alone

with Curtis, especially not in a small space like a truck, but I also wasn't about to let that nervousness show. He'd probably like that, me squirming, and I wasn't scared as much as just not sure I wanted a field trip with everyone's favorite cranky lumberjack.

"I'll pick you up here at two. Be ready to work, but we'll be back before your dinner rush." Curtis looked me up and down like he wasn't quite sure I was capable of "work".

"I'll be ready. And thanks."

"No problem. You get the veggie burgers in yet?"

"Yep. But any chance of tempting you with my special—"

"Veggie. Burger. Lots of onions. Fries."

"Please," Nash added for him with a laugh. And clearly I had a problem because I dearly wanted to hear that word from Curtis. *Please. Please.* What would his voice sound like broken and pleading? Would it keep the melodic quality? Get higher? Lower?

Obsessing over that kept me busy back in the kitchen while I made his food. And yes, I totally snuck a peek after Mason delivered their plates, just to see if Curtis made that blissed-out face again. He did. And it only caused me to wonder—since he'd called my food merely all right—what would he do with something utterly divine? And damn if I didn't want to be the guy to find out.

THREE

Curtis

Nash volunteering me for shit had me in an even worse funk than the one I'd been in since the new year had started. Friday my whole body was tense, every muscle, every nerve ending, every *thought*, like it knew I was supposed to be heading to Bill and Tom's and wasn't. I tried hard to remember my manners, though, and sent two books the cashier at the kid gift store downtown said were popular. I hadn't *always* been a cranky bastard. Pessimism seemed to be my default now, the tattered blanket I wrapped myself in when the world met my low expectations.

Saturday I followed my usual custom even though there was a drizzle going and traffic would likely be light. I woke up early, set up several works in progress at the gas station. I'd had the pumps removed years ago, but the building's past life was still unmistakable. The awning that used to shield the pumps was probably my favorite part of the structure, as it allowed me to ignore the drizzle, lose myself to hours of carving. I'd found over time that tourists enjoyed watching me do my thing. And me? I didn't much mind an audience. When I was in the right mood, it could be fun showing off, and it often led to sales.

Sweat rolled down my back as I worked on a huge eagle. I loved doing birds, loved watching them emerge from a tree trunk all proud and regal, loved their energy and personality as I put the final details on—the eyes, the ruffled feathers, the right curve of the beak. No tourists stopped, so I spent hours getting the guy right. Eventually, my head got a little swimmy. Crap. I'd forgotten to eat. Again.

I went around to the makeshift greenhouse I had out back. This time of year, not much wanted to grow, but I had some hearty greens, a few onions. I made myself something approaching a salad and headed for my shower. I'd traded a plumber friend some statues for his help rigging a shower in one of the two bathrooms. I had no patience for a full rehab. Been there, done that with the house. All I needed was a way to get the grime off, so it was a strictly basic affair, and I didn't linger.

That done, I padded to the storeroom I used as both closet and pantry. I told myself to grab something, anything, but my hands refused to cooperate, instead wandering to the back of the closet to my leather. *Leather Night.* That was tonight. I fingered my favorite leather jeans, the ones I would have worn to Bill and Tom's with one of my harnesses under it. In the smell of the leather, so many memories lingered. Troy. Others. Bill.

Damn. I wanted to get fucked up, wanted to be pushed out of my head until the memories were dust.

They'd be back, of course. They always were. But a sweet escape... Man, I needed that. And I hated the club scene. Hated. But I disliked those apps even more. And sure, there were people I could call, but like Bill and Tom, they'd all known Troy, and I just couldn't deal with sympathy.

Maybe there'd be someone new at this thing. Someone from out of town, possibly. Someone who didn't know Troy or me or all my business. If nothing else, maybe I could get my dick sucked. It wouldn't be what I really needed. But I could pretend.

So I pulled on my leather pants. Wasn't quite feeling it for a harness, so I went with a vest I loved that laced up the back and sides. Double bicep gauntlets because I wasn't entirely sure what mood I was in other than needing *something*. Boots needed a quick polish, and I tried hard not to dwell on all the times I'd done this for Troy, taking pride in taking care of his leathers.

By nine I was fed, dressed, and antsy as fuck. I debated whether to drive or walk. It wasn't like I'd be bringing someone back *here*, and I was intending to drink. How much would be determined by how slim the pickings were. But in the end, I decided to drive. I could always walk back and return for the truck in the morning.

The tavern parking lot was as full as I'd seen it in months, lots more motorcycles and jacked-up trucks than usual. To my surprise, the guys had a bouncer working the door. And damn it. I knew him. Sam Shelburne, longtime friend of Troy's. Big guy who drove a CVO Harley and owned a bike dealership up in Coos Bay—he was an ideal choice for the front door. But still no one I wanted to talk to.

"Curtis! Motherfucker, what you doing out of the cave?" He left his stool to give me a hearty back-slap. "Cover's five bucks, but no worries if you're short."

"I've got it." I pulled out a five, let him stamp my hand like I was a teenager at a rave.

"Ronnie's inside. You find him, he'll get your first round. Damn, man. Been too long since we've seen you." He shook his head. "There's a ride coming up. You should come."

"I don't ride anymore." It was the truth. All my love for biking and our friendship circle had died with Troy, but I still tried to look apologetic. Sam was good people. Just not *my* people any longer.

Coming here had been a terrible idea, but a group of people were behind me, so I had little choice but to go into the tavern. The lights were lower than usual, and a DJ was set up to the side of the dancefloor, spinning a remix of a classic rock tune. I headed straight for the bar. Adam Ringer was working the bar as usual, and he looked to be in his element, handling multiple orders at once. I kind of admired how he was wearing his flannel and jeans, absolutely no nod to the theme night.

"Double of Jack. Neat," I ordered when it was my turn. A local brew would be my usual choice, but a beer felt a bit too social for my mood. Besides, I welcomed the burn, the only friend I was truly happy to reconnect with.

And sure enough, several others came up to say hello, including Sam's Ronnie who tried to get my drink, but I waved him off.

"You hear about Bill and Tom? Damn happy for them." Ronnie wore a classic "X" harness, studded collar, and leather pants. I'd seen him in far less, but, like most of the crowd, he seemed to be taking it easy—not as many ass-less chaps or jocks as I'd seen at other leather events and more people were standing around chatting than dancing or groping. "When are we gonna get your ass back on a bike, man? There's a ride—"

"Sam told me." I took a long sip of my drink, let it burn all the way down. "I don't ride anymore."

"You should. Troy would want you back up on the horse. You know that," Ronnie chided.

I did know, but I just shrugged.

"Whatcha in the mood for tonight? Want me to introduce you to some of the newer guys—"

I did not need or want a wingman. "I'm good. Just here to support the business. That's all."

"Civic pride? You?" Ronnie laughed like I was the funniest thing ever. "Or maybe you wanna come back with us?"

Oh, I needed a pity fuck even less. And Sam and Ronnie had never had the right vibe for me. Too damn cuddly and into each other. "Nah. Thanks, though."

A young guy in a leather vest and pants walked up to us, greeted Ronnie. He had slicked-back hair and the air of an eager pup who wasn't yet attached to someone to keep him in line. Ronnie made the introductions, introducing the guy as Kicker, which I doubted was what his mama named him, but the group had always been big on nicknames.

"You wanna dance?" Kicker licked his lips as he looked me up and down.

I didn't, not really, but I also needed to get away from Ronnie before he started wandering further down memory lane. Kicker didn't know me, didn't know Troy, so in that sense he was perfect.

In every other one, though, he was a trial, dancing too close, big liquid eyes like he was just waiting for me to take charge. Which I could have, I suppose. I had come with the idea of getting my dick sucked, and Kicker seemed like he'd be on board with that plan. But he danced like an overeager baby goat and smelled like bad aftershave and suddenly I was tired. So very, very tired. I needed something else. What, I wasn't sure, but this wasn't it.

———

Logan

"I think it's a huge success," Mason raved as he came into the kitchen a little before midnight to check on an order. "We're definitely doing this again."

"I agree. We've been hopping." I wiped my face off with the edge of my chef's jacket. Fuck it. I was hot and we were minutes from closing. I stripped off the jacket— nobody was gonna care if they saw me in a black T-shirt. "Food orders have slowed a bit in the last hour. I let Horatio take an extra-long break, see if he wanted to dance a bit before cleaning with me."

"You're a nice boss." Mason laughed. "I saw him out there. Told Adam to keep an eye on him. Everyone seems really nice, though. It's a far friendlier crowd than I would have expected."

"How's Bobby holding up?"

"Tips are good. She's been nervous, but she's doing great." Mason collected the order of fries, probably the last of the night. "I'll let it be known that the kitchen's closed now. I'll be back to give you a hand wrapping up."

"I've got it. But thanks." I was wearier than usual, for reasons I didn't really care to examine. I'd peeked out at the crowd a number of times, and Mason was right. The event was a big success. But all the leather daddies and their boys made my stomach hurt, made me remember the Portland scene and my disastrous forays into it after Seth and I finally broke up for good two years ago.

And it didn't help any that Curtis had come out after all his protests that he wasn't interested. I saw him dancing with some slick twink who was gazing at him like he was a choice cut on prime-rib night. I didn't like the vest Curtis was wearing—the laces made me think of shibari, him with his hands behind his back, knots going straight up with black rope. He'd never ever go for it, of course. Probably laugh himself sick at the idea.

And the absolutely last thing I needed was to start having fantasies about Curtis of all people. Images of dominating big, toppy alpha men was fine for private daydreams, but in reality, guys like Curtis *never* shared such ideas and tended to get downright hostile at the suggestion. It was almost like I couldn't help it, though —something about how competent he was when carving, how larger-than-life he could seem, made me want to harness all that energy for myself. But I was trying to be smarter these days. Set attainable goals. I wished that other scenarios turned my crank even half as hard, as it would make my life so much easier. All in all, I was happy for the bar, happy for the business, but I couldn't help the weird melancholy that had settled over me.

And it persisted, even after Mason went back to the main room and I started cleanup. I had a stack of cardboard that needed to go to the recycling out back, and I needed some air, so I gathered it up and headed to the bin. The parking lot was still half full, so I took my time walking back, admiring the different bikes and trucks. *Someday...*

"Well, hello, kitten." A deep voice sounded from behind me, and I whirled to discover a large, wide man who appeared to be a good twenty years older than me. He had greasy gray hair and a motorcycle club vest with a ton of pins on it. "Why didn't I see you earlier?"

"Busy." I moved to pass him, but he stepped in my way, effectively pinning me against the building.

"Now is that any way to play?" He finished with a chiding noise that made my palms itch.

"Not interested." I tried again to get free, but he moved when I did.

"You got a daddy, boy? Someone to take care of you?"

Damn. The dude was persistent. And also, by the smell of him, drunk off his ass.

"Not a sub." My heart sped up. This was Portland all over again when visiting leather bars had earned me all sorts of unwanted attention. But now I had my friends to think about, the business. I couldn't go putting him in his place just because he pissed me off and made me nervous.

"Oh, sweetheart, you just haven't met the right daddy," he crooned, and leaned in. And fuck this. I could deal with the fallout later. I had had enough. I grabbed his arm at the same time I kneed him in the groin, using a well-practiced twist to make him howl in pain as he crumbled to his knees.

"Ow. Ow. Ow. Motherfucker. Now you've made me mad."

Of that, I had no doubt so I didn't release his arm, keeping my position of control, looming over him. "Not. A. Sub. I'm a Dom, you overgrown idiot. Now, you going to leave me alone?"

"Uh-huh." He nodded emphatically as I tightened my hold, working every nerve of his pressure points.

"Good." I released him and stepped clear.

"Leroy!" someone yelled right as the big man charged at me like some deranged linebacker. And I didn't think. Out of reflex, I foot-swept him and used his momentum to flatten him.

"Leroy Davidson, you big fool. You're going to get the police called, fighting in the parking lot." Curtis came striding over, nimbly stepping between me and Leroy, who was struggling to sit up.

"He started it," Leroy spat.

"He did not." Curtis laughed, and he had a nice laugh —full and rich. It might have been the first time I'd heard it. "I heard you hit on him. Saw him say no. And I was coming over to tell you to knock it the hell off when he handled his business, put you on your ass. Now you getting on home?"

"Yeah." Leroy let Curtis help him up. "Might be a bit…tipsy."

"Ya think?" Curtis shook his head. "Bob? Can you give this drunk asshole a ride?"

It was then that I realized that we weren't alone — there was a group of people gathered by the nearest truck, all staring. *Shit.*

"What the hell's going on?" Sam, the big guy Adam had asked to work the door, came rushing over, Mason fast at his heels. "People are saying there's a fight?"

"Ain't no such thing," Curtis glibly lied. "Little disagreement, but folks are moving on. Someone needs to see Leroy on home, though. Too wasted to drive."

"Logan? You okay?" Mason asked.

"I'm fine. Gonna go back to my kitchen now." I spared a last hard stare for Leroy before slipping in the rear door, back to my safe place, where I took several deep, cleansing breaths.

"What the hell happened?" It didn't take long for Mason to follow.

"Nothing. Some drunk guy made a pass at me. He was too wasted to take no for an answer."

"Oh, Logan." Mason didn't know about my interest in being a Dom, but he had seen the shiner I'd gotten last year in the leather bar dust up. I'd explained it away as some guy who didn't want to be rejected at a bar I hadn't named, but in retrospect, I probably should have just claimed I'd walked into a door because it had made my friend that much more protective. "Maybe we don't want to do another night like this — "

"You kidding? This is our best Saturday night in three months. One drunk asshole doesn't mean ditching our business plan."

"But we also can't have you fighting customers in the parking lot." Mason's voice went all stern. "I heard people say you flattened him."

"I took care of myself. That's all. I wasn't trying to start a fight. I was *avoiding* one."

"Self-defense isn't going to matter much if someone calls the cops. That could be bad. We're trying to keep a good reputation. I get that the guy was hassling you, but—"

"It won't happen again." I found my water bottler over on the shelf and downed it. "Promise."

"I know that you've got a black belt in whatever—"

"Aikido."

"Yeah, that. But I don't like you having to use it. Maybe Adam was right and you're vulnerable—"

"Fuck, no. Just drop it." I turned my attention to cleaning the grill. I just wanted to get the hell out of there, and the faster I cleaned, the faster I could be at home, under my shower, washing this stupid night off.

"Here. I can do the last of the cleanup." Tone more apologetic, Mason came over to the stove. "You've had a long night. Let Adam and me close. Head on home. Unless you want to wait and ride with me?"

Ordinarily, I'd object, make sure I did my share of the work. But I was just *done*. "I don't need a ride. I guess I'll head out."

"Go." Mason pushed me toward the corner where my bike gear was stashed.

"Okay. Okay." The ride home would be short, so I didn't bother with the full get-up—just the helmet, reflective jacket, and some Velcro straps for my pant legs.

My bike was locked to the little enclosure that shielded the recycling and trash Dumpsters, and I really didn't like crossing the now-mostly empty lot again.

My senses were already on red alert when a voice said, "Hey, kid."

I turned to find Curtis coming out of the shadows.

"Not a kid." I supposed I owed him for intervening in the Leroy mess, but I wasn't feeling particularly grateful.

"*Logan.* You got a minute?"

"What do you want?" I made my voice harsh as possible.

"You."

FOUR

Curtis

I had better come-on lines in my arsenal, but that one just slipped out. And judging by Logan's slack jack and wide eyes, he was just as shocked as me. Hell, I didn't even know exactly why I was still there, why I'd waited around to talk to him. Up until he'd flattened Leroy, I hadn't particularly liked the kid, but something about the way he'd handled the situation had earned my respect — and my dick's notice. I'd liked his commanding tone, his hard stares and regal posture, all things that really did it for me.

"Just wanted to talk a second," I clarified when he still didn't speak. "First off, wanted to make sure you were okay."

"I'm fine." He continued to look at me critically, like I was some new species of bug, one that was annoying his ankles. And damn, but I hadn't known he was capable of that stare, and part of me liked it. A lot. "I already told

Mason I wouldn't fight again. Sorry if he was a friend of yours—"

"Leroy? Hell, no. We go way back, but I wouldn't call that piece of shit a friend. You did what you needed to do, handling yourself. Damn impressive."

That was the truth. I'd been bored silly all night, drinking a tad more than I should have and waiting it out so I could drive back. Then the kid chef had made old Leroy squeal in pain and my dick had woken the fuck up. But it was also what I'd seen in his eyes. Hardness. Anger. Pride. *Enjoyment.*

"Thanks." A muscle worked in his jaw.

"You liked it, didn't you?" I pitched my voice low, seductive.

"I don't know what you're talking about." A flush crept up his neck.

"It's okay. I'm not gonna tell a soul. But you liked putting a hurt on him."

He nodded sharply. "Not in *that* way—"

I laughed. "In *exactly* that way. You like handing out pain? You serious about what you told Leroy? That you're a Dom?"

"I am. And if you're here to give me shit—"

"Me? Aw, hell, nah. I'm here to see if you've got more in you."

"More?" Damn it. He really was going to make me spell this out.

"You wanna put a hurt on someone? Still got a head of steam built up? Well, I'm here for that."

The critical look was back, but it was more thoughtful now. "You want pain?"

"And lots of it." I nodded. Now we were getting

somewhere. It was what I'd been jonesing for hard for two weeks now, what I hadn't really expected to find tonight. I was damn picky, and I didn't much feel like playing with someone who'd known Troy and me after the whole Bill thing. Too much baggage. But strangers were dicey business, as I knew all too well. So I'd figured on getting my dick sucked and leaning heavy on my fantasies to get off, but then little dog here had gone all alpha on Leroy, and my senses had perked up. He might do nice. Green and malleable enough that I could keep control of any scene, not be taking any crazy risks, but pumped full of enough adrenaline to dish out what I wanted.

"But you're…" His eyes narrowed, zeroing in on my arms. Ah. He spoke code enough to notice the placement of my gauntlets. "You're a sub?"

"I switch. But I'm a pain slut. You can get any master/slave fantasies right out of your brain, because I'm not into that. But pain? Control? Bondage? Bring it on."

"Now?" Oh, his face was so damn expressive. I loved that about him. I'd be able to tell what he was thinking, which was good. And right then it was like I'd proposed Christmas in July, complete with all the trimmings.

"Well, I'd prefer not in the parking lot." I laughed, trying to turn on my little-used charm, show him I meant the offer. "Your place?"

He was quiet, but his eyes kept moving, like I could see the wheels turning. Finally, he said, "Thirty minutes? I need to ride home and shower off the stink of the kitchen. I smell like fryer grease. But we can talk more there about what exactly you want."

45

I wasn't too awfully picky about smells myself nor did I fancy much conversation, but I nodded. Best to let him get comfortable with the idea. "You want a ride? We can toss your bike in the back of the truck."

"No thanks." His eyes went back to wary, like he didn't quite trust my offer, like I might be about to pull a big joke on him. And I hated that wariness, wanted to stomp on whatever had put it there.

I held up my hands. "I'm serious about this. I wanna play tonight. One-time thing." That needed saying, so I put some firmness behind the words. "But I want what you can dish out."

"Thirty minutes. Be ready." He skewered me with another of those hard stares before unlocking his bike.

"Will do." I watched him take off and took my time getting to the truck. He lived on the same sleepy street as Nash and Mason, and, on further consideration, I really didn't want either of them knowing my business. I'd lost my damn head, and I sure didn't need Nash's opinion on that. So I parked behind a vacant house two blocks away and slowly walked over, trying to give him his time without second-guessing myself and calling off the whole deal.

But then I remembered the look he'd leveled on Leroy. Yeah, I wanted me some of that. My ancient cell told me it had been exactly thirty minutes since we'd left the tavern, so I stepped up to his door and knocked. When he answered, he didn't say anything. Just stood there looking at me, toweling off his sandy hair, in gray dress pants with bare feet and a bare chest. And okay, really, I wanted him for the sadistic glint in his eyes earlier, but I couldn't deny that he made an appealing package outside of his ridiculous chef and biking outfits.

He was more muscular than I'd given him credit for —ropey forearms, lean but defined biceps and chest. And while no one was going to mistake him for a bear, he had more chest hair than I'd imagined, a light smattering across his pecs. Rosy nipples. And the expensive pants were a nice touch. Course I would have put him in leather myself, maybe some tight jeans, a vest, wrist gauntlets...

"You coming in?" Another hard stare.

Oh, yes. "Yup." I followed him into the living room. It had the same couch Mason had had when I'd helped Nash move his stuff out, but the wall art was new—giant classic movie posters on both walls and a neat row of plants in front of the window. "How do you want me?"

"Right here." He backed me against the door, using his body far more effectively than I would have thought, crowding into me. A shiver raced through me. Maybe this was going to be more than I'd bargained for. And then he leaned in, fingers trailing down my bearded jaw, and I knew with certainty that it was.

"You really want to play?" he asked in a husky whisper.

"Oh, yeah." Another shiver. I liked him like this, all confident and bossy, with just a hint of vulnerability that really did it for me.

"Good." He angled his head and I just managed to dodge his mouth. I wasn't sure why I did it—more instinct than anything else, but my heart hammered, and suddenly letting him kiss me seemed far riskier than letting him whale on me. His lashes were impossibly long, mouth far lusher than it had any right to be, and the way my stomach clenched, wanting to know what he tasted like, made me nervous. And I didn't do nervous.

"I'm not here for kissing." It came out gruffer than I'd intended, and I felt the immediate loss of his warmth as he stepped away. I was being ridiculous, and I almost wanted to yank him back, but before I could, he paced away.

"We should probably talk about why you *are* here. Wants. Limits. Safe words." He crossed his arms over his chest, and I couldn't decide whether he was making a conscious effort to be more intimidating or if he was either cold or nervous. Or maybe all three.

"We won't need a safe word." I waved that notion away. My insides clanged around, a weird feeling of loss, like maybe I should have let him kiss me, see where things would have gone if I'd let him be spontaneous. I *should* have been happy he was treating this like a transaction, and yet I felt like I was missing out on something important. It was my own doing, so I straightened my spine and tried to keep my voice light. "And why don't you show me your toy chest, and I'll tell you what I'm in the mood for."

His eyebrows went up. Uncrossing his arms, he pointed at the couch. "Sit. First, I don't have a toy chest."

"Nothing?" I sighed instead of sitting. "You *sure* you're a Dom? If you were just putting it on for Leroy, like I said, I switch. I can give you the training-wheels version of kink, see if you like it more than you think…"

"*Sit.* I know what I like." He all but growled at me. "I may be inexperienced, but I don't need the training-wheels version of anything. I'm pretty damn sure my hands can give you what you're after, and if you need something else, I've got belts and plenty of kitchen implements. I'll tell you, though, this isn't a buffet."

Damn, but I liked him hard and mean. I sat on the couch, let him loom over me, arms crossed. "I like belts. Your karate moves were impressive, but I'm not looking to spar. Your hands—"

"Are more than enough to get the job done. Now, are you going to keep interrupting me? We need to talk limits, not you shopping my offerings like it's a Target."

I cracked a grin at that. "I don't need a safe word, and I doubt you're gonna stumble on my limits."

"I won't play with you if you don't have a safe word." He stared me down, clearly meaning business. "And I want to know these limits, even if you don't seem to think I'm capable of finding them."

Uh-oh. Baby tiger was insulted now. And I honestly wouldn't put it past him kicking me out as his mouth had narrowed to a thin line, his eyes steely flecks. And okay, fine, I wanted what all that hardness promised to deliver. So I'd let him work through his BDSM 101 primer on kink negotiation.

"Didn't say you weren't capable of it, just that my limits seldom get tested. And we can do red as the safe word if it makes you feel better to have it." I wouldn't use it, but I'd throw it out there for him.

"It does. Limits? And since you seem to have a mile-long wish list, how about preferences?"

I cracked a smile despite myself. He was *fun.* "Okay, okay. Don't break the skin if you can help it, but I'm tested and negative for everything, so don't freak if it happens. No breath play or stuff around my neck. No piss or bodily fluids that aren't cum."

His face was so serious, I almost expected him to be taking notes the way they do with allergies at the doctor's office. "And preferences? Things you like a lot? Hate? This is your chance to tell me how you'd like things to go. And I know you've got *opinions* so don't say 'none,' or I'm gonna assume that's free rein for me to get creative."

Him being creative hardly sounded like a hardship, so I was half tempted to say "none" just to see what he'd do. But it had also been a long damn time since someone had seemed so eager to get a scene right for me. It was a luxury almost, being asked. Troy, well, he'd always just *known.* And Bill, he had his own ideas, ones I was usually okay with as it got me what I wanted. Good for everyone and all that. "Fine. You asked, kid—"

"*Logan.* You don't have call me Master or Sir if you're not into that, but you'll call me Logan. No more kid. I'm twenty-seven. I know I look younger, but I'm sure as hell not a kid. And while we're playing, you'll at least pretend to respect me."

"I can do that." Man, I liked him all ruffled. The angrier and more commanding he got, the more it worked for me.

"Now. Last chance. What do you like?"

"Pain. Back. Ass. Thighs. Chest. I'd rather you not go at my feet and hands—need to be able to stand and work tomorrow. I'm not opposed to fucking, but that's not really what I'm in the mood for." I'd bottom for him if that's what he had his heart set on, but for whatever reason, I was reluctant to go there with him, same as with the kissing. Some part of me seemed to want to hold back even as the rest of me was chomping at the bit to see what he could offer. "Same deal with bondage. I love it, but no offense, I don't know you all that well. Not sure I want you trussing me all up. But feel free to keep up the bossy 'tude. That works for me. I like orders, but I'm not crazy about humiliation. If that's your bag, though—"

"It's not," he said quickly. "At all. And we don't have to fuck or tie you up. How do you feel about being held down? Me grabbing your hands?"

Karate or no, I was pretty sure I could take him, so I nodded. I might not have given the same freedom to a different hookup, but I didn't want to think about why that was.

"As long as it's not my neck, grab away."

"And how do you like to come?"

I couldn't remember the last time someone had asked me that. It was usually an afterthought in scenes with Bill, something that happened, but wasn't the primary reason either of us had been there. But Logan looked so earnest, like knowing that was the key to the whole thing for him. I opened my mouth, intending to be flip and tell him it didn't much matter, but what tumbled out instead was something much closer to the truth than I liked.

"Make me wait a good long time. I fucking love getting off from the pain—rubbing on something or jacking myself off."

His eyes took on a gleam that made me smile. "I can work with that. Any injuries or triggers I should know about?"

"Avoid my kidneys—I've pissed blood before and would rather not again."

"Got it. You ready?" He couldn't quite hide the eagerness in his voice, which I liked more than I should have.

Finally. I grinned up at him. "You know it."

"Good." His voice went lower, harder, made something warm and delicious unfurl in my gut. "Strip."

FIVE

Logan

I half expected Curtis to object or make more smart remarks. Or to wake up and realize this was all a weird-ass dream. *Curtis* wanted me to dominate him. Wanted me to hurt him and make him come. My fantasies about taking a larger, more aggressive man and making him submit were within reach, including the ones about *this* man, with all his charisma and power. He wanted me, and that was heady stuff.

Curtis didn't laugh or crack another joke. Instead, he yanked off his boots and socks before standing and pulling open his vest. It had hidden snaps down the front, but the side laces made me think again about rope, and I was a little sad that he'd taken bondage off the table for this encounter. But I was glad I'd gotten him to be clear about what he wanted, giving me some parameters to work with.

He set the vest on the far end of the couch. He had even more tats than I'd realized—colorful sleeves going down both arms, a big back piece of feathery wings, and a flame-spitting motorcycle piloted by a bird on his chest. He had hair on his chest, but it didn't obscure the bright color and details of the tat.

"Nice," I said, pointing at the chest tat. "You've got a great artist."

"I know a few. You in the market for ink?" He grinned wickedly.

The New Year's resolution I hadn't told anyone about popped into my head. "I might be. I've got a few ideas."

"Yeah? Best person I know for virgin ink is this chick over in Roseburg. She'll go easy on you, but her work's top shelf."

At the mention of the word "virgin," my spine stiffened. "Pants. Off."

Curtis paused with his hand on his fly. "You done this before?"

"Done enough." I wasn't going to outright lie, but I also wasn't about to turn this into a confessional. I'd studied aikido for fifteen years. I'd also been practicing knots for about that long, getting serious about bondage-style knots and ties within the last two years or so, after Seth and I broke up and I'd admitted to myself what I really wanted out of sex. Since that time, I'd attended a shibari workshop in Portland, where I'd practiced on clothed fellow participants, and that had been fun. Ditto the BDSM lectures I'd found. Portland was nothing if not accepting of kink.

But finding this, a real person willing to let me dom them had been...elusive. It didn't help that all my fantasies revolved around guys like Curtis—beefy, muscled men. And I didn't like the app or personal ad scene—not only was I gun-shy after my disastrous leather bar visits, but trying to describe what I was after had made me want to slam my head into a wall until I'd temporarily given up, decided to focus on this move to Rainbow Cove.

"I'm not going to call this off if you say no." Curtis's voice was gentler than I'd ever heard it. "You being green isn't a turn-off."

"I've done some tying up," I admitted, tongue having apparently decided to confess after all. "But my ex thought I was *too* into that, so we never took it further. I haven't done a formal scene before, but I've spent the last few years figuring out what I like and doing research."

"Research, huh?" Curtis grinned. "That sounds fun, unlike your ex. He was missing out. And for this, I'm going to suggest you go slow, ramp it up gradually. I can take a lot, so no worries there. Your arm will give out before me."

"Is that a challenge?" I glared at him. "Get the pants off, arrange yourself over the edge of the sofa, and get comfortable. You're going to be here awhile."

"Yes, sir." Curtis gave me a filthy smile. He was enjoying this far too much. He dropped his pants, giving them the same careful treatment as the vest, putting them on the end of the couch. No leg tats, but he was muscled all over, a meatier ass than his frame would suggest, and a fine, fine cock. He was hard, which was good. It let me know he wasn't kidding about pain and control being a turn-on or about wanting it from me. I kept thinking of ways this could go very badly for me, but seeing him hard soothed me in a weird way.

He arranged himself kneeling on the couch, ass out,

long back extended, head pillowed on his arms resting on the arm of the couch. He looked comfortable, like he'd done this before, and that further quieted the fish flopping in my gut.

"Good. That's good." I paced the length of the couch, admiring him. His joke earlier about my needing a toy chest had me wanting to invest in every paddle and flogger I'd bookmarked. He'd said this was a one-time thing, and I fully intended to make it count, but man, what I could have done with some pre-planning.

Testing, I gripped his shoulder, mindful to stay clear of his neck, and pressed. The effect was immediate, him yielding to my grip, sinking further onto his arms. Sweeping a hand down his back, I let myself admire all the muscle and power on display for me. He smelled like leather, sweat, and some sort of herbal soap. It still felt surreal, like any second he'd change his mind or tell me he was kidding. But his muscles vibrated under my touch.

Anticipation.

I let my hand rest on his shoulder blade. With my thumb, I found the pressure point there, the same one I'd used to fell dozens of opponents over the years. And I dug in. This was another experiment, one to make damn sure he was on the same page with me.

"Oh, *fuck*." His voice dropped, exactly how I'd pictured it, getting lower and more gravelly.

I used my other hand to brace his hip so he didn't try to collapse or kick out. But he didn't throw me off. If anything, he relaxed into the touch.

"Yeah. Fuck. That hurts."

"That would be the point." I laughed, managing to

not sound like a diabolical cartoon villain. I pressed harder, far past what I'd be able to get away with in sparring.

"*Fuck*. Fuck." Without warning I released the spot and he exhaled hard. "Shit. You're a beast."

The praise made me smile, made me crack my knuckles before tracing the crest of his hipbone, finding the pressure on the sacrum. This time I dug in hard from the get-go.

"Ah. *Yes*. Okay. *Ah*." I released and he panted through a few breaths. "Okay. Point made. Your hands are a weapon. Hope you don't mind loud because that's just how I get, and I'm not the most into gags."

"Get loud as you need." I fucking loved it, lived for the sounds he was making. Thank God this wasn't an apartment. When I watched porn or fantasized, the noises were my favorite part of the whole scene, the way subs could transform pain into pleasure, the way their voices would change into begging and whimpering. I loved the idea of being able to do that to someone, being able to take this strong, confident man and reduce him to nothing more than needy moans.

I ran a hand over his ass, loving how muscular and rounded it was, but I continued my exploration to his thighs, thumb finding the little-known pressure point toward the inside of the leg.

"This one's gonna hurt," I warned before putting my weight into the press of my fingers.

"Damn it. Fuck. Ah. Ah."

I liked the curses, but my favorite was the way he'd descend into just groans the longer and harder I went. The pressure-point game was fun, so I did a few other spots, just to see him react. Simply these noises, his reactions, were far better than any sex I'd had. With Seth, things had always been...scripted almost. The list of what he wouldn't try or found distasteful was longer than that which he would do, so we'd fallen into quiet routines that led to orgasms, but it didn't give me the same rush that domination did.

Curtis *needed* me, needed what I could give him, couldn't do this for himself, and that ramped up my arousal. Each sound of his told me how much he was into this as did the tremble in his back muscles, and being able to do this for him, push him like this, give him what he craved was what I most loved about domination. He'd probably have some faint bruising tomorrow from how hard I was going, but I really wanted to see some serious shades of red.

"Ready for the real fun?" I asked in a low growl.

"Yes. Fuck. Yes." Sweat had already started to bead up along his hairline.

Crack. I let my hand fly, connect with the meat of his pale ass. His whole body undulated from the blow. A faint pink tinge colored the area, and all my senses hummed. The air smelled like sex, even though we'd barely gotten started with what I wanted to do. Anticipation gathered in my mouth, making me need to swallow hard. The big, powerful man had let me do that, let me mark him. I wanted more of that. Right that moment. And amazingly, he seemed to want more, too, rocking subtly toward me. It was magic almost how pain could be transformed into something we both wanted and craved, pleasure for us both. I loved how he was trusting me to do this, to create that magic for him.

I spanked him again, twice more in rapid succession, harder each time, and he groaned. "Oh, fuck. You're… stronger…than…you look."

"And you look damn good with my handprints on you."

"More."

Oh, yes. "I'm in charge," I said sternly, returning to the sacrum pressure point with my thumb. "And that was a little warmup. I'm going to go harder now."

"Bring it."

"You're so damn cocky." I shook my head as I stroked down his back. "I'm going to make you count. Don't mess up."

The counting games on most spanking porn videos were dumb and tiresome, but the reality of him spread before me, whole body tense, mouth slightly parted, like he was ready to say the number, was hot beyond belief.

I went as hard as I knew I could maintain with a decent rhythm, and he moaned and cursed before spitting out. "One."

We got to five before he added, "Lemme touch my dick. Please."

"Oh, fuck no." I laughed. He'd said he liked to work for it, and I fully intended to do exactly that. I rattled off another three with just enough time for him to get the numbers out. My palm was stinging like I'd petted nettles, my bicep burned, and my lungs and heart heaved like I'd just biked a century, but I'd never felt so euphoric as looking down at all that red and pink skin on his ass. This was headier than the rush of doing a five-course meal to perfection, managing each small detail, tweaking the experience for the recipients. That sense of being able to manipulate the details was something I hadn't even realized I needed, but I couldn't deny the way my pulse was thrumming at being able to create this scene for Curtis.

"Please. Fuck. I'm so hard." He was breathing as labored as me, and his voice was ragged.

"Let me see." I ran a hand underneath him, down his sweaty chest, stopping just above his dangling cock. "You come when I touch you, it's going to be five more. Harder."

"Incentive," he rasped.

"Ten," I countered. "With the belt. And you don't get them if you've come."

"Won't shoot," he promised, way more contrite now.

His cock was a pulsing bar of iron, damp at the tip, generous plump head, thick shaft. And knowing he was this hard for *me*, because of what I'd been doing, what he wanted me to keep doing, had my own cock throbbing.

"Let me suck you," he wheedled. "Before the belt. Let me suck you off."

"Tempting." I stroked him, slow and leisurely.

"I'm good at it."

"I'm sure you are." I withdrew my hand. "But right now, much as I want to know what talents your mouth has, I want to see you wearing stripes more. And I promised you ten. You take ten, you can touch your dick."

"Fuck, yes." He stretched, making the handprints on his ass dance. If this was a dream, it was the best I'd ever had, bar none. Curtis was on his knees, ass blotchy pink and red, wanting *more*.

I undid my belt, dragging it across the fabric, letting

him hear it unfurl. I'd practiced a little bit with the belt on my own thighs and calves, tried a lot with pillows, and seen tutorials aplenty, but my hands still shook with unwelcome nerves. Thank God his eyes were closed and had been for a while. I took several deep breaths.

"I need you to speak up if I go too hard." I made it an order, managed to mask some of my uncertainty.

"I want this. Want you." Curtis's words went a long way to reassuring me. He sounded buzzed, which was what I was going for, but he also seemed sure of his own desires and needs. "Warm up slow, if you need, but I'm not gonna break."

"Good." I let the belt snap through the air. The whole room became electric before the leather connected with his already pink flesh.

"One." His groan was an intimate thing, not unlike a lover about to climax. Fuck. I wanted more. Just like that. I waited to watch how his skin reacted—a deeper flush of red, but the skin wasn't broken and no alarming welts.

"More," he urged, further showing me that I hadn't gone too far. A deep sense of satisfaction settled over me. He wanted this, wanted my marks. The man who made his living leaving indelible marks in wood was willing— eager, even—to cede control to me. This. This was what I'd fantasized about. Waited for. I varied where the next several blows landed, doing a few on his upper back, and his moans started to mingle with curses and pleading.

"Five. Please. Oh, fuck. No more."

I paused, loving how far I had him on the edge but wanting to give him ample opportunity to safe word if I'd pushed too much.

"I think you can take it. Just five more. Then you get to come. And you're doing so damn good. So fucking hot."

"Yeah. I can." He gulped like the air was water in the desert and his whole torso shone with sweat. Mine did, too, I was sure. "Can't. Count."

"That's okay," I soothed. "I'll count for you. Just five. I promise."

I counted off the next three, and he groaned over and over like he was a porn star getting fucked hard.

"Nine." I let it land right on the worst of the bruising on his ass, expecting more cursing, but he seemed beyond that now, almost keening.

"And ten." That one hit right where his thighs met his ass. His groan was so low and broken that I thought for sure he'd come, but his dick was hard as ever, dripping precum.

"You did it. So good." Throwing down the belt, I reached for his dick, bending over so my lips were against his ear. "Come for me now. You earned it."

I worked his cock with my right hand, running the left down his back and ass, pausing at each red mark. As soon as I reached the big bruise on his ass, he started to shake and his cock swelled in my grip. I pressed down on the sore spot with my thumb. "That's it. Come on, now."

He came with a mighty shout, shudders rippling through him. Collapsing fully onto the couch, he kept groaning, "Fuck," softly, over and over.

"You did so good." I wiped the sweaty hair off his forehead, half tempted to kiss him there. He seemed to be sinking into subspace, a trance-like state where I wasn't sure whether he was about to drift off or what.

And while my own cock was screaming at me for relief, the urge to take care of him was stronger than the need to jerk off onto his marked flesh. Instead, I raced to grab a bottle of water, a towel, and some aloe lotion with arnica that I used after bike falls.

"Here. Drink." I crouched next to him, holding the bottle while he chugged half of it. "Slow. No puking."

"Won't." His voice was slurred.

I cleaned him off with the towel, and he was remarkably pliant, letting me move him this way and that to get at the mess on his stomach and the couch. Then, after he settled on his stomach, I worked the lotion into him, starting with his shoulders, inspecting each bruise, making sure I hadn't accidentally broken the skin. The whole time, I offered him soft praise, the sort I'd been waiting years to hand out. Giving him the pain we both craved had been sublime, but being with him like this might have been my favorite thing out of the whole encounter.

I was especially gentle with his ass. No broken skin, but he was certainly going to feel it tomorrow. Pulling a blanket off the back of the couch, I draped it over his legs.

"You can rest here as long as you want." I stroked the uninjured parts of his back some more.

He cracked open an eye. "I'm only putting up with this aftercare business because I came my brains out and still can't feel my feet."

I recoiled like he'd slapped me. "It's part of it. An important part."

"Not something I need." His voice was still slurred.

"Some do, though. So, you know, A-plus for effort on your part, kid."

"I don't want an effort merit badge." My voice came out far harsher than I'd intended.

"Why don't you come over here, let me suck your dick?" He still didn't have both eyes open. "You earned it."

"I'm good." I meant it. I'd beat off to memories of tonight for months. But I didn't need a sleepy, sloppy blowjob from him, not when we were back to the calling-me-kid business, and he seemed to be in dire need of a nap. He might not *think* he required the aftercare, but I saw it as a big part of my job and responsibility—giving him what he needed, not simply what he thought he wanted.

If he were to ask me what *I* wanted most, it would be for him to sleep and then maybe have a much less kinky round two, where I still got to come all over his marked flesh. That would be my ideal. But I knew instinctively that I wasn't going to get it, that he'd be gone after the briefest of sleeps.

Oh, well. I'd rather lose my chance at an orgasm and get the opportunity to see him just like this, eyes closed, face slack, soft sounds escaping his mouth. *I did that.* Pride, every bit as potent as a climax, surged through me. And with it a small hint of sadness. He'd said one-time thing, and he'd meant it, but damn what I wouldn't give for seconds.

Curtis

I woke up alone on the couch, soft covers pulled up around me, and a pillow under my head. Damn. Boy Wonder didn't do things in half measures, that was for sure. It wasn't unusual for me to need to sleep a good scene off, but this was the first time in a long time I'd had such…caretaking. And I didn't like it. I got that he was trying to follow whatever kink guide he'd found on the Internet, but I didn't do aftercare. And he'd been almost…worshipful in it, cuddly even, crooning praise and rubbing me and making me feel all sorts of safe and comforted. Things I'd rather not feel at all. Comfort was for other people, not me. Comfort was something you could come to rely on if you weren't careful.

But he was new, so I had to make certain allowances for him. And oh yes, he'd been brand-spanking new. I smiled at my own pun as I sat up. He'd sidestepped the question of whether it was his first scene, but it had been, I was sure of it. Nerves had rolled off him in big breaker waves before he started his pressure point torture, so much that I'd been sure he was about to call the whole thing off.

But then he'd pulled himself together and *how*. Each point he pressed seemed to give him more confidence until he was in total control of the scene, voice hard and commanding, authority and not nerves coming off him, hands steady and firm, demanding, even. Just his pressure-point work had pushed me hard, thrown me up against that blissful white zone that pain could bring. By the time he got to the belt, I'd been there, buzzing hard, white place calling my name until it consumed me even before the orgasm, a high unlike any other. He could have gone for a hundred lashes at that point, and I

65

wouldn't have stopped him. I'd been so certain that I could control any scene with him, but in that moment when he told me I could take more and I believed him, I handed everything to him. And flew.

When I'd finally come, it had only made things that much brighter, wringing me out. I'd expected him to have me jerk off, so his hand had been an unexpected treat, but also one more comfort I didn't want to come to depend on. Which was why I groaned when I saw the note stuck under the fresh water bottle by my boots. His handwriting was neat but loopy.

Went to bed. There's coffee in the pot, ready to brew, and you're welcome to shower. Fresh towel in there. You're also welcome to join me in the bed :) But if you head out, thank you. That was amazing. ~L.

There was a world of hope in that smiley face, so much that it made my chest hurt. For the briefest of seconds, I considered showering, crawling into what was undoubtedly a warm bed, waking him up with the blow job he really had earned. He'd be sleepy and appreciative and I'd get to watch him come apart. And because I'd already pegged him as a giver, I'd get to come again, too, probably with lots of touches and cuddling and praise from him. *Nope. Not gonna do it.* I came back to reality, *my* reality, and dressed fast before heading into the chilly January early morning. I'd have to see him again soon, I was sure of it, but the least I could do would be to make sure my armor was firmly back in place.

SIX

Logan

Sunday morning started with the best orgasm in recent memory. On my own, of course. I'd heard Curtis leave in the wee hours but hadn't come out to make an awkward situation that much worse. I'd left the note, and he'd made his choice. Simple as that. No reason to feel hurt, and I could certainly be adult about this.

So even if my chest pinged, I'd gone back to sleep and, when I woke up again, I'd had a raging hard-on. I'd replayed Curtis's sounds and expressions from the night before, working myself slow until I simply couldn't stand it anymore, imagining myself coming all over his marked flesh. *God, I want that.*

With that little indulgence out of the way, I'd showered off and headed to the tavern for Sunday prep. On the bike ride over, I kept telling myself that I needed to forget the night before. Think of it like a really great dream. Or maybe a vacation. A spectacular island I only got to visit once.

But it was hard as I kept coming up with scenarios I'd love to try with him. Rope. Cuffs. Wooden spoons. Floggers. Paddles. Kissing. That last one especially. I hadn't even tasted his skin, and that seemed like the worst kind of oversight. *No seconds.*

I locked up the bike and braced for what was sure to be a tidal wave of concern from my friends.

Sure enough, Adam was first to spot me. He was doing inventory in the bar area but stopped to flag me down before I made it to the kitchen. "Next time you need to take out boxes on a theme night, you get me. Or have Horatio do it."

"Mason's caught fish that weigh more than Horatio. I can handle myself."

"Yeah, but Horatio's got street smarts. His brother and dad both ride with one of the motorcycle clubs."

"I have a black belt—"

"From some shiny studio in the Portland suburbs. I love you, man, but you gotta admit you've been…sheltered."

"Just because I didn't grow up here with you and Mason doesn't make me sheltered. And sure, my parents were comfortable, but I've been around. We traveled a fair bit for vacations. I've seen some dicey areas."

Adam snorted. Out of everyone in my friendship circle, he seemed to hold my parents' money against me the most. Like it made me soft. Or like it had somehow protected me when that couldn't be further from the truth.

Mason came out of the kitchen. "What Adam's *trying* to say is that we're worried about you. You're just not the most intimidating dude—"

"You look like a TV ad featuring cherubs." Adam was more blunt. But they were wrong. I'd intimidated Curtis plenty last night, had him on his knees, begging, holding still for my blows. The memory made my stomach quake, in a good way, a giddy little flutter.

But this was why I'd never confessed my desire to be a Dom to either of them. They'd laugh themselves sick and then try to talk me out of it. Gently on Mason's part. Ruder on Adam's, but the effect would be the same—no one taking me seriously, yet again.

"I loved that we did Leather Night," I said firmly, trying to move on from talk about my appearance and ability to defend myself. "Are we in the black for the month now or what?"

"Or what," Mason groaned. "The last few months have been terrible. Our theme nights are keeping us afloat, but it's like the Titanic over here."

"Which of us is Jack?" I laughed even though I was pretty sure it was me. Adam and Mason had gone to elementary school together and were tighter than many brothers. If anyone was getting shoved off the last piece of floating debris, it would be me.

"We're all in this together, and we knew the first year or so would be rough, especially the off-season as we work to build up more local trust to make up for the drop in tourists. But this is hard." Mason shook his head. "I wish I'd taken more business classes."

"No substitute for real-world experience." Adam gave a bitter laugh.

I got some last night. I thought of all the kink lectures and books and demo videos I'd consumed over the years. Nothing could have prepared me fully for my first scene.

It was all great knowledge to have, but there really was no substitute for real-world exploration. Now the only question was how to get more of it.

But I needed to stop letting my mind wander and pay attention to our state-of-the-business discussion.

"Do we need another cash infusion?" I asked. We'd gotten a small-business grant from the state, some loans, and each of us had put up some savings. Of the three of us, I had the best financial situation. Adam was living with his sister and her kid to save money and took on the occasional odd job for extra cash. Mason had his family to worry about. But I had a small inheritance from my grandfather that I'd been living on and fewer expenses. "I could ask—"

"No to Bank of Mom and Dad," Adam said, reviving an old argument. They'd let me put up my own money but hadn't wanted my parents as investors.

"We might have to think about it. Seriously." Mason rubbed his head. "We need to make it to Memorial Day weekend. Easter and spring break should give us a bit of a bump, but it may not be enough."

"What about doing a Valentine's weekend special with the B&B? Special dinner, drinks, dancing, and then a room at a great price?" Adam suggested. "That could be the February bounce. I know my mom will go for it. I'll text her now."

"I love that idea. I'll work up some menu ideas that sound elegant but aren't too pricey. But I can still talk to my parents, get the ball rolling there."

"Do it," Mason said, giving Adam a warning look before he could object more. "Let's find out what all our options are. And I'll work on getting some publicity for the Valentine's dinner—maybe we can get some locals out, too, go for a more mixed crowd."

It was time to prep for lunch, so talking was curtailed until later. My special was a cheddar beer soup, perfect for the dreary weather and my not-so-great mood. After the moderate midday rush, I found Mason.

"Do you want me to fill in for you later?" I asked. "I know the schedule says I'm off tonight and then tomorrow afternoon for that wood pick-up, but I can move things around if you want." I had no idea if Curtis would even show for the wood-delivery thing, and my money was on "no," but of course I couldn't tell Mason about that. But I was antsy and not really wanting a bunch of hours in front of me to do nothing.

"No way. I want the kitchen." Mason smiled. He was usually the one to take over the kitchen when I had time off. We'd gone to the same culinary school, and Mason had decent cooking chops even if his forte was manage-ment stuff. "Nash is bringing Lilac in for dinner, and they can't wait to see what my special is going to be. And I really do need the nights off I'm scheduled for later in the week, so let's not rearrange."

"Okay." I was more than half-tempted to stick around, offer to be his sous chef, but he shooed me out of the kitchen. For some reason, I didn't want to head straight home. What I wanted was to lose myself in something—a sparring match, a long ride, sex, cooking. But I had yet to find a local dojo I liked for my aikido training, and it was too slick and rainy for anything more than a brief trip on the bike to be palatable. That left sex, and after last night, I had no desire to go through the trouble of trying to find a hookup. I wanted to revel in my memories of Curtis some more before I ventured back to the largely vanilla flavors I'd sampled for years now without a ton of success.

Down to cooking. My personal fridge was a little barren these days. Last night after Curtis fell asleep on the couch, I'd realized I didn't have much more than coffee to offer him if he stuck around for breakfast. And for a chef that wouldn't do. Also, I needed to get started coming up with some ideas for the Valentine's Day dinner. I could have done that at the tavern, of course, but there was something comforting about cooking alone in my own kitchen, no one bustling in and out, no opinions until I asked for them. So instead of heading home, I made sure I had room in my panniers and biked the few blocks up to the grocery.

It was a small store with limited options. In the time that I'd been living in Rainbow Cove, I'd already learned that parsley and cilantro were their only fresh herbs, pasta strictly a dried affair, higher end cuts of beef and pork not a thing, and bread sadly lacking outside of sandwich loaves. I missed Portland more every time I shopped.

Oh, well. I needed to be cost-conscious with the Valentine's menu anyway. Go with something that people loved but that wasn't as spendy as a filet. Something suitable for this weather of layers and—

That's it.

Layers. Like a tagine. Or ratatouille, but the store had no eggplants. Or maybe something with phyllo? Spinach pie? But they didn't carry phyllo, which left me trekking back to the pasta aisle. I was daydreaming about classy, upscale lasagna when I almost bumped into—

"Curtis?"

"Kid." He gave me a wary once-over, like I was about to hug him or do something else equally horrifying. "You not cooking tonight?"

"Not at the tavern. I'll be cooking at home tonight." That sounded suspiciously close to an invitation, so I added, "Testing recipes. We'll be doing a special night for Valentine's. Mason's cooking at the tavern, though, if you wanted to stop in."

And now I was rambling and needed to just stop. I gave him what I hoped was a bright-yet-distant smile.

"I don't."

"Understandable. Crappy weather." I was proud of myself for making such mundane small talk. No need to refer back to or even think about last night except every other second. To distract myself, I scoped out his basket. I couldn't help the nosiness. I was a chef. I always wanted to know what people were cooking. Besides, I'd heard that he grew most of his food. He had some canned tomatoes and a few bags of beans. "You doing a vegan chili? I've been thinking about making that soon as a special. You want my recipe? The secret is cocoa—"

"*Kid*." Curtis silenced my rambling with a stern look. No one watching us would ever believe that this guy had been on his knees, willingly—eagerly, even—for me. "I make beans. Once a week. Same way for about fifteen years now. It's just food."

Just. Food. I swear it felt like a slap, him rejecting my attempts to be friendly. And it was never just food. It was joy, warmth, happiness, texture, sweetness, heat—a thousand sensations in a single meal.

"Oh. Well. Have fun making it." The awkward place I'd worked so damn hard to avoid had now arrived in the form of a too-long pause and us both looking away, but feet not moving yet.

"See you around." Curtis moved first. "Tomorrow at two, right?"

Ah. I supposed we were still on, after all. Making Flint unhappy by backing out of our deal must have been a worse prospect than spending a few hours with me. "If you want."

"We don't want you cold. That rental of yours must get nippy." *Finally.* Finally there was a spark in his eyes, some reminder that last night was not a total figment of my imagination. He knew exactly how drafty the little house got, which was why I'd been so careful to cover him with blankets. His mouth quirked. Not a smile or even a hint, but there was something there. "I'll stick around, give you a lesson on lighting the stove the first time. Nash won't forgive me if I let you burn the neighborhood down."

"I don't need..." *Lessons.* Real-world lessons. Like Mason had been going on about. That was *it*. "Second thought, that sounds good. See you then."

I offered him a cheery wave before heading away with my cart. I had the beginnings of a plan now, and it was going to be great. Better than my dinner ideas, even.

SEVEN

Curtis

The kid—and it benefited me to think of him as one no matter how much he claimed to be twenty-seven—wanted to trade recipes. *Ha.* I had no doubt his chili would be the best stuff I'd ever tasted, but I went home, alone, no recipe in hand, and put a bag of beans in a large pot of water to soak. I felt a bit like I'd squashed a butterfly back there at the store.

He'd been trying so hard to play it cool, whereas I'd gone straight to grumpy-ass and didn't look back. It hadn't helped that I could still feel him with each move-ment, still remember how he'd made me soar. Maybe I'd make it up to him when we got wood. Be…well, not nice, but more considerate. Too nice would give him the wrong idea, but I also didn't need to be cruel.

I spent Monday morning on a bunch of small tasks that needed doing—servicing my truck, working in the green house, cleaning tools. While I loved the high of finishing a big sculpture, little routines were what grounded me. Brought me peace.

I was at the tavern at exactly two, and the kid hurried out the back door right as I got out of the truck. Boy Wonder had clearly talked to Ringer about what to wear to haul wood. He was wearing a too-big flannel jacket and too-new jeans along with sneakers. We had to get this boy some *boots*. And there I was thinking about him in leather again. Not-so-cranky was all well and good, but I couldn't go getting a *thing* for the kid.

"Ringer loan you work gloves along with his coat?" That came out a bit harsh, so I made myself smile.

"Yeah." He flushed like he hadn't noticed my smile. "He said your friend lives off in the hills?"

"Yup." I headed back to the truck.

"This is your truck?" He seemed a tad surprised. Guess he'd figured me for driving some ancient piece of shit. But in my line of work, a good truck was a necessity, not a luxury. I routinely hauled heavy loads, so I had an F350 diesel with a towing package for when I needed the trailer.

"This rig would make Adam jealous." He smiled as he climbed in. He smiled a lot, and it was hard to ignore the effect all those dimples had on me—prickling tender bits of my insides, making me cranky and nostalgic both.

"It gets the job done." I shrugged off the compliment.

We made our way out of town, up the old mill road to catch a country road that would lead us into the woods where Johnny lived. It was a decent trek. I wasn't good at chatter despite being more social than people gave me credit for, so it wasn't a surprise when Logan reached for the radio.

"Doubt you'll get a signal," I warned.

"Yeah, but don't you have your phone plugged in?"

"Nope." I laughed and pointed at my phone, an ancient flip model that Troy had bought me years ago that I'd never seen reason to upgrade.

"Oh, man." His reaction was comical, all wide eyes and head shaking. He really was the most expressive creature. "Wish I had a cable. We could use mine."

"Something tells me you and I have very different tastes in music." My laugh escaped without my consent, damn it.

"I'm not a club rat if that's what you're thinking." He sounded mortally offended. "I listen to all sorts of things. Classic rock, even some like the stuff I've heard you blaring when you're working outside."

"Thank you kindly for pointing out that I'm older than dirt."

"You're what? Forty like Nash? That's nothing." He waved away our age difference like it was a pesky bug.

"Forty-two actually." And I felt every one of the fifteen years separating us with each of his easy smiles.

"But you went to school with Nash, right? Are your folks still around here?" He was simply making pleasant conversation. He didn't know my history. I could lie, tell him some pretty tale, and he wouldn't know the difference. Instead, the truth bubbled up.

"Dead."

"I'm sorry for your loss. That sucks."

"Don't be. They were both raging alcoholics that make Mason's relations look like a TV-show family. And that was before the meth." Apparently the truth didn't want to be pasted over.

I glanced over at him, expecting more wide-eyed shock and horror. Or worse, pity. But his eyes were soft and compassionate. "That sucks. No siblings to share the load?"

"None that I'm aware of."

"I'm an only kid, too. Not saying I know what it was like for you, but I hate it sometimes, not having a sibling to talk to."

"Eh. It was okay." I'd hated that, too, but I was also a realist. Chances were high that whatever brother or sister my parents churned out wouldn't have been the most understanding of souls. And honestly, even if they'd been decent, I wouldn't wish my parents on another person. And then, because I was done talking about me, I asked, "Your parents back in Portland?"

"Lake Oswego, but Dad works in Portland, yeah." He named a ritzy suburb which confirmed a lot of my assumptions about him. "They're not happy with me so far away. Like I said, a sibling would make it easier. I'm all they have."

Yup. Another suspicion confirmed. Boy Wonder wouldn't be sticking around, especially if the tavern couldn't make it. I turned onto the dirt track leading up to Johnny's place. When the cabin came into view, he gasped, and I had to laugh. It looked like Johnny was preparing for a zombie invasion with stacks of wood everywhere. More wood than house, really. His selection of trucks was neatly lined up, and various other pieces of heavy equipment completed the logging camp look.

"Wow. It's a real log cabin. How cool." He grinned like I'd taken him to Disney. "Did he build it himself?"

"Him and his old man, yeah."

"Think he'd let me peek inside? I've always wanted to see one up close."

"Knock yourself out, kid. I'm sure he'll give you a tour if you want."

Sure enough, Johnny and the dogs were out to greet us before I even got parked. Despite his remote location, Johnny was plenty friendly and he had a back slap for me and a hearty handshake for Logan.

"You bring cash? My card reader don't work out here."

"Yup." The kid peeled off a stack of twenties so crisp they crackled. "Here you go."

"Excellent. Let's get y'all loaded." Johnny was all smiles after getting paid. He led us to the nearest stack of split wood.

"Tell me a little about your operation here? I love your cabin." The kid continued to look like he'd landed at a theme park, eyes darting this way and that.

"Yeah? You wanna see my newest hauler?" Switching direction, Johnny led us to a shiny logging truck. "This baby's gonna earn her keep."

Logan circled it and kept Johnny busy with all sorts of questions, like a kid on a field trip. And of course, Johnny ate it up. Didn't take more than a little hint from me before he was showing off the cabin, pointing out his new solar panels on the roof.

"Oh, wow. You've got solar. And for your water as well." Boy Wonder looked at Johnny like he'd invented the sucker.

"I've got some, too." I just couldn't keep quiet in the face of the mutual admiration society I was witnessing.

"Oh, you'll have to show me." He gave me a dazzling

smile, same one that had apparently rendered Johnny brain dead. "Someday when I get my own place, I want to go all eco, passive solar, the works. It's so awesome that you got to design your house."

Much as I suddenly had the urge to throat punch Johnny, I couldn't help but be entertained by the kid's enthusiasm. He'd be back in Portland someday, building in some subdivision with a woodsy name. And that made me a little sad. I sure would have liked to see what he came up with.

"You can't have a cabin that's all kitchen," I joked at him.

He stared for a long second, like this was the first time I'd been funny. Which, okay, maybe it was. But I was *trying*. Especially with Johnny oozing lumberjack charm over there.

"Can, too." Logan winked at me.

"You cook at the tavern, right?" Johnny looked Logan over like he was one of the daily specials.

"Yup. Come in sometime. Tell Mason or Adam that I sent you, and we'll comp your dessert."

"I might just have to do that." Johnny headed back outside. I walked a little closer to Logan than was strictly necessary and glared at Johnny's back.

"What?" Logan whispered. "Sorry if this took up too much time."

"It's fine. Let's get loaded." Between the three of us, we got the truck full of wood quickly, Logan pulling more weight than I would have thought. He was far stronger than he looked and a good hard worker.

"Come in this week," Boy Wonder urged Johnny as

we got ready to go. "I'm going to do a beef pot pie as the special on Thursday, I think. You might like that."

"I might indeed." Johnny had a back slap for each of us, and I had a long warning look for him. From what I knew about the kid, Johnny was far, far from his type, but I still didn't like the idea of either of them trying it on.

I decided I better fill the kid in as I headed back to the road. "You might want to be careful with your invites. Johnny's a rope Dom. Plays with both men and women. He wouldn't mind lashing you to that pillar in his living room."

"Wow." He blinked a few times. "I...uh...wasn't hitting on him. Only meant that I thought his place was cool."

"Oh, he was happy to show it off." My laugh was a touch too bitter. "Just...tread careful."

"Why does everyone seem to think I can't handle myself?" He groaned and let his head fall back on the seat.

"I've got little doubt you could, actually," I admitted. "But I'd rather not have to explain to Nash why you laid out Johnny with some karate kick take-down move."

"Thank you." He beamed like I'd handed him a gift instead of the truth. "And I can be polite, too. He hits on me, I'll simply say I'm not interested. That usually works except with drunk assholes like Leroy."

I didn't like the sound of that "usually," didn't like the thought of him in situations with jerks who wouldn't take no for an answer. I let myself stew on that all the way back to town. It wasn't until we were unloading that he started talking again.

"That business with Johnny reminded me of an idea I wanted to talk to you about." His words were a little too careful. He'd deliberately waited to spring this idea on me until we were at his place and I couldn't kick him out of the truck. Not that I would have, but I was instantly on edge, beard prickling.

"Oh?"

"I've got a proposition for you. A bargain, if you will." He set down his latest armload of wood and turned to smile at me. "I want lessons."

"Lessons?" I considered him carefully. No way did he want carving lessons.

"Kink lessons," he clarified. "I want to know how to be a better Dom for the next time I get to do it in real life. I think you're just bossy and opinionated enough to give me tips."

"You want tips?" I set my own load of wood down next to his in the ancient firewood rack on the side of the house.

"Yes." He nodded eagerly. "I know you said the other night was a one-time thing—"

"And meant it."

"But this wouldn't be dating or anything like that. Just you walking me through some pointers and doing a few more scenes."

"Do I look eager to hold Dom 101 classes?" My eyes narrowed, but I had to admit, his idea wasn't without appeal. A regular source of play was something I sorely needed, but I wasn't convinced Baby Dom was worth the hassle. Or the risk. "And how is it that you got to twenty-seven without these...lessons you seem all fired up for?"

He groaned. "I've always loved the idea of being in charge, giving orders, but I had this boyfriend. Kind of an on-again-off-again thing that started our junior year in high school and went until last year. My parents *loved* him, so I kept going back to him. But he's seriously the most vanilla person on the planet. Won't even entertain the idea of anal."

"The same one who didn't find being tied up fun?" I was starting to get a picture of this stuck-up idiot who most certainly had not been worthy of someone with Logan's creativity.

"That's the one. And anyway, I'd sneak porn, a lot of it kinky, but it was only once we broke up for good that I really let myself explore the idea of being kinky myself. I started dabbling in some lectures and workshops, but when I went to a leather bar in Portland, I ran into a Dom who made Leroy look like a basket of puppies."

"Fuck." I did not like the idea of Logan in danger.

"And this guy had friends. Got into a bar fight, which kinda turned me off the idea of trying to find a sub for awhile. And I...uh...have rather specific tastes." His neck flushed red.

"Oh? Now I'm curious."

"I like bigger guys. With muscles. Guys who look like Doms at first glance. Anyway, you don't need all my baggage. I just need to figure out how to get people in the lifestyle to take me more seriously. I thought you'd be great at giving me pointers." His smile was still encouraging but starting to waver a little.

I looked him up and down. It was damn easy to see what Johnny had found so appealing about his angelic looks. Even now in his too-big jacket, he looked nineteen, not twenty-seven.

"Get yourself some decent boots. Think about some leather. Cut the hair. Grow a beard or goatee if you're able. A few tats wouldn't hurt."

He was silent a long time, and I thought for sure I'd wounded him. Finally, he nodded. "That's good. That's the sort of thing I need to hear. My ex manages an upscale menswear store, and my mom has this thing about my hair, so I've always gone for the preppy look. But it's probably time for a change."

His eyes were soft and sad, though, and my stomach clenched. Fuck. I had hurt him.

"Listen. You gotta do you. Leather's not just a look, it's something that's in your soul. It's who you *are*. You can get all the tips you want, but unless you really feel it, you're just gonna be faking it, and that's no good, either."

He licked his lips. "I think I *am* leather. I just have a really hard time letting it out. Cultural conditioning and all that."

I nodded like I knew what the fuck he meant with the big words. But I could tell him more about me. "When I see leather, my pulse hums. I put it on, I get hard. I fucking love leather. But maybe for you it's more a suit or something like that. I know plenty of Doms who like looking all snazzy and aren't into the leather as much. You gotta find a look that works for who you are."

He made a face. "Suits don't do it for me as much. I daydream about tats. Leather. I'm just scared of looking like a poser."

"You won't. You'll look like you." I couldn't say how I knew that. I just did. There was something in this kid that wanted out. I wasn't exactly sure what it was yet, and I was the worst person on earth for this pep talk, but I felt compelled to try. "Own it. Life's too damn short to not go all in on who you are."

"You're right. That was my New Year's resolution this year. To be myself more. Maybe get a tat and to figure out how to be a better Dom. How to get a sub."

"It's not going to be me." I tried to gentle my words some, but he still frowned.

"I know that. I just want lessons, so that I can get a sub of my own. Real-world experience. I want to be ready. And yeah, the look thing can be part of it. Maybe with you advising me, it'll be easier to make changes."

I didn't much care for the vision of him with a sub of his own, probably some gym rat twink even more fresh-faced than he was with the muscles Logan seemed to crave but no common sense grounding either of them.

"What's in this deal for me?" I told myself it was merely curiosity keeping me from shutting him down flat.

"Pain. Plenty of it and whatever else you want me to try. See, you're bossy and this is your chance to get what you want from a scene. All your preferences accounted for." He smiled widely like he had my number. And he wasn't wrong. I'd had enough scenes go sideways over the years that I was picky about who I handed the reins to. And it *had* felt like a luxury the way he'd quizzed me so carefully about what I wanted and then delivered exactly that without pushing for anything else.

But I didn't do luxuries. Luxuries were even riskier than giving up control to the wrong person. "What else?"

I was prepared to put him in his place if he offered cash, but he laughed and surprised me again.

"You mean besides the fact that it would be fun and you know it? I'm not dumb enough to offer to pay for lessons, but I was thinking I could cook for you. And honestly, you'd be doing me a favor there, too, letting me test more of my vegetarian ideas on you and use up some of our leftovers."

His cooking was way more of a luxury than offering me my choice of items at the kink buffet. And fun... Lord, I wasn't sure I could handle fun. I needed to say no to this bargain right away, before it could work its venom into me.

"It's winter. Your garden's got to be pretty limited, right?"

"I make do," I lied. It was limited. On so many levels. With Bill out of the picture and me not wanting to go on the hunt, it was likely be a long cold spell on all fronts.

Maybe watching Logan blossom into himself would be worth the risk. A public service almost. I thought of what could happen, him getting the wrong mentor, and my blood temperature dropped thirty degrees, especially when I thought about what he'd said about the bar fight. He had a world of potential as a Dom, but the wrong person could ruin all that, or worse, destroy his confidence.

And it was that image, the high likelihood of him getting taken advantage of, that had me nodding before I really knew what I was doing. "I guess we could have a lesson or two."

EIGHT

Logan

"You'll do it?" I honestly hadn't been sure whether Curtis would agree to my proposal. He was awfully unpredictable. In fact, his eyes shifted around like he was considering whether to retract his agreement.

"Nothing permanent. But like you say, you've gotta learn the basics sometime. You're making a good start, though, that's for sure."

I beamed under his praise. "The scene was good for you, then?"

"Now you're just fishing. You know it was." He laughed. I really liked his genuine laugh—not the sarcastic one he trotted out a lot, but the real one that seemed to bubble up from deep inside his chest. "I'm not here for an ego trip. I'll tell you if you screw up."

"Good." I wanted that. I was serious about getting better at this, getting all I could from his experience. "And I'll think what you said about my look—"

"It's not a *look*." His tone was serious—the same one he'd used when he'd described how leather was in his soul. His words had been almost poetic. And I'd known instantly what he'd meant.

"I know." Sometimes I'd look at tattoo art or pictures of guys in leather and the longing would be almost palpable. I wanted that to be me—wanted the cool ink and the buttery soft leather wear, wanted to be the kind of guy who could do those things with confidence. In my obsession with older movies, that was always the type of hero I was drawn to—the give-no-fucks badass with a smart mouth and cool wardrobe. But fear had always held me back from trying it, and I'd worried too much about what others in my life would say. Seth was also so particular about his preppy menswear that he would have been horrified by my leather leanings. And my brief forays into the scene in Portland had shown me that there were plenty of people who would be fast to label me a poser even if I did try to embrace that side of myself.

"It's not about getting the right Halloween costume to be a Dom. You *are* a Dom. You did a fine job in those fancy pants of yours. It's about letting out whatever is inside you, projecting that to the world."

"I want that," I said with the force of years of trying to find the courage to venture out of my comfort zone. It felt like I'd spent my entire relationship with Seth suppressing my inner Dom, and now that side was demanding its turn in the sun.

"'Course some boots wouldn't hurt a damn thing." His mouth curved and it took me a second to realize it was a real smile, not one of the fake ones he pasted on pretty often.

"I own a pair," I admitted. "Leather pants, too. And I'm going to take the plunge, order some other gear."

His eyes lit up. "You're taking requests on that, right?"

"Absolutely."

"I love floggers. I can show you how to wield it, but after seeing you with a belt, I think you'll be a natural. Get yourself a nice balanced combo flogger for that empty toy box."

"It's not *completely* empty," I admitted. I seriously couldn't believe we were standing here in my side yard having this conversation. "I own bondage rope in a few different colors and thicknesses. I've done shibari work-shops, and I'm good with knots."

"Noted." He rubbed his beard. "How about we work up to that?"

Oh, I liked the sound of that, liked the idea of multiple lessons a lot. "Absolutely. I want to work with your limits and preferences."

"You sure are eager." He laughed again.

"So when should we start?" I checked out my phone. "I've only got about an hour before I've got to be back for the dinner rush."

"Ha." His pale eyes sparkled. It was a nice look on him, full of good humor. "Probably not long enough for a scene, but I did promise you a wood-stove lesson, and I think I owe you something."

"Oh?" Brushing off my arms and legs, I led the way to my side door, really hoping the "something" might be a kiss.

"First, the stove. Then, if we get it working, I owe

you a blow job. And lesson one, I want you to top the hell out of me while I do it."

I swallowed hard. That sounded *amazing*. And like nothing I'd ever had. "I can do that."

Conscious of time, I tried to pay attention as Curtis got the fire started in the wood-stove insert in the fire-place. I had some newspaper and kindling ready to go after the guy had come to inspect the stove last week, and Curtis added a few pieces from the wood we'd brought. He didn't make a terribly big blaze, as I had to leave soon. Also, we both seemed to have other things on our minds. No wonder there.

It did make the room instantly warmer, though the heat I was feeling was probably caused by the images Curtis had planted in my head. *I want you to top the hell out of me while I do it...*

I'd had some oral sex over the years, but I wasn't sure much of it would be considered me being dominant at all.

However, this was supposed to be a lesson, and I was game for trying out a few of my fantasies. I tossed the jacket I'd borrowed from Adam on the couch and remained standing. Curtis was still crouched, poking at the fire.

"I think that's good." He turned toward me with expectant eyes. *Game on.*

"You can stay on your knees." I gave myself permission to be as stern as I wanted. No need to worry about being nice. He liked harsh, and God knew, I liked delivering it.

He knee-walked the two steps between us until he was directly in front of me. Fuck. I liked him there. A lot.

"You want my cock?"

"Oh, yeah." He was breathing hard—and I knew it wasn't because of any effort in lighting the stove. I stroked his shoulders, stopping at a pressure point to dig in. "Mmmm. Ow. *Ah.*"

His eyes fluttered shut as he gave himself over to the sensation, leaning into the touch, torso brushing my legs. Damn, but I loved what a little pain did to this man. I used the grip to urge him closer. He rubbed his face against my pelvis.

"Get it out," I ordered. "I'm being nice, not binding your hands. Don't make me regret giving you use of them."

He moaned softly before undoing my belt and fly with deft fingers and tugging my cock out. I was rock hard and aching, just from having him like this.

"You said you're good?" I moved my hand from his shoulder to bury it in his hair which was thick and bushy and remarkably soft. I kept my grip light, in case this was a no-go zone like his neck. But he moaned again, deliberately moving against my palm.

"I am. Promise." His breath was warm against my dick. His tongue darted out, licking a stripe around my slick head. Fuck. His tongue was just as agile as his fingers.

"I want to go hard." I tightened my hand on his head to make my point clear.

"Yes," he panted. "Do it. Use my mouth."

All my fantasies split open, right there. Big guy, begging for my cock, hungry for me to take control. He sucked the tip of my cock into his warm mouth, beard tickling sensitive tissues. He held back from going further, eyes locked on mine, waiting. Rocking my hips, I slid forward, giving him plenty of time to decide he didn't want me to go too deep, but he welcomed me with a lusty growl, sucking hard. His hands on my hips tugged me deeper, until his lips were at my base.

"That's right, take it." I started a slow rhythm, both to learn what he was capable of and to keep from coming too fast. He had a very active mouth, sucking and licking, as I set the pace. "Put your hands behind your back."

He obeyed me immediately, clasping his hands at the small of his back. Even without binding him, it was a submissive position, one that put him more at my mercy as he couldn't send me signals with the grip of his hands on my hips. That compliance felt even better than his mouth. I liked being in control of things like sauces and my bicycle, liked it when situations went my way, but this, having another person let me direct them, willingly giving up the same control that I treasured, was a huge rush.

"Good. So good," I praised. "You want me to fuck your mouth? Go harder?"

He moaned his assent, so I sped up my thrusts, using my grip on his head to hold him steady. He seemed to like it when I tugged, groaning around my cock. He was sucking hard on each upstroke, chasing my cock, and no way was I going last.

"You want me to come? Show me how much."

Oh, yeah. He doubled down on his efforts like I'd handed him a bomb to defuse and a thirty-second timeline. His tongue did this flutter thing that was just *money* against my cockhead.

"Oh, fuck. That's it. You are so good for me. Gonna get me off."

He hummed his approval and that was all it took. I fucked hard and things got sloppy as we both lost finesse. I came with a low groan. My knees shook and my back spasmed as orgasm rocketed through me. *Power.* His position. His ready obedience. My hand in his hair. The freedom to fuck his face as fast and hard as I wanted, knowing it was what he wanted, too. All of it combined to make me feel as powerful as my first century ride, adrenaline spiking. The sensation was as unexpected as it was delicious, a new level to the familiar sensation of climaxing.

"Good. So good," I chanted as he sucked me through the aftershocks. When I got too sensitive, I pushed him away.

"Please." His hands were still behind his back, eyes closed, mouth swollen like we'd kissed for hours. He seemed to vibrate with need. Need that made me feel even better than the orgasm. Me taking charge had done this, had reduced him to this.

"You wanna come, too?" I stroked his hair, gentler now. "You did so damn good. You earned it. Go on, now, get your dick out."

"Thank you." His breath released in a whoosh as he wrenched his fly open, pulling his cock free. He stroked it with a frantic hand, like I might yank this reward away if he didn't do it fast enough.

I tightened my grip again, going from gentle to demanding. "Come on now. Come for me."

"Yes." He moved his head so I had no choice but to tug harder. "Fuck. That. Right there."

I reached down, got my other hand on his shoulder, and dug into the pressure point I'd started with.

"Fuck. Fuck. Fuck." He came all over his fist, breathing hard. I gentled my hands, stroking him through his shudders.

"Good. So good for me." I smoothed his hair back.

"God. Your thumbs should be registered weapons," he groaned. "And awesome touch with the hair-pulling. You've got this great way of reading what I'm up for. Keep those instincts."

Oh, yeah. I'd totally forgotten he was going to rate my performance, give me tips after. I'd gotten so caught up in the moment, I'd forgotten it was supposed to be a lesson. Felt real as hell, that was for sure.

"Thanks." I shrugged out of my T-shirt, offered it to him for cleanup, and gave him a hand up. I wanted to kiss him, taste my cum on his mouth, but he'd slipped into evaluation mode.

"Just so we're clear, praise kink isn't my thing, but you're good at it. You'd be great with a newbie sub with that."

I didn't want a newbie sub. I wanted *him*. Specifically, I wanted to collapse on the couch with him for some post-sex kissing and touching, but I'd asked for this so I just nodded. Also, I suspected that he liked the praise more than he was letting on—he'd sucked harder each time I'd complimented him and seemed to sink into my gentle touches as much as the harder ones. But I wasn't going to point that out.

"So…" He sized me up. "You gonna make that order? Give me a call when you've got some new toys to break in?"

"Absolutely." I had no doubt that he probably owned floggers and whatnot, assuming Troy had been kinky, but I sure as hell was neither asking nor wanting to use something of his dead lover's. I'd get right on the rapid shipping, soon as my shift was done. "And you're good with a leather flogger, right? No need to get a special vegan one?"

He laughed, low and lusty. "No. I fucking love leather. Fetish I guess you could say—I love the smell, the feel, the look. I know that's weird for a vegetarian, but I don't avoid meat out of a political statement."

"Oh? I always figured it was an environmentalist thing for you."

"Hardly. My old man was a big-time hunter and fisherman when he was sober and sometimes when he wasn't, and he insisted on taking me. And I've got the weakest stomach on the planet. It wasn't pretty. He kept making me go. I've got no problem with others eating meat, but the taste makes me gag."

"That's too bad. About your dad, I mean."

"Eh." He shrugged. "It was what it was. And the reason I go more full-on vegan than vegetarian is it's cheaper and easier on my gut. Never cared for eggs at all. And dairy and my wonky stomach don't get along the best."

"You should give me a list of foods that irritate your stomach—I do want to cook for you. And I'd hate to make anything worse."

"Kid. We're not doing a medical-intake form here. It's just food."

He'd said those words before, and it made me sad for him. I wanted to cook food for him that would transform his attitude, return joy with food for him. And I wanted to throttle his parents. His upbringing seemed dire and bleak and far removed from my own suburban security.

"Logan," I reminded him. "And one of these days, I'm going to change your mind."

He shook his head and sighed like I was pesky puppy. He leaned in and I thought I was finally about to get that kiss, but he just reached around me to retrieve his hat from the couch. Curtis might not think he wanted praise, gentleness, tasty food, and kisses, but I was going to find a way to work them all into our lessons, sooner rather than later.

Curtis

I was losing my damn mind. That was the only reason I could see for why I'd agreed to Logan's little plan, why I'd been on edge last few days, waiting for a text message from him. He'd specifically made sure I could get texts on my phone before we parted on Monday, and now I was checking the damn thing all the time like some teenager with a crush. Which I wasn't. And to be honest, the kid didn't really need my help.

He'd taken over that blowjob like a pro. I fucking loved giving head, but there was something about having my mouth owned and being controlled that made me rock hard. It was his voice that did it for me—he had this low, firm tone where it seemed to curve and caress me, same as his talented hands, demanding yet gentle at the same time. It was addictive, and I didn't do addictions.

I also didn't do dog and pony shows, and yet there I was Thursday morning, wearing clean, sawdust-free clothes, beard and hair reasonably tamed, ready to perform for the corporate man. Thanks to Mason and the guys at the tavern and their whole gay-tourism plan for Rainbow Cove, big investors were considering reviving the long-defunct resort on the edge of town. They had grand plans for a spa, putting green, renovated suites, upscale everything. All to appeal to happily coupled love-birds of the rainbow persuasion.

And because I did like the green color of that rain-bow, especially when attached to cold, hard cash, I was trying to get them to consider a major commission from me. The investors were meeting with various local arti-sans, looking for ideas for the grand lobby as well as smaller pieces for the more lavish suites and the spa. The Portland contingent, led by Mason's friend Brock, was scheduled to stop by around ten. They were starting their tour at one of the local galleries, and my hope was that they'd be sufficiently bored by Etta Garvis's paint-ings of the same damn Osprey nineteen ways that they'd be ready to talk wood.

My phone chirped right as I was reviewing my sketches. I'd never figured out how to make it vibrate or do something remotely pleasant with a text, so instead it made a sound not unlike one of Etta's damn Ospreys.

Packages arrived. You want to come over tonight around ten?

Damn, that was fast. And even through the phone I could sense his eagerness. Part of me wanted to hunt and peck out a reply right away. Wait. No addictions. I couldn't go getting all eager.

I made myself set the phone aside, wait impatiently for the corporate invasion.

The group considering the art arrived in a black Escalade. Mason's friend Brock introduced Naomi, who would be overseeing the project with him and eventually be manager of the resort, and Martin and Paul from the architect and interior design firms respectively.

"It's good to see you again." Brock had the sort of fake friendliness I despised. We'd met maybe three times, mostly at Chamber of Commerce meetings, which I also disliked. "What do you have for us?"

I showed off my current selection of sculptures, most of which were outside, under the awning. "This is what I do. I carve. Large pieces mainly. I did some sketches for you of things I'm thinking for your lobby."

I hated how my hand shook on my sketchbook, hated how I felt in the face of these fancy-pants people with their big degrees and expensive suits and narrow gazes.

"Anything with *color*?" Naomi cast a skeptical eye on the largest of my current pieces, a giant eagle emerging from a stump.

"I let the natural woodgrain show. I've never painted my work." I tried to be diplomatic, but my distaste must have shown because she frowned further.

"I'm not sure whether the rustic trend is still in," Paul added. "We wouldn't want to date our look."

"A big installation is timeless. Iconic, you might call it. I'm not talking little pieces." I waved a hand at my selection. "I'm talking big. Dominating."

I finally got them to glance at my sketches, but it was hard to read their blank faces. They probably taught that look at fancy-pants school, handing out disdain right alongside the MBA. What I'd been visualizing was an installation in the center of the lobby, my biggest yet, numerous pieces combining to create a nature scene with local birds, bears, trees, even a fish or three. It wasn't so much the money that had me nervous — I'd seldom wanted a commission more because of the driving desire to craft this installation. My sketches had taken hold of my imagination, and that need to create had me on edge. I wanted this, and I tried hard to not want much in this life.

"And the price?" Brock gave me what I supposed was an encouraging smile.

I quoted a number that darn near made my already tetchy stomach want to hurl. It would be my biggest commission, but I also wasn't going to undersell myself. I had numerous carving championships under my belt, and the guys at the big championships charged staggering prices compared to me. Plus, wood kept going up in price. And I'd want the absolute best for this piece. The group nodded, not reacting to the number.

"We're considering a number of directions for the lobby." Naomi explained what I already knew. "We'll be in touch soon."

I nodded and walked them back to the car, trying to calm the roiling in my gut. Fuck. I hated feeling like this. Small. Desperate. Eager. Just like the kid…

Wait. That was it. I knew exactly what I needed. Soon as the Escalade disappeared down 101, I found my phone. A good scene would push all these feelings aside, get me settled back into myself, make my skin thicker, so to speak — I needed to shrug off this all-consuming want. If the investors went a different direction, so be it.

Wasn't personal. Except it felt like it might be, and that just wouldn't do.

I'll be there, I typed and hit send before I could second-guess myself. Logan would help me set this right. Only trick would be not needing him more than I needed that commission.

NINE

Logan

I worked until nine and rushed home to set the scene for Curtis. It didn't matter that this was technically a lesson. I still wanted it good for him.

I laid out everything we'd need in the bedroom. I told myself doing the scene there instead of the living room made sense because the bed would be easier to work around than the couch, but the truth was that I wanted Curtis in my space, wanted my sheets to smell like him, wanted the chance of sleeping together afterward.

He'd said he liked the idea of me in boots, so I ignored my bad memories of the scene in Portland and put on my heavy black boots and leather pants. If leather was truly a fetish for him, I might as well get over myself and indulge him. I knew I was going to get sweaty during the session, so I skipped a shirt again. That, and the wood stove had my little place nice and toasty.

Curtis knocked on the door right at ten. His heated gaze made me happy I'd gone with the leather look.

"Nice. I like the boots. We gotta get you a vest or a harness to match."

"I'll consider it." Also under consideration? How I should greet him as I ushered him into the house. We still hadn't kissed, and that seemed presumptuous for a hello. And I knew without asking that Curtis wasn't usually a hugger. So instead, I held out my hands for his coat, a black leather motorcycle jacket instead of his more-often-used plaid flannel one. Under it, he wore a close-fitting black tee and black jeans. "I've got everything ready in the bedroom, unless you're hungry, in which case I've got vegan apple crisp for you."

"Eager." He laughed. "I'm good on food. Let's see what the mailman brought you."

I'd stripped the bed down to a clean sheet and lowered the lights in the bedroom—bright enough that I'd be able to see what I was doing, but dim enough to be soothing. My purchases were arranged on the sheet— three different floggers, each with different properties, a paddle, and some quick-release cuffs.

"Well. Someone was busy." Curtis picked up the softest of the floggers, one made from deer leather. "This one is good for warming up the skin, but for real bite, you'll want to use one of these." He motioned to the two combo flog-gers—made with a combination of suede and oiled leather, one with twenty shorter falls, the other with forty longer ones. "Good quality. You wanna see the difference in feel?"

"You want to test them on *me*?"

"Of course. You need to know what the sensations are that you're creating. I'm not going to give you a long flogging, but you should let me demo each."

"I've practiced with the belt on my legs some—I know what pain feels like."

"Good. Now you'll know what this feels like, too." He motioned for me to get on the bed. I'd had a plan for this evening and being a test dummy wasn't it, but at the same time, I didn't want him calling it off, either.

Don't be a wimp. "Okay." I stretched out on the bed next to the implements.

"You look like you're headed to the electric chair. Trust me. I'm not going to take advantage here. One stroke of each, right across the upper back, no wrapping."

"Wrapping?" Him telling me what to expect helped. I loved his voice, the way it reassured without being patronizing. And he had a really good point—I should know what this felt like to my sub. I trusted him, more than I did a lot of people, actually. Given that I was asking him to trust me a lot more, being willing to try this seemed like less of a big deal.

"Wrapping is when you accidentally catch the sides of the body, and it stings like crazy. Try to avoid that— I'm enough of a pain junkie that I don't mind it as much as some, but it can jar even me."

"Okay." I tried to sound resolute.

"This is the all-suede soft one." He danced the falls around on my back, tickling me. "Knowing you, you probably already practiced on some pillows."

I snorted because he wasn't wrong, and I wasn't sure I liked him knowing me so well.

"So this is a regular hit—I'm not going all-out, but I do want you to feel it." He snapped the flogger back, and

I braced for the impact. It wasn't terrible—it stung like sunburn but faded very quickly.

"Not bad," I managed.

"Ha." He rubbed my shoulder. "You don't have to like it. But you see that light sting with a little thud behind it? That's what the sub feels. You're not going to get a ton of sting or thud with this soft one, even if you go hard, but you'll see with the next flogger, too—a lot more of each sensation. You can feel the difference. This is the twenty-fall, short flogger. I'm aiming right for your shoulder blade—this one's easier to target a particular area."

He cracked the flogger and I hissed in a breath even before it hit. It stung like crazy—like a slap with sandpaper, but again, not unbearable.

"So start softer with that one and move around?" I asked when I could speak without fear of squeaking.

"Yeah. Use this one in a more targeted way. And now we'll try the last one—it's my favorite kind. Lots of heavy falls, lots of sting, great thud. Enough of this and you'll really feel it. The number of falls spreads out the sensations, makes it easier to take much more."

I knew this one was going to hurt, but he dragged the tails up and down my back a few times before drawing back and releasing a blow.

"Ow. Fucker." This time I couldn't stop the curse. So much for seeming tough.

"Yup. That one's got some bite to it." Curtis sounded pleased with himself. "Okay. Up with you. Whack the pillow a few times so I can see you're not wrapping the falls, and then you can get even with me."

"Oh, yeah." I rocketed off the bed. I let him correct

my stance and grip, same as I'd let an instructor at an aikido class direct me, but inside I was itching to get on with it. He made me hit the pillow more than a few times, clucking when the falls wrapped or I snapped too fast.

"Okay," he said at last, pausing to finger the Velcro cuffs on the bed. "What about these? You wanting to cuff me to the headboard?"

"They're quick release," I explained, demonstrating. "You can just flick them with your thumb to get free, but I thought they might be a fun warm-up to doing bondage sometime."

"You sure are fired up to get to the rope, aren't you?" He laughed and ruffled my hair. Him back to treating me like a cute-but-annoying kid was the final straw. I was getting it cut that week.

"You're going to look amazing all tied up," I countered. And he would. All those muscles and tats at my disposal, dark rope crisscrossing his flesh. I couldn't wait.

"Flattery's going to get you nowhere. But I suppose we can try the cuffs."

"I'll make it good," I promised. "Now strip."

And this would be good. I'd make sure of it.

Curtis

I could tell the exact instant the kid shifted from lesson to scene, voice going lower and harder, spine stiffening as he ordered me to strip. After sitting on the bed to remove my boots, I pulled off my clothes and waited for his next instruction.

"On the bed, knees or stomach, your choice, but arms in front of you." He didn't disappoint, giving me more of that deliciously sinful voice. And I liked that he gave me a choice. Seemed to be his style, to allow a little play, even as he seized the reins.

I chose to lay on my stomach, both to give him a better target, and because I wanted to drift on the sensations and not have to worry about holding a position too long. Logan fastened the cuffs around my wrists before attaching them to the wrought iron headboard. He fussed, getting me a pillow for my head and upper body, testing the restraints to make sure they held, running a finger around the edge to check circulation. One thing about the kid, he sure was thorough.

Then he did the oddest thing—he dropped kisses down my spine before straightening. Damn. That felt as nice as the soft flogger would, but I needed him to not go getting any romantic ideas.

"God, you look so good, laid out for me like this." He stroked down my sides before picking up the softest of the floggers. Proving himself a fast study, he repeated what I'd done—dragging the tails up and down my back to tease—before drawing back. The first blow was a soft one, but he quickly followed it with more, dialing up the volume of intensity with each pass until he found his stride.

I moaned as the sensations built, tugging on the cuffs to keep myself steady. I didn't want to wiggle too much while he was still figuring out the flogger, but he seemed attuned to my slightest motion. He was so damn good at reading me, figuring out what I wanted. And what I wanted was exactly what he settled into—an unpredictable, not-too-hard rhythm that warmed my skin up slowly, awakening new nerve endings with each hit.

He'd been damn cute when practicing blows on the pillow, but turned loose on my body he was nothing short of masterful, each stroke of the flogger getting me closer and closer to that blissful place where I no longer had to think.

"You can go harder." I wanted more, wanted to get there sooner, wanted him to chase the last of the cobwebs of this long day out of my head.

"Lesson part is done," he said firmly. "I'm in charge right now. And I love going slow like this. Your skin is just starting to turn the best shade of pink."

"It's not a sunset," I grumbled.

"It is to me." Without warning, he snapped the flogger hard, more sting than thud.

"Fuck." I liked how the sting started sharp and then eased into something hot, making my nerve endings sing. He repeated the motion again, making me crazy trying to predict where the sting would land next.

"I'm switching to one of the other two. But you have to guess which it is."

"Mmm. Okay." My brain was pleasantly fuzzy, like I'd had a few shots. I figured he'd do the same order I did, so I was braced for the swift, localized impact of the smaller flogger. I wasn't prepared for the harsh lick of all forty long falls against my already sensitive skin. "Fuck. Fuck."

The next blow did weird things to my wiring, made me go cold and hot at the same time, and sweat broke out on my skin.

"Well? Which is it?"

"Forty...falls." My words were slow to cooperate.

"Very good." His praise washed over me, finding every tender spot, soft as silk. "You're so good for me. Ready for more?"

"Fuck, yes." I could tell from his tone that he was going to go harder, and I both dreaded the bite of the falls even as I craved it. I liked that he wasn't doing the counting game again, instead dropping blows with random, sharp stings on already heated muscles.

Sizzle. A particularly hard strike landed right across my back piece tat, and the sharpness faded into a deep, lingering pain. And fuck. I was there. Floating. Another blow came, and it barely registered. This was the place I craved. No more thinking, just existing from electric touch to electric touch, the pain both grounding me and setting me free to soar. I was glad for the cuffs as they were the only thing keeping me from melting into the mattress.

"So beautiful." Logan was murmuring praise even as he moved to the other side of the bed, working me over from the opposite direction. I rocked my hips, grinding into the mattress, not seeking to come, not yet, but it simply felt so good to move, to spread the sensations out, letting the bite of the flogger translate into good feelings for my dick, letting the pleasure and pain mingle. I lived for each new hit, moaning during the wait for the next strike. This was my drug, my church, my everything.

"Okay, okay." The mattress sagged as he knelt next to me. He squeezed my ass, and I moaned, wanting more of the flogger. "You've done so fabulous. Tell me what you need. You want to come?"

"You can fuck me." My words were slurred. I

honestly wasn't sure what I wanted, just that I needed him, needed more, never wanted to come down from this session.

"Nope." He slapped my ass lightly. "We didn't talk about changing that limit beforehand, and besides, when I fuck you, you're going to be begging for it, not just giving me permission."

"Want whatever you want." My voice was demanding, a needy thing I didn't recognize.

"Good answer. I'm going to use the smaller flogger now, and I want you to keep rubbing off on the bed. Get yourself off, and then I want to come all over your marks."

"Yes. Please." I wanted that, wanted his cum on me, wanted that mark, too. And knowing he wasn't going to stop until I came was freeing. No counting. No waiting games. I loved rubbing off while getting flogged, and his permission had me groaning even before the first hit. The smaller flogger lit me up, sharp flicks of pain on top of the earlier blows.

"That's it, gorgeous. Let it feel good," he urged. "Fuck. I wish there was a way to beat you and suck you off at the same time."

I was almost too far gone to laugh, and a harsh barking sound escaped my throat. "More. Harder."

My dick dragged against the smooth cotton of his sheets, some impossibly soft blend, and I was so close. The need to get fucked was building in me, and I let out a frustrated moan.

"Want it. Want you to fuck me."

"Yeah? You still want that when you're not flying high on sub space, then next time, I'm going to fuck you so good. After I flog you senseless again. Fuck, but I love you like this. All strung out for me."

His next targeted strike landed across the deeper blows on my upper back. "Close. So close."

"Do it. Come for me." The smaller flogger dropped next to me on the bed, and I almost sobbed with relief as he picked up the big one. Hard, rapid-fire blows now, sending me rocketing back into that blissful, empty place. I didn't need to come. I could live forever right here. But my body had different ideas, hips bucking hard as he urged me on.

"Now. Come now," he ordered, landing a vicious strike on my shoulders. And I was powerless, body obeying him, the sensation of my climax starting in my toes, working up my calves and legs, balls lifting and tightening, then cock spasming as I came all over the bed. I shuddered over and over, relief, pleasure, and pain all mingling, the most potent of highs. I was barely aware of the sound of his zipper, him kneeling on the mattress again, the slap-slap of his hand on his cock.

"Fuck, your back is so gorgeous. Wearing my marks. Love the sounds you make."

"Come on me." If I couldn't get a fuck, this was the next best thing, him marking me this way, too. I loved knowing the scene had turned him on so much, that I had pleased him.

"Fuck. Yes. Yes," he chanted as hot cum hit my raw skin, making me moan again with an aftershock of my own.

He collapsed next to me, face slack with pleasure. But he didn't stay down long at all, going back into fuss mode, unhooking my cuffs, rubbing my wrists and fingers before cleaning off my back with a damp towel. He had more of the herbal scented lotion he'd used last time, and he applied it with gentle fingers. I didn't like how damn good it felt, his touch and soft words of praise.

"I really don't need all the aftercare," I grumbled.

"Yeah? Well, maybe I do," he retorted. "I'm not sure I can do this without it, actually. This is a big part of it for me, taking care of you afterward. It makes me feel good inside, like I gave you exactly what you needed and like I'm…I dunno…*rewarding* you."

He had given me what I needed, in ways I hadn't even expected, but I didn't say that. "You're the first one I've met with a kink for aftercare."

"Is it that bad?" His hands kept working in more of the soothing lotion.

It was on the tip of my tongue to say yes, to make him stop. But something held me back.

"Nah. Knock yourself out." I was supposed to be helping him become a good Dom, and he was going to be amazing for some sub. Someone who deserved nice words and gentle touches and all this praise. I wanted to gut-punch this nameless sub already, but I also didn't want to quash all the goodness out of the kid. The world needed more like him, even if I didn't.

So I made myself not protest his caring. But I also tried not to like it. It would be only too easy to come to need this. To crave it more than the scene. To come to depend on him would be the stupidest thing I could do, and yet, I still felt myself sinking into the blissful post-session haze, wrapping his affection around me even though it was sure to carry a price.

TEN

Logan

We'd had three sexual encounters, but Curtis and I had never kissed. This was starting to really bug me, especially after he'd done another middle-of-the-night exit.

After I'd taken care of him, I'd stripped and settled in beside him on the bed, intending to only rest while watching over him, making sure he didn't have any sub drop. I'd read about that, and it sounded nasty. I'd figured I'd get him to eat the food I'd made for him as a midnight snack or maybe take it with him if he was intent on leaving fast after his nap. And I'd been planning on a goodbye kiss.

But he'd looked so peaceful dozing there that I'd ended up drifting off, too. When I woke up later, he was gone. No way was I giving up on our lessons, though— there was still so much I wanted to do with him. Kissing. Bondage rope. Fucking. When he'd offered fucking, I'd been very tempted to take him up on it. But he'd been flying in sub space—glassy eyes, slurred words, limp muscles—and the last thing I wanted to do was ignore his limits and have him regret it later.

Thanks again for the lesson. I had food for you, I texted him in the morning before heading to the tavern. *Want me to drop it by?*

His reply didn't come till I was in the tavern parking lot. *I'm good.*

I groaned aloud. Of course he was fine. Of course he didn't need me. Of course he didn't want my food. Or aftercare, for that matter. And that had turned out to be one of my favorite parts, taking care of my sub. Sure, I apparently had a sadistic streak, and I did love marking his skin, hearing his groans, and watching him writhe, but a big part of it for me was the trust. He trusted me to make it good, to not go too far. That kind of trust was awe-inspiring and humbling. And I had loved rewarding that trust, lavishing gratitude on the sub, and reminding myself that I wasn't some kind of monster. I was a Dom, doing what his sub needed.

But in all my fantasies and plans I'd never pictured a sub as contradictory as Curtis. He pushed me. Tested me. And I wanted more. However, I wasn't going to force my attentions on him, either, so I didn't reply right away. I locked up the bike and headed into the kitchen.

"You're later than usual," Mason observed. He was making bread, which was part of our morning routine. I handled most menu items, and he baked any buns and breads necessary for my creations.

"Overslept." I wasn't going to claim a busy night. My arrangement with Curtis obviously wasn't for public consumption.

"Good for you. You work too hard. We need to get you a hobby or something." He offered me a tight smile as he dumped dough ingredients into the industrial mixer.

I have one. If he knew the amount of time I spent studying kink, he'd probably laugh himself silly. Which was why I wasn't ever telling him.

"I've got enough." I shrugged. "And I'm lucky to love my work. How many people get to say that?"

"True enough. And speaking about loving what we do, have you spoken to your parents yet?"

"This week's been busy. I was waiting for a good time to broach the topic with them."

"Could you?" Mason flipped the mixer on. "I'm going through the bills, and it's carnage in there. I know Adam would probably rather you toss in the rest of your inheritance, but we can't completely drain you. It might be better to take on a more formal investment."

"It's Friday, so my dad is probably working from home. I'll call in a moment," I promised.

"I've got a business plan to show them, numbers and estimates, all that." As we worked, Mason discussed the amount he thought we needed, the advertising he wanted to do with the cash infusion, and the state of the bills.

After he got the dough shaped and rising and headed back to his small office, I made the call I'd been putting off. My dad picked up quickly, as I'd known he would. It was rare for him or Mom to make me wait. We covered the pleasantries. Yes, I was enjoying myself. Yes, I was eating well. Yes, I was making friends. The last wasn't as much of a stretch as it had been the previous time we'd talked. Curtis counted as a new friend, right? I mean, he was one I couldn't tell anyone about, but he had to qualify as something more than an acquaintance.

"How's business?" I asked. My dad ran a company that dealt with digital medical records—I'd never completely understood what they did, but it kept our family comfortable.

"Excellent. We landed a few new contracts recently, so that will keep us busy." There was a squeaking sound like he was leaning back in his chair. "Can't wait until spring. These winter rides are brutal. How are you holding up?"

"Managing. Not getting as many miles as I was in the fall, though." We shared a love of road biking. One of my favorite memories was the summer he surprised me with a trip to watch the Tour de France.

"Still haven't found a local dojo for your aikido? I ran into Master Duncan at Whole Foods recently—he and the rest of the dojo miss you. As do we."

"I miss you, too. But we're doing good work here. My menu has been getting raves."

"I'm sure it is. Can't wait to hear what comfort foods you're bringing to the gray days. And you know who else would probably love to hear about your menu?"

"I'm not talking to Seth right now."

As usual Dad ignored me before continuing. "I saw him at his parents' New Year's party. He was alone—"

"We're not getting back together." Both my parents had been so thrilled when Seth's family had moved in junior year. It was all just so perfect—our dads golfed together, our moms shopped, and Seth and I were a matched pair. Except for the part where he was a master emotional manipulator, undercut my self-confidence, didn't like any of the things I liked in the bedroom, and took years to get free from thanks to almost a decade of insincere apologies and parental pressure.

"You were such a *good* couple." Dad sighed. "And he always loved your cooking. Which is just one more thing your mom and I miss, too. No one around here does a burger like you. What would you say to us coming down next weekend? Drive down Thursday night, and then go back Sunday."

They'd already visited me a few times since I made the move, so I wasn't surprised by the request. He'd treated me to a flight home with a local charter from Coos Bay for Christmas so I wouldn't have to make the five-hour drive.

"That would be excellent, actually, because the guys and I wanted to talk to you about something. What would you think about investing in the restaurant?" I tried to channel my new confidence into this conversation, but instead I felt like a thirteen-year-old asking for a raise in allowance.

"Oh, Logan, you know we'd love to help, but if the business is struggling, maybe it's time for you to look for chef positions closer to home? Or perhaps you'd like to think about going back to school?" Although they'd paid for culinary school and suffered through all my cooking experiments in junior high and high school, my parents had made it clear they'd wanted me to attend a four-year university and have a more typical college experience. Like Seth had. Never mind that that was the last thing I wanted.

"I want to make this work." There. I managed some

firmness to my tone. "I love what we're building here. Let me show you when you come."

"I do love hearing you so enthusiastic. I'll keep an open mind about investing when we come down, but I want you to keep an open mind, too. Think about whether cutting your losses and coming back here might be the best choice for you. I worry about you, down there in the middle of nowhere."

"Dad. I can't abandon—"

"And it doesn't have to be an either-or thing. We could invest in your friends' business, and you could come back home. Where you fit in more. We miss you terribly."

Jesus. If it wasn't Mason and Adam worrying about how I could handle myself, it was my parents.

"I get along just fine," I lied. It wasn't like I could tell them how I'd felt like a poser with the leather night crowd or how I'd levelled Leroy. And truth was, the preppy look that I'd mimicked from Dad and Seth really didn't fit in as much around here with all the flannel and canvas and denim. I was more than ready for a change, and Curtis's words had been the kick I needed, but Dad wasn't going to understand.

"I just worry. Humor your old man. At least think about seeing if there are more openings than last time you looked?"

No. Somehow I couldn't make the word come out, and an "I'll see," popped out. *Weak.* "But you'll consider investing?"

"I'll talk to my broker, see what's liquid right now, and I'll let you and your friends give me the pitch when we come down."

"Good." I hated how I forever felt like a little kid with my dad. He loved me. I loved him. But I just needed *someone* to see me as a capable adult. Hell, even Curtis, with all his "kid" business, seemed to have a hard time with that concept unless we were in the middle of a scene. And since I couldn't be in a scene 24/7, it was about...how had Curtis put it? Projecting the me on the inside to the outside world. Maybe it was time to put more effort into that. Take more risks.

Curtis

I managed to avoid the kid until Tuesday. It meant turning Nash down for a weekend lunch, but seeing as how I didn't want to trip his curiosity about Logan, it was probably all for the best. And I knew I was being a bit of a coward, avoiding the kid, but our last session had rattled me. I'd woken up to him all cuddled my side, and I'd liked it. I'd wanted to stay, and that wouldn't do. So yeah, I was laying low.

But Tuesday afternoon Logan showed up at my place. He was on the bike, and he pulled off his helmet and grabbed a container out of his saddle bag contraption before walking over to my work area. I'd been cleaning up the carving on a troll, a bit of whimsy for a customer with a big garden over near Eugene.

"I need a taste tester," he announced. "The guys are sick of hearing about my ideas for the Valentine's dinner, and I need an opinion on my vegetarian option."

"You know my opinion is that Valentine's is bunk. Just serve salad or something. The couples will be too busy thinking about getting laid later to care." I tried not to let on how nice it was to see him. Being cranky was easier than giving in to the urge to hug him.

"I hate the holiday, too. But we need the business." He leaned against the awning's column.

"You? Hate Valentine's day?" I would have figured him for the hopeless romantic type, dreaming up special surprises and pining for someone to spoil.

He sighed and looked away. "Some kids played a horrible practical joke on me back in junior high. Ruined the holiday for me. And then Seth—my ex—always claimed it was too commercial and never wanted to celebrate. Seems like a big excuse for people to get hurt feelings."

"Little bastards. Junior high is the worst." I instantly hated those kids. Logan was too nice to be so cynical. *Look who's talking.*

"Eh. It's okay. But anyway, I need you to taste this butternut squash ravioli, tell me if I'm on the right track. It's still warm." He held out the plastic container and a disposable fork. His guarded expression said he was expecting me to turn him down flat.

Which was why I found myself accepting the food, opening the lid. It smelled heavenly—like sage and garlic with sweet undercurrents.

"I suppose I could take a taste," I allowed, telling myself it was only polite, like accepting one of Janice's offerings.

"Thank you." He beamed at me, and I noticed his fuzzy upper lip and chin for the first time.

"What's up with your face?" I asked as I got a forkful. "You lose your razor?"

"I'm trying to grow a goatee. So far it's just a lot of itchy stubble, but I think it'll look cool. Eventually."

"This is why I don't shave the beard. Regrowth sucks." I laughed before tasting the food. And damn, I barely suppressed a moan. It was that good. Velvety sauce. Sweet, well-seasoned filling. Pillowy pasta.

"Good?" he asked, still smiling.

"It'll do. Be sure to charge decent for it. Feels like fancy Portland food, so it probably needs a fancy price." I ate another forkful. Damn. This stuff was amazing.

"Fancy's excellent." His sly grin said he hadn't missed how I was wolfing it down. "Anything I should change?"

"Bigger portions." I couldn't help the joke. Just couldn't. Something about him cut past all my grumpy barriers.

"Awesome." God, his smile could power the whole coast. He rubbed at his chin. "And so this itchy-face phase passes?"

"Yup." I laughed again. I seemed to do that a lot around him. "You're not doing it because I gave you a hard time, right? Your face is fine without it."

It was as close as I was gonna get to saying he was damn cute.

"Nah. I've been thinking about changing my look for a long time, actually. You were more like the push I needed. Now I've gotta get my hair cut. I might have to drive up to Coos Bay—all the places in town seem to cater to the perm-and-color crowd."

"Hell, you just want it short? I've got clippers. I can save you the twenty and the trip, do it now."

"Really? That would be awesome. I've been thinking military short, like some of the guys I've seen at aikido competitions. Not bald, but no more floppy in my face, either."

"I can do that." I really couldn't say why I was offering a reason for him to stay longer. I supposed I just wanted to thank him for the food. "Let me go grab them. We can do it out here, keep the mess with all the sawdust that needs sweeping anyway."

I finished the last of the food and headed inside to get the clippers from my bathroom, bringing them, a towel, a mirror, and a selection of blade covers back outside.

"Sit." I indicated a stump I had yet to carve. It was near the electrical outlets on the side of the building. "You serious about this? It's just hair, and it'll grow, but you don't need to go proving anything."

"Maybe I want to prove it to myself." His mouth was a narrow line as he sat. "Let's do this."

"Okay." I draped the towel over his jacket. "I'm going to start with the longest setting, then you can decide how much more you want me to take off."

"Cool. My parents are going to freak when they see me. They're coming this weekend."

I paused with the clippers in the air. "Your folks are coming?"

"Yeah. And before you can ask again, I'm sure. Get on with it."

"Bossy." I started with the back of his head.

"Speaking of my parents, I might bring them around on Friday or Saturday. I'm trying to show them more of the area."

"I don't do meet-the-parents," I said firmly. "That's not what...this is."

"Simmer down." He rolled his eyes. "Didn't say I

wanted them to meet *you*. My mom's really into art, and I thought she'd find your stuff interesting. Maybe get you a sale."

"Business is fine," I lied. "Don't need you stumping for me."

"Well, you happen to add some local color. If you're carving outside like you do, she'll find that fascinating. And I'm trying to get them to invest in the area. I need them to have a fun weekend. So you can just deal." He trotted out his bedroom voice, all confident and commanding.

"Suit yourself." I was careful to not take my frustration out on his head, making neat passes and sending his blond hair raining to the concrete. "You guys need the investment to keep going?"

"Yeah." His voice was resigned. "Mason probably wouldn't be happy with me telling you, so keep it under your hat. My parents could help if they weren't so freaking worried about me fitting in here."

"What do they care?" I went slow around his ear. "You fit in just fine."

"Thanks." The back of his neck flushed. "And they're just protective. They know what a hard time I had in school. That prank I mentioned? That wasn't half of it. The bullying started in junior high and kept up into high school."

"Kids can suck." I hated the thought of anyone picking on my— No. Not my guy. *Not gonna start down that path.* "That why you started karate?"

"Yeah. My parents thought it would help my confidence. And it did. But the bullies didn't care—they kept up their vendetta until they finally got expelled sophomore year. It was miserable, and my parents are always worried that I won't find friends. They were so relieved when I met Seth that it wasn't funny. And then they were a wreck when I moved to Portland, worrying all over again."

"They can't keep you safe forever," I said even though I wished I could go back in time, keep him safe from the damn bullies, make sure no one ever crushed his sunny spirit. My heart ached for his younger self.

"I know. It's a bit...smothering at times. They love me, but it's exhausting being the center of their universe."

"I'm sure." I really couldn't imagine. I'd been so far from the center of my parents' world that it wasn't funny.

"Sorry. I shouldn't be unloading on you about my past."

"It's fine." I meant it. Hearing him talk made my stomach warm, and I ate up the little details about his life even if I wanted to go knock some teeth out over his hurts.

"Anyway, I'm glad you enjoyed the food. You're my toughest customer, so that means something."

"Oh, I am not." I wasn't sure I fit that label. "I don't mean to be picky."

"You are." He laughed. "I get it. You like what you like."

"No. That's not it." I steadied my hand as I shaped the hair on the crown of his head. His hair was so soft and silky that I could happily mess with it all day. "I'm trying hard *not* to be picky, see?"

"How's that work?" He sounded genuinely baffled.

"You've never been poor." I didn't say it as a curse,

just truth. "I mean, really poor. Not sure where food's coming from or when it'll be there again. I learned early on not to become attached to food. No point in having a favorite cereal or flavor of ice cream when you never have it. And pining for more than what you've got is pointless. So between my stomach and being poor, I try not to get all worked up over food. Long as there's some in front of me, I'm good."

"That's so sad. No one should have to be hungry. Ever. But you've got enough now, right?"

"Yeah. I get by. My garden sees to that."

"Then why not let yourself enjoy food? It can be such a pleasure. And pleasure is good, right?"

Of course, the king of aftercare was going to think that. For all he liked to dish out a hurt, he wasn't one to hold back on indulgence and little luxuries.

"Can't go getting dependent. Soft. I don't want to start needing something only to have it ripped away," I admitted. I'd never said that aloud to another soul before, and admitting the fear had me feeling like the air temperature dropped twenty degrees.

"Oh, Curtis." Logan frowned. "That's awful. I'm so sorry you got such a raw deal. That sucks, not trusting the world."

"Since when has it given me reason?" I scoffed. "It gave me shitty parents. Shitty school years. Gave me the best man in the cove only to rip him away. Explain to me again how I'm supposed to trust the world?"

"I'm…not sure." His voice was smaller, all that confidence gone, and I missed it immediately.

"Sorry. It's the truth. The world and me, we don't get

along." I softened my tone. "But you go right on believing in the good. World needs more like you."

"Thanks. Except the world needs *you,* too. Even if you don't think so."

"Ha." I dusted off his ears and shoulders. "That should do it. Take a look." I held out the mirror. He'd been cute as a teen pop star before, adorable really. But now, he was hot as fuck. If he asked me. Which he didn't, and I wasn't about to volunteer the compliment, either.

"I love it." He turned his head this way and that. The long lines of his face and neck were much more evident now, good bone structure giving him an air of authority he hadn't had before. The goatee was only going to enhance things. Make him look older. Tougher. More like the person he was in the bedroom. And why that made me a little sad, I couldn't say. Wasn't like I could keep him all to myself forever.

He might be my favorite secret, but like I'd told him, I knew all too well the perils of becoming attached. Our eyes caught, gratitude and approval shining in his, God-knew-what in mine. His head tipped against my shoulder, and it would have been so easy to kiss him. Too easy.

"We should probably get you back to work," I said gruffly, moving away. I didn't let myself look to see if there was disappointment in his face. There was plenty of that, down deep in my soul. I didn't need to add his. Keeping him from getting too attached was a kindness. Really. And maybe someday I'd even believe that.

ELEVEN

Logan

Curtis didn't invite me in for a fuck after the haircut, not that I'd expected him to. I'd needed to get back to prep for the dinner rush, and he'd seemed spooked by our near kiss, so it wasn't the time to press. And yes, he'd been about to kiss me, and we both knew it. He liked me a lot more than he wanted to let on, so I was content to let him go back to being gruff. I'd wear him down eventually. And speaking of Mr. "It's Just Food," my heart broke every time I thought of his childhood self, scared to have a favorite cereal. I wanted to shower him with the tastiest food, make sure he always had an abundance of whatever it was he wanted most, the secret desires he hadn't shared yet.

But he didn't text Tuesday or Wednesday, which left me all antsy by Thursday night when my parents arrived late after I'd finished at the tavern. They'd both worked full days and then headed out afterward, making them cranky and tired as I welcomed them into my house.

"Logan. What did you do to yourself?" My mother could not have sounded more dismayed than if I'd been in a full-body cast. "Your gorgeous hair!"

Ah, yes. She was probably the reason I'd had essentially the same haircut from two to twenty-seven, only varying in degrees of shagginess.

"It was time for a change." I tried to sound decisive, but I had a feeling we'd be revisiting this several times over the course of the weekend.

"You look like a Wanted poster." My father's critical eyes swept over me, taking in the hair and the growing goatee, my faded jeans, white T-shirt, and heavy boots. I'd been wearing the boots more, finding them more comfortable for long kitchen hours than the sneakers.

"It's just hair." I tried to channel Curtis's attitude.

"It'll grow." Dad sighed. "I guess we should be grateful you never went through the blue hair and tattoos phase like so many kids."

"I don't know. A tat might be cool." I dipped my toe into waters I planned to tread in the near future. She'd hate it, but it was past time that I stopped letting her opinions on my appearance matter so damn much.

"Logan. Stop joking." Mom shook her head at me. "You have the most gorgeous skin. Cover models would kill for your complexion and tone."

"Mom. Please." I led the way to the second bedroom that I'd turned into a basic guest room—queen bed, bed-in-a-bag set I'd ordered online, and some prints from *The Endless Summer* and *The Beach* on the wall. It was nothing like their well-appointed master suite back home, but they said they were happier staying with me than at the B&B.

Luckily, they were both tired after the long drive, and they went to bed shortly. I thought about texting Curtis, just to check in, but then I thought about how I'd feel if he didn't respond, so I didn't.

In the morning, I took them with me to the tavern, where Mason delved deep into facts and figures for Dad, laying out the business plan, the funding we'd already had, the advertising he wanted to do with a cash influx.

Dad didn't immediately say yes—he wanted to think about it. He needed to check in with his office and get some reports done, so he and Mom worked from my place, and after the lunch rush died down, I took them for a drive around the area. We went up to Moosehead Lake and then took the beach road, appreciating the bluffs and coastal views. Back in town, I pointed out all the small businesses, trying to impress them with the local character. We visited one of the art galleries, and Mom bought a painting of some ospreys.

Although chilly, it wasn't raining, so after stowing the painting in the trunk of Dad's Lexus, we walked down the row of shops on 101—stopping in the taffy place, the wind-chime store, and the jewelry gallery. Playing tourist was kind of fun, but I really just wanted them to love this place as much as I was coming to love it. And commit to helping the business. I didn't want to have to go back to Mason empty-handed.

From the upscale jewelry place, I could see Curtis's converted gas station. He was working out front under the awning, something he typically did on weekends. The piece he was carving was large, maybe half a mature tree, and he was attacking it with a chainsaw, sawdust flying everywhere.

"Come on. I want you to see the chainsaw carver. His stuff is really cool." I motioned for my parents to follow me, Mom's wedges clicking on the pavement as we approached Curtis's place. He had finished the troll he'd been working on Tuesday. It had a place with the other finished pieces in front of the station, a "sold" sign hanging around its thick troll neck.

"Oh, I love this." Mom inspected the troll. "And the birds."

"A bit…rustic." Dad's tone was skeptical—he'd sounded the same all day. He just wasn't seeing what I did in Rainbow Cove.

"The artisan certainly is fierce." Mom leaned close to me so that I could hear her over the buzz of the chainsaw.

Curtis wasn't just fierce. He was magnificent. In deference to the temperatures, he had on a wool cap and a red plaid shirt along with thick safety goggles and ear muffs, every inch the iconic lumberjack. He moved around the piece he was working on with complete command, angling the saw in different directions. I wasn't only impressed—I was proud. All that power and mastery and he still chose to submit to *me*. It was more than a little humbling.

Slowly, the image of a person started to emerge from the wood, an old man's craggy face. Curtis was so deep into the zone that I wasn't sure he'd registered our presence. I sure as hell wasn't going to interrupt a man with power tools. Just watching him was a delight. But I could sense my parents' impatience. Right as I turned to lead them back to the car, the saw shut off and Curtis walked over.

"Kid." He nodded at me as he pulled the safety gear off.

I'm taking that out of your ass later, I beamed at him with my eyes before introducing my parents.

"I want a troll," my mother said to him. "Just like that one over there. It'll look so cute in my garden, don't you think, Ed?"

My father grunted but dug out his wallet. "You require a deposit for a custom order? We can pick it up next time we come visit Logan."

"Fifty percent down. Cash or check."

"You need a card reader," I observed, still smarting from the "kid" remark.

"I get along just fine." There was a rebuke in his eyes. "Those phone card readers are full of fees and hassle."

"Plus you'd have to get a new phone," I joked, then remembered I probably wasn't supposed to know what type of phone he had. My mother gave me a curious look.

"Nope. Gonna be buried with this one," Curtis tossed back, but the warning was still in his expression. Fine. If he didn't want to publicly be my friend, no one was going to make him. I let Dad write him a check and fill out a photocopied order form and then followed them back to the car.

Dad was grumbling about Mom's impulsiveness but then switched his attention onto me. "How do you know the wood carver?"

"He comes into the tavern with Flint—Mason's guy. And he helped me get firewood for the house."

"Hmm. Doesn't seem like your type of friend at all."

You'd be surprised. "We're not really friends."

That wasn't a lie. Curtis's warning look had made it clear that he didn't want to deal with an association with me. Which, okay, I guess I understood and could live with. However, I wasn't done with him. Not by a long shot. But I also didn't have illusions about this being something with a future. He wasn't ever going to be a meet-the-parents guy, and seeing as how my dad hadn't seemed impressed by him at all, I should probably have been relieved by that. Not having this weird want in my gut and strange melancholy that settled over me.

Curtis

I was going to burn my damn phone. To start, I had to turn Nash down for food at the tavern. Twice. Then, I had the kid and his fancy-pants parents looking down their noses at me not taking credit cards. Like I needed one those little fiddly phone things a lot of the artists at fairs had now. Gah. Last thing I wanted was more math and numbers in my life.

But the last straw for my phone came Sunday when a text arrived. *Parents headed home. You owe me a lesson. I'm off today at two. Thought I might stop by.*

I literally growled at the phone. I wanted to see him in the worst way. Wanted the release of a scene. Plus, he'd inevitably have food with him, and my winter greens were getting awfully tiresome. But that want was dangerous. It was why I hadn't gotten together with him since our last scene. I didn't like how I was coming to crave *him*. His laugh. His hands, alternately punishing and tender. His praise, which I tried so hard not to need and still felt like a drug. I'd been doing scenes with Bill for years. Never once craved him personally. The pain? Sure. But I didn't moon around thinking about whether he'd like my latest sculpture or what he might cook for me or what we might talk about like I did with Logan. The kid. Needed to keep that straight in my head. But it was hard, when I enjoyed him so much more than I'd expected—our conversation when I'd cut his hair had been every bit as pleasurable as our kinkier encounters.

As it happened, though, I was working on the troll for his mother that morning. So it wasn't need that had me replying. Or so I told myself as I typed out a response. *You want to see your mom's piece? Should have something ready around then.*

Of course, Boy Wonder was fast with the reply. *I'll be there.*

A drizzle had been coming down all day, but I wasn't surprised when he came on the bike, not the car I'd seen in his garage.

"You cold?" I asked as he got his helmet off and the bike stowed under the awning. "I've got a pot of coffee on. Passably fresh."

"Thanks." His smile was more welcome than the missing sun. "But I'm good."

"Yeah, you are." I gave him a once-over. The goatee was really starting to come in now, and his new haircut really did suit. I'd done the sides shorter and left a bit more up top. He looked like some Hollywood guy prepping for an action flick. He was still slim, but something about the new look made him seem taller. Tougher. Hotter.

"Let me see what you've been working on? I want to text a pic to Mom, if that's cool."

"It's not done yet, so you be sure and tell her it's in progress, but feel free." I led him over to where I had all my gear set up. I'd roughed out the body of the troll, so now it was down to the detail work. "He's starting to take shape. I should have him finished next week, get him a coat of wood protector and polyurethane so he won't rot in the garden."

"He's perfect." Logan snapped a bunch of pictures, crouching low to get a good angle, giving me a nice view of his ass. Taking a quick glance down the street, I reached down and squeezed his muscular ass. "Hey!"

"Sorry." I grinned at him. It was weird—something about being around him made me smile, but I was also far grumpier around him than I was with other people. Even with Nash, I could usually put up a front, not let too much of my true emotions show. But Logan felt different, and that unnerved me.

"You are not." He shook his head at me. "But really, my mom is gonna freak at how good this is looking. How did you even get into carving anyway?"

"Had a neighbor growing up. He hated my folks but took pity on me some. Slipped me food and taught me how to whittle." I still remembered how elated I'd been at the gift of a pocket knife. Still had the sucker, too. "From then on, I always had some little creature going. But it wasn't until I met Troy's old man that I learned about chainsaw carving."

"He was a carver?"

"Yup. Logger, too. Worked with Johnny's dad. He got me jobs after high school, logging with them, and then after seeing my whittling, he taught me the basics of carving with a saw."

"Sounds like a great guy."

"The best. Salt of the earth." I'd grieved his death from a heart attack far harder than my father's overdose. "Anyway, I started doing it with scrap pieces, and when that started selling, I got more serious. Did competitions. Learned from the guys who won. I still take a logging job here and there, but the carving's become my main work."

"I love it. You're so damn talented." Logan strolled down the row of my pieces, stopping every so often to touch or take a picture.

"Eh." I shrugged off the praise. "I just work hard. Lot of practice."

"And how'd you get the service station to use as a gallery?"

"Troy's dad again. He had a buddy who owned the joint, and when it went belly up, he sold it to Troy and me for a song. It's good real estate on 101."

"Yeah, it is. Plus it's quirky. Tourists like quirky."

I snorted. "I could give a rat's ass about quirky. I'm just not about to replace a functional building with something prettier. That's all."

"What did Troy do?" The kid paused next to a sculpture of a bear cub, one of my favorites. His words were cautious, like he knew he was wandering into dangerous territory.

Usually I kept Troy tight to my chest. Didn't like sharing him with outsiders. And locals already knew our story, knew better than to ask too many questions. But somehow, the kid always had a way of getting me talking.

"Put himself through school as a trucker. Got a business degree and then used his dad's life-insurance money to open a trucking company with some buddies. They did good business." I couldn't help the pride that slipped into my voice.

"He sounds like a great guy," Logan said softly, petting the top of the bear's head.

"One-of-a-kind," I agreed, throat going tight.

"And his parents were cool with you guys? That's awesome."

"Wouldn't say they were cool, exactly. They loved Troy. Simple as that." They'd loved Troy, and he'd made it clear to them that I wasn't going anywhere, so they'd dealt. And I wasn't ever going to stop being grateful that they hadn't cut us off. "It helped that we'd been friends first. They knew me. His dad had already been getting me work at that point. Think they pretty much suspected after a time, so maybe it wasn't that big a surprise."

"That's how my parents were, too. They love me. They found out when I was in junior high—all the bullying made it so I had to tell them. But like you said, I don't think it was that big a shock to them."

"Sucks about the bullying. Hope you laid a few of them out when you got your karate skills."

"I promised my parents I'd only fight if I had no choice. Self-defense only. Three of them came at me freshman year and cornered me behind the gym. I didn't throw a punch, but I did knock them down to get away."

"Good for you." I didn't like the way my heart sped up at the notion of him in danger.

"Can you show me around the place? I want to see

your winter garden." He seemed over heavy emotional talk, and God knew I was, too.

"Sure." I led him into the building, trying to see things through his eyes, hoping he didn't find me lacking. I hated caring what he thought.

"This is my work room, more or less." I used the counter for writing invoices and stored checks and cash in the old register until I could be bothered with a bank run. The rest of the room was taken up with my equipment hanging on racks and assorted smaller pieces that I worked on in the evenings.

"Awesome." He went from piece to piece, touching and looking, like a kid at one of those hands-on museums. In the far corner, the counter that had held food displays and a drink dispenser now had a basic two burner cooktop and a sink. He inspected that, too, and I had a feeling his chef side was cringing at the lack of oven and amenities.

"Back room is where I sleep." Felt somewhat weird, showing him that, so I quickly added, "You wanted to see my garden?"

We went outside, past all the wood on the side of the building to the homemade greenhouse I had.

"Oh, this so cool." He admired my winter crop of greens and onions. "Someday I'm going to have a huge garden. Enough for me and then herbs and stuff for the restaurant. Mom gardens, but it's mainly ornamental plants."

Man, I loved his big dreams. I nodded. "Garden to go along with your eco house? You're going to be busy."

"Yup." Undeterred, he smiled at me. We came out of

the greenhouse, and he pointed at the tarp against the back of the station. "What is that? A motorcycle?"

"Yeah." I didn't stop him when he went to take a peek, but I also couldn't quiet the sudden roiling in my gut.

"Oh, this is *sick*. Better than the bikes out in the lot on Leather Night. It's yours?"

"Yeah."

"Wow. Would you take me for a ride sometime?" His voice had all the same wonder that it did when he talked gardens and houses. My chest ached with the force of wanting to be something more than what I was for him. "I've always wanted to try a motorcycle, but none of my friends are into them."

"Nope. I don't drive it much anymore."

"You don't?" His face fell, and he let the tarp drop. "Why—*oh*." His mouth made a perfect circle. "That's how Troy died?"

Damn. He saw too much. "Yup. Drunk driver up by Coos Bay. I've only ridden a few times since. Just... can't, I guess."

"Understandable." He rubbed my arm. His sympathy felt both itchy and welcome—a wool sweater on a cold day. It was big and scary, letting him see even that much of my private grief.

"You want me to give you a lift home?" I switched topics abruptly, heading over to where the truck was parked. "We can toss your bike in the back."

"Uh..." His mouth quirked like he was thinking hard, trying to keep up. "You wanna go to my place?"

"That's where you keep the rope, right?" I looked him up and down, making my meaning clear. I needed away from this place, away from these memories and feelings, away from my own head. And he was the right one to get me there. Funny how I wanted to run, but not from him. "You're so all fired to get me trussed up. How about you tie me to the bed and fuck me until I can't think?"

His eyes went wide. "Hell, yes. You're on."

TWELVE

Logan

Curtis wanted me to tie him to the bed and fuck him. And I knew a huge part of it was that he didn't want to talk about his dead lover anymore and was tired of my questions. But there was heat in his eyes, and he brought my bike over to the truck with purposeful strides. He certainly *seemed* intent on this plan, and I sure as hell wasn't turning him down.

I helped him heft the bike into the truck bed even though he was a guy who routinely lifted entire trees and could undoubtedly manhandle one bike.

"You have stuff at your place?" he asked as he swung into the cab.

"Yup." I'd purchased some condoms and lube in a fit of hopefulness. And bondage rope I already had plenty of.

"Good." He drove like he walked and worked—sure, confident, and just this side of reckless, like he couldn't help but go fast.

When we parked at my place, he glanced down the street in the direction of Mason and Nash's place with a frown on his face.

"Mason's at the tavern. Lilac's with Mason's dad. Think Flint is working today," I reassured him.

"Wasn't worried." He looked down that direction again, eyes narrowing.

"Liar. But you could just say we're friends if someone asks. You don't have to tell them about... anything else."

He snorted. "Nash isn't gonna buy us as friends, sorry."

"Hey." I took affront to that. "I make a good friend. Nothing too weird about two guys getting together for a meal or a movie or something."

"Never said you weren't friend material. Nash and I have been friends for over twenty years now. He sees my truck here, he's gonna know we're fucking."

"Fair enough." I gritted my teeth as I got out of the truck. I wasn't so sure that Nash would automatically know and disapprove, and I didn't like Curtis dismissing the idea of a friendship so easily. It ticked me off that my dad had essentially thought the same thing—that friendship with Curtis would be a bad idea. Who the fuck cared what other people thought? For whatever reason, I liked him. Liked spending time with him. And despite all his protests, he needed a friend. It didn't have to be any more complicated than that.

"You want me in the bedroom?" he asked as I unlocked the door.

I want you any way I can get you. "That'll do."

I followed him down the short hall to my bedroom

and went to the closet where I'd stored my bondage rope and other supplies on the top shelf.

"I like you in black." Trying to lighten my mood, I grinned at him as I tossed a couple hanks of black rope on the bed. I added a pair of scissors. "See? I can cut you loose at any point."

"K—*Logan*. I'm not going to safe word on you. I want this." Dropping the kid label meant every bit as much to me as the trust he was placing in me. I loved when he said my name. He unbuttoned his flannel shirt. "Honestly, I'm more worried about the fact that you haven't topped than your knot-tying ability."

"I never said…" I sputtered.

"Never play poker with me, kid." He laughed as he pulled off his shirt. And just like that I was pissed again.

"*Logan*. And that was a dirty trick. You could have just asked."

"Yeah, but my way was more fun." He winked at me as he finished undressing. "And I don't mind. Just go slow, don't be afraid to get off once before we fuck if you're worried about going off like a rocket, and—"

"I'm not," I snapped, even if that wasn't bad advice. "Although giving your mouth something to do is starting to sound excellent. But first, I want to tie you. Kneel on the rug." I had a thick blue throw rug on the floor by the bed, and it would work to save his knees.

"No ties that go around my neck," he warned as he complied.

"I won't touch your neck," I promised. "Did something bad happen to you in a past scene or you just don't like your neck touched?"

His eyes got distant. "I've done some breath play.

141

Mainly with Troy because I trusted him. It can be hot as fuck. Until it goes sideways with a crazy-ass top who trots out choking without warning. I had bruises for weeks. And now I won't go there."

"That's awful." I stroked his hair. "I'm so sorry that happened to you."

"Eh. I'm over it," he said even though he clearly wasn't. "Get on with the tying."

"I'm going to do a variation of a box tie," I explained, so he'd know what was coming. I hated that other top who had hurt him, wanted to flatten him. But even with that impulse, I was still eager to get on with our scene. I had hours and hours of kink research to finally put into practice. "Arms behind your back but crossed, not straight. Make sure they're comfortable before I start. The rope will come around your shoulders and torso before circling your biceps and then binding your arms together."

"Okay." He watched me unwind a hank of black rope. "You going to bind my legs too?"

"Just the arms." Even as my nerves jangled, my brain kept humming along with stuff I'd like to try. Some day I wanted to get him in a full frog tie on the bed, fuck him on his back, but I wanted him to have more range of motion for this first time. Plus, I liked the ability to have him move if I so chose.

"Sounds good." He stretched his arms and shoulders a few times and assumed the position I'd described, arms behind his back, crossed. Using gentle motions, I made his hands lay flat on his forearms, wrists facing each other. This position was called the Takate Kote, and I'd been in love with it ever since I'd seen it demonstrated at a workshop. It managed to be both elegant and complicated without being crazy difficult to execute.

I started with a three strand cuff around the wrists and then pointed the knot at his neck so I could do the torso part of the tie.

"I'm surprised you don't need to look at a picture on your phone," Curtis said with a laugh. Man, I loved his genuine laughter, how warm it made my gut, how it worked its way past all my nerves to relax me. He made enacting my fantasies *fun,* and I loved that easiness we shared.

"Don't make me paddle your ass before we fuck." I wrapped the rope around both upper arms in a double pass, adjusting tension so it was even between all the lines.

"Exactly how bad do I have to get for that?" He winked at me, sparking a fresh wave of warm feelings in me. "Because I can insult—"

"Paddle it is." I locked the upper chest strap in place by catching all four strands before starting the lower chest band, just below his pecs. "When I practiced this at the workshop, the sub was silent. No laughing."

"I'd tell you you're damn good at this for a novice, but I really want that paddle."

"Oh, you're getting the paddle. After you blow me." My voice was firm, but I couldn't resist smiling at him.

"Such a punishment." He licked his lips.

"You're such a bratty sub." Both upper and lower chest straps fastened, I got to do my favorite part, grabbing the rope through the crook of his elbow and using the cinch that created to define the bands around his

ANNABETH ALBERT

biceps. It looked hot as fuck, and he wasn't getting free anytime soon.

"And you love it." He wasn't wrong. I did love him like this, relaxed and joking, just bratty enough to justify the paddle, but still giving up control to me. A truly quiet sub might be too intimidating for me—with Curtis, I always knew where I stood, and he kept me from getting wrapped up in my own head. And even though I'd fantasized about it for years, the reality of tying up a bigger man was far hotter than imagined, all his muscles rippling as I worked, tats playing peekaboo with the rope.

I repeated the cinch under his upper arms, being careful with the tension to make sure everything was even, nothing twisted or digging in. The simple, clean lines looked great, and I made sure his wrists were well supported before tying everything off.

"You want to see a picture of the rigging from the back?" I grabbed my phone from my pocket.

"Nah. I trust you. I can tell your tensioning was spot-on. I'll let you do my legs sometime if you want—you've got a knack for this. Turns me on."

I loved knowing that. Tying him up was awesome, but it was even better if he liked it as much as I did. The fact that someone like him *wanted* this from me was never going to stop giving me a thrill. "Now you get to work on your patience."

I undressed slowly as I circled him, inspecting my work from all angles. First my shirts came off, then boots, and finally my jeans. I kind of liked staying clothed while he was naked, but this was going to be easier for what I had planned.

"Gimme." He jerked his head in the direction of my cock.

"What did I say about patience?" Gripping my cock at the base, I gently slapped it against his cheeks. His idea about coming fast so that I could enjoy the fucking more was a great one, not that I was going to give him credit. I gave him just the tip to lick, standing far back enough that he had to work for each taste.

"More," he growled. "Please."

"Ah. There's my favorite word." I gave him a little more, sliding the shaft across his waiting tongue before retreating. "You want to get me off this way?"

He moaned his agreement, sucking on my cockhead.

"Good. Do it fast and I'll give you that paddling you seem to want so much. Make your ass all red before I fuck you hard."

He went right to the flutter-suck with his tongue that had worked last time. I had more confidence this time, too, fucking his mouth fast. He moaned around my cock when I went deep and chased me on the retreat. I loved looking down at him all bound up, too. The same muscles I'd seen flexing and working while he carved were all my disposal. And all the command and charisma he usually flaunted were replaced with supplication, so much that it made my breath catch. The trust he put in me was every bit as potent as his tongue action.

"That's it. Gonna get me there." I put a hand in his soft hair, both because he seemed to love it and also to steady him as I went faster. Much as I loved owning him like this, I didn't want to accidentally choke him. "You love this, don't you? Being bound for me? On your knees?"

He groaned low, making my balls tighten. Another hard suck and I was right on the edge.

"Here it comes," I gasped as the climax hit. It was fast and swift, like a clean takedown in an aikido match —knocking the wind from me. Our eyes met, and that further stole my breath, the way he looked at me like I was his whole world, like he had no better purpose than to get me off. "Fuck. So good."

"You're lucky I don't go comatose like you after coming." I stroked his face and hair, loving the contrast of smooth skin, fuzzy beard, and silky hair, reveling in that look in his eyes as he waited for my next order. "I've still got plenty of energy to make your ass sting."

"Counting on it. How do you want me?"

"On the bed." I had to help him up, and then I arranged him face down on the bed, pillows raising his ass for me. It gave me a perfect view of his rigging. I did a quick circulation test to make sure the shift in position hadn't caused any issues. "Arms okay? Nothing too tight?"

"Peachy. Fucking love this. Bring it on." His eagerness for pain was the stuff of my dreams. I'd always found the idea of inflicting pain on a willing partner absolutely intoxicating, and the need in Curtis's voice made my chest tighten. He needed this from *me*, and I wasn't going to let him down.

I fetched the paddle from the closet and then stood next to the bed so that I could spank him with my full range of motion. I'd practiced with the paddle on both the arm of the couch and my own thigh, and while there was a definite sting to the leather paddle, it spread the pain out in a way that made it more manageable.

Rather than counting, I played with him, starting very softly and building intensity with each blow until he was moaning and his skin was starting to pink up. It didn't take much before my dick was hard and aching from the sight, ready to go again.

"More," he moaned as I landed a particularly hard strike. I loved the smacking sound the paddle made, loved the way his ass bounced from the impact. I didn't give him too many blows — I wanted to make sure the sex wouldn't be too painful, to enhance the sensations, but not make it an endurance marathon.

"I'm going to fuck you now," I told him, voice firm even as my insides trembled. *Finally*. I was really going to do this. After years of Seth's active dislike of even the idea of fucking, it had taken me a while to get comfortable with wanting that, and after we'd broken up, I hadn't been in too much of a rush to find a hookup who would let me top. What I'd wanted was something more than the garden variety hookup anyway. I'd wanted *this*, a partner at my mercy, giving up control to me, wanting my domination every bit as much as I craved giving it. And if I was honest, I wanted connection, too. The sort Curtis and I shared, where I genuinely liked and respected him, where I enjoyed his smart mouth and dry jokes and hidden depths

"Go hard." His voice had the drunken quality it took on when he went deep into the pain play. I loved being able to do that for him.

I grabbed the condoms and lube from where I'd stashed them in the nightstand. Putting the condom on first, I then coated my fingers with lube. I rubbed circles around his rim, loving how that made him moan.

"Don't need prep." Curtis's rocking hips called him an impatient liar. He was liking this plenty. "Just go. *Please.*"

"I do love it when you beg." I worked my slick finger in, but in truth, I was every bit as impatient as him. There would be other chances to really torment him with fingering and rimming until he was crazy out of his head, but right then every cell in my body was crying out for me to fuck him already. I added more lube to my cock before lining up. I couldn't resist a bit more teasing, though, rubbing up and down.

"Need a map?" he groaned.

"Cranky and bossy?" I slowed my motions down even further. Using the hand that wasn't holding my dick, I slapped his still-pink ass. "I think not."

"Please. Fuck me. I need it."

"Well, I suppose. Since you said please." I managed to sound completely disinterested even as my body was clamoring to thrust. Somehow managing to contain that urge, I slid forward slowly. Groaning, he pushed back against me. He was tight, far more than I'd expected, and warmer, too. And I was really glad I'd already come once, because three seconds of my dick gloved inside Curtis's fist-tight hole—shit, this was *Curtis* I was fucking—and I would've shot. I rocked slowly, shallow motions that gradually took me deeper.

"More," he moaned. I had to use a hand on his hip to stop him from riding back. With my thumb, I pressed on a pressure point. "Ahh…*fuck.*"

"I'm in charge," I reminded him. Reinforcing my control, I fingered his bindings.

"Yes. Fuck. More. Please." Each broken, ragged

syllable from him made my cock throb. His ass was still hot from the paddling, and I liked how it felt against my thighs as I finally slid all the way in. Fuck. He'd let me do that, let me spank him until his skin heated. My pulse pounded. It felt like I'd been waiting my whole life for this moment, for a partner like him. My hands returned to his bindings, tracing them as I started to set a rhythm.

"*That.* That."

"You like?" I pulled him closer, careful to not yank too hard, but using the rigging for leverage.

"Fuck, yes. Harder."

For once, I followed his demands, mainly because my body was taking over, and it needed the same thing. I tried to aim for the angles that made him moan louder.

"Fuck. *Logan.* You're gonna get me there. Wanna come."

My whole body surged at the sound of my name. "Not yet," I warned.

"Need it. Please. Touch me."

Just because I could, I slapped his ass. "Like that?"

"Fuck. My cock. Touch my cock. *Please.*"

"Ah, there's the word." I slid a hand under his belly where he was rutting against the pillow. Harder than I'd felt him, he was leaking precum and groaned as soon as I touched him. "Not gonna take much, is it?"

Things were too tight for effectively stroking him off, but just my hand there seemed to be doing it for him. "God, tell me. Tell me I can come."

"You can wait." I sped up my thrusts. "Wait for me."

"Fuck. Yes. That's it. Want you to come, too, Logan. Fuck me hard. Please."

Oh, fuck. His begging was doing it for me, knowing I

had reduced him to babbling and low groans. I needed him to come, wanted to feel him go. "Now. Get yourself there. Fuck my hand."

His ass bucked as he thrust against me and the pillows, and he moaned over and over. His whole body went tense, ass clenching me hard, and I felt him shudder several times before his cum coated my fist. And the pulsing of his ass was all it took for the last of my control to evaporate. I thrust frantically. Once. Twice.

"Coming. Fuck. I'm coming." In him. I was coming in him. This was Curtis, the guy I liked more than I should have, the guy who made me feel things I'd never really thought possible. And he'd welcomed this from me, wanted this, *needed* it as much as I had. The thought forced another spasm from me.

"That's it. Give to me." His voice was shredded now, and he was still shaking with his own orgasm. He collapsed into the bed, squashing my hand, and taking me with him in a heap. Trying to be gentle, I eased out of him. "Fuck."

"Sorry."

"Don't be. Fucking incredible." He'd gone all limp and pliant and didn't protest as I cleaned him up and carefully untied him from the bindings.

Rubbing circulation back into his arms, I dropped kisses across his shoulders. "You were magnificent."

"Magnificently tired." He yawned. "You wear me out."

"Good." I smoothed lotion over the fading marks on his ass. "You sleep. I'm going to make you dinner."

"Don't need..." He didn't finish the thought, snuggling into the clean pillow I'd given him for his head.

"Yes, you do." I kissed the back of his head. I hadn't been lying—this taking care of him was one of my absolute favorite things. And now I was going to watch him sleep and daydream about what I could cook for him. Heaven. I knew it wouldn't—*couldn't*—last, but I was determined to wring every last drop of joy out of this day.

THIRTEEN

Curtis

Logan's bed really was the best—soft sheets, an abundance of pillows, and fluffy comforters he'd draped over me. Far more luxury than one person needed, yet I'd been powerless to do more than drift away on the cloud of good feelings post-sex. I woke up from my nap, not sure how long I'd slept, but more content than I'd been in a long time. So much so that it was almost unsettling, how good I felt. The most amazing smell was drifting into the bedroom—tomatoes, basil, something Italian, I bet.

Pulling on my jeans first, I went in search of Boy Wonder and whatever he was making. At a certain point, hunger won out over principles and resolutions to not let myself get attached to his cooking. And right then, my stomach was rumbling.

"That smells incredible," I said as I entered the small kitchen. He had on some soft music and was stirring a pot with a little smile on his face. Like me, he was in jeans, no shirt, and bare feet. So fucking adorable. And I wasn't supposed to be thinking that, but it was true, and I was still buzzing on endorphins from the scene and couldn't push the thought away.

"Thank you." His grin was dazzling, and before I realized what he was after, he'd abandoned his stirring in favor of trapping me between the door frame and counter. Standing like this, I realized for the first time that we were very nearly the same height. His slighter build was deceptive and—

Whoa. His lips slid over mine. This was unexpected, and it had been so damn long since I'd been kissed that all I could do was gasp. I maybe could have handled an aggressive I'm-gonna-own-your-ass kiss easier, but while assertive, Logan was painstakingly gentle and cautious. But not timid or fleeting, either. No, this was an exploration. Little slides and sips and sighs, each of which melted another layer of the icy armor I wrapped myself in.

"What was that?" I asked as he pulled back with a grin.

"Long overdue." There was a softness around his eyes that made me uneasy. I'd known that his first time topping might rattle loose some feelings, and I didn't need him to go getting any romantic ideas about what this wasn't. But before I could set him straight, he continued, "And you complimented my cooking spontaneously. That's a first. Figured I better shut you up before you came to your senses."

"Lucky for you, you fucked me stupid. I'm too hungry to turn you down." More than hunger for whatever he was making. I was too starved for attention like his, too long without kisses. And when he leaned in again for another kiss, I met him eagerly, letting him nip and lick and deepen the kiss to something that revealed how damn hungry I really was.

"Fuck. You're going to make me burn the sauce."

"Can't have that." I pushed him away. I needed a moment to collect myself anyway. I had no business kissing him, adding complications to an already complicated...whatever this was. I wouldn't precisely call him a fuck buddy or hookup, but I wasn't sure why labels I'd used regularly in the past didn't work here. "What are you making?"

"Pasta alla Norma. Vegan version without the cheese on top for you. It's got eggplant, tomatoes, basil, and garlic. You liked the ravioli, so I thought Italian might be nice, and pasta's one of those things that sucks to make for just one."

"I'm not sure I've ever had eggplant," I admitted.

"It's rich and meaty. If you like the mushrooms in our veggie burger, you'll like this." He dumped a package of noodles into a pot of bubbling water. "And I had to get the eggplant on my last trip into Coos Bay, so be kind. I'm trying to decide if it would be worth the hassle to make this the special one day."

"Hey, I'm not mean," I protested. "And I do like mushrooms some."

"Ha. Okay. Not mean. Cranky. Do you drink wine?" He held up an open bottle. "I added a little red wine to the sauce, but it's a good Oregon Pinot Noir, too nice to waste. I'm going to have some with my food. My folks brought a few bottles with them."

Wine was far fancier than I usually got, but Troy had

dragged me on more than one ride through the Willamette Valley vineyards. He'd liked it more than beer with special-occasion foods.

"As long as it's not Chardonnay, I'll try it," I allowed. He already had it open, so me being rude wasn't going to serve a purpose other than bringing back that kicked-puppy look of his that I hated. "That stuff tastes like burnt wood to me."

"You just haven't had a good one." He laughed and grabbed two wine glasses from a cupboard by the stove. This was far, far too intimate for me. He had the little table set with large flat bowls, the kind they used to serve pasta at restaurants. He even had place mats, woven ones out of various colors of straw.

"Nice setup." I waved my hand around his space.

"Eh. It'll do for now."

"Until you get your dream place." My chest pinched again at the thought of him in some eco-friendly wood cabin with a big garden and welcoming kitchen and some blessed person to share it with him. It was another reminder that these lessons wouldn't last forever. He was destined for things other than me, so I might as well enjoy him while I had him.

"Someday." He handed me both glasses of wine. "Here. Put these on the table while I drain the linguine."

"Ungh." I couldn't help the groan as I sat. He'd lit my ass up good. I loved the ache from the paddle and the fucking.

"I'd apologize, but I kinda like seeing you squirm." He laughed. In short order, he drained the noodles and tossed them with the thick sauce. Watching him cook was a pleasure, the way he concentrated and hummed along with the music while sprinkling in salt and some green herb. Reminded me of the zone I got into while sculpting. He dished up plates for both of us, adding a generous amount of cheese to his and garnishing mine with what looked to be parsley.

"When did you know you wanted to be a cook?" I asked as he sat down opposite me.

"I guess I was around thirteen or so. The bullying was really bad, and I'd come home and lose myself for hours in cooking shows on TV. Sounds stupid, but they were what I needed."

"Not so stupid. I used TV, too," I admitted. "When shit was bad with my folks. I could count on old sitcoms or *The Simpsons*. Necessary distraction."

"Exactly. And the TV-show chefs were always so happy and had a nice dish at the end. I wanted to be like those chefs, bringing people together with a meal. Spreading joy. I convinced my mom to let me start messing around with recipes from the shows. The rest was history. I loved being in the kitchen. It became my solace."

I got that. Carving had been that for me, too. "Well, you're damn good at it."

The pasta was tender without being mushy, while the sauce was chunky and rich. He'd called the eggplant meaty, but it didn't remind me of any beef or chicken. Closer to bread than meat, it was velvety and tasted heavily of garlic and onions.

"You like?" His twinkling eyes said he already knew the answer.

"It'll do." I couldn't help smiling back before taking a small sip of the wine, which really did complement the food perfectly with its robust taste. "If you put it on the menu, tell Mason or Ringer to talk up the wine idea. That'll bring you some more dollars if folks drink with dinner."

"I love your ideas. I already told Mason about pricing the ravioli right and doing bigger portions."

"Did your parents agree to invest with you guys? That should help more than any tips from me."

"Eh." Logan groaned. "I wish it were that easy. Dad wants to think about it. They're visiting next month to get the sculpture from you and to talk with us more."

"That's a start, right?"

"I think what they really want is me to move back to the Portland area. They miss me."

I'm going to miss you, too. Whenever he finally did return to his fancy Portland life, I'd miss his cooking and his smiles and his homey little place. And fuck, I didn't want that. The wine turned sour in my gut. I missed enough damn people in my life. I didn't need to miss him, too. Maybe the only solution was to collect some memories to keep me warm after he left, to try to soak up as much of his sun as I could now.

Logan

By some minor miracle, I'd managed to get Curtis to agree to food and another lesson on my next early night, Thursday. We'd been text-flirting the first part of the week, or at least as flirty as Curtis got, me tossing out ideas for the lesson, him countering with suggestions of his own. We were talking predicament bondage, which was something that intrigued me a lot.

So when a message came in after lunch on Thursday, I didn't think much of it until I glanced at my phone. *Gotta cancel tonight. Sorry. Hurt my foot.*

Damn it. Knowing Curtis, it could be anything from an accidental amputation to a log landing wrong and crushing it.

How bad? I replied, but no answer came. I wasn't content with that, so as soon as I finished up at the tavern, I headed to his place. A thick rain had been coming down all day, so I'd taken my car that morning, a rarity for me. I parked next to his truck. No Curtis out front, but also no pool of blood, thank God.

"Curtis?" I called, rapping on the glass door. No answer. It was unlocked so I poked my head in. "Curtis? You here?"

"Hey, kid." He was sitting on the only chair in the space, a stool in the corner, foot propped up on a stump while he whittled some little thing. "I'm fine. Promise. You didn't need to hurry over. Just banged up, that's all."

"What happened?" I crouched in front of him.

"Slipped getting a load out of the truck bed. Wasn't thinking or something. Lost my footing. Banged my shin and hip, too, but the ankle seems to have taken the brunt of it."

He had the boot off, so I inspected it. His whole foot was swollen and puffy. "This looks bad. Can you put weight on it?"

"Not much. That's why I canceled on you. Probably shouldn't try to drive on it, but I'll be fine tomorrow."

"You need the urgent-care clinic. I think it could be a break."

"Eh." He shrugged. "I hate doctors. All they're going to do is poke at it, make it hurt worse."

"No, they're going to take X-rays which is what you need." I moved to pat his shoulder. "What's so bad about doctors?"

"When I was little, we never had the money to visit a clinic. And the few times I was sick enough to have to see a doc, they were always suspicious of my parents. Felt like I was one report away from foster care."

From everything I'd heard about his parents, I wasn't convinced that would have been the worst outcome, but I understood childhood fears. I nodded and rubbed his shoulder. "I've heard good things about this urgent-care clinic. Let me take you."

"It's not that bad. You could rustle me up some Tylenol, I suppose." He was pale, mouth a thin line, forehead knit with obvious pain.

"I don't think so. *Curtis.* Your foot is twice its usual size. Over-the-counter painkillers aren't going to cut it. We're going to urgent care." I used my Dom voice on him.

"Not sure I can walk to the truck." He sighed.

"I'll help you. And I've got my car. That'll be easier for you to climb into." I moved so I could give him a hand up. "Just lean on me. We'll take it slow."

Being all muscle, he was heavier than he looked, but we managed with him leaning on my shoulder. I assisted him into my passenger seat and locked up the building for him. "You don't have to do all this," he protested more than once.

159

"I'm off work. Nothing better to do," I joked, trying to get him to smile. "Might as well cart you around."

The urgent-care clinic was located just outside downtown in a low building with a large parking lot. Adjacent to the lot was a helipad for Life Flight. Since we didn't have a full-fledged hospital, all the serious injuries went to Coos Bay's big regional hospital.

Curtis being Curtis, he refused the idea of a wheelchair and continued using me a crutch to make it to the clinic's reception desk. She got us in a triage room pretty quickly. I went with him because he was still protesting the wheelchair despite not being able to put weight on the foot. The medical assistant took his vitals and said the doctor would be in shortly.

"You didn't need to come with me," he grumbled as we got him situated on the exam table.

"It was that or watch you squash the nurse, you stubborn—"

"Knock. Knock." A man entered the room, the tag on his white coat announcing him as Doctor Strauss. He wasn't that much older than me—maybe early thirties with dark hair and almost elfin features with an impish smile. "Stubborn is my specialty. I hear someone's going to need X-rays. Let's take a look, see if we can get some painkiller on board before too much longer."

"I'd be fine with Tylenol." Curtis frowned, wincing as the doctor bent to inspect his foot. "Ow. F—heck. Heck."

"Uh-huh. I think we'll do a painkiller shot, tough guy, unless you've got any allergies or other reasons not to." The doctor continued his prodding as Curtis groaned.

"No allergies," he gritted out.

"Good. It could be just a bad sprain, but I want to see some X-rays before I say for sure. Let's get you in the queue, and I'll see you again in a bit. Veronica will be in with that painkiller shot. And I want you to let her use a wheelchair to get you over to imaging. No more using your…partner as a human crutch."

"Oh, we're not boyfriends," I quickly corrected him, even if I was coming to wish that were true. Our pleasant Sunday had been close to perfect—kinky-as-fuck sex and sweet dining together and a long, slow kiss goodnight that promised another round later this week.

"No way is he putting up with my ass," Curtis joked while still wincing. That wasn't true. I'd happily put up with his cranky side if it meant more days like Sunday.

"You're not so bad," I protested, because I couldn't let him go thinking that I was the one holding back.

"You guys are fun." The doctor gave us both a bemused smile. "Take care. I'll see you again later."

Curtis continued his grumbling when the nurse brought in the painkiller shot but managed to be civil to her and the X-ray tech. We had a long wait for the X-rays to come back.

"You want my phone?" I offered as I picked up a cooking magazine. Nothing on the table of magazines in the waiting area looked likely to appeal to Curtis.

"For what?" Curtis frowned.

"A game or the internet? Here, let me show you this fun game I downloaded." Digging my phone out of my pocket, I leaned in so I could teach him the finer points of the fish-raising game I liked.

"This really worth the price of that phone?" He shook his head even as he clicked around. I could tell the painkillers were kicking in because he was smiling more than usual and complaining less and didn't seem to care how cozy we probably looked sitting close together like this.

"Well, the games, email, pictures, Instagram... Lots of reasons to join the new century, old man." I bumped his shoulder.

"Who you calling old?" There was more heat in his eyes than I would have expected given his pain levels.

"Your X-rays are ready." Veronica came to fetch Curtis right as I was about to continue the flirting.

"You want me to go with you?" I asked even as I went ahead and stood. I really wanted to hear what the doctor said.

"Guess you might as well." Curtis's dopey grin was cute. Veronica wheeled him into the room, and I took the side chair after helping Curtis get on the exam table.

"Good news." Dr. Strauss came back in. "It's not a break. Probably just a bad sprain and—"

"I told you." Curtis glared at me.

"It's always a good idea to be safe rather than sorry," the doctor soothed. "Let's get you in a walking boot and on crutches and reevaluate in two weeks. I'd like to see you stay off it for a few days, though, even with the boot. The more rest you get, the faster it will heal."

"I don't need rest. I've got work to do." Clearly, the painkillers hadn't smoothed *all* Curtis's rough edges.

"He'll rest," I assured the doctor.

"Good. Listen to your friend," he said to Curtis. "He's a smart guy." The doctor's gaze lingered on me a few seconds longer than it should have. "Wait. I know where

I recognize you from. The Rainbow Tavern, right? I ate there last week. Amazing food."

"Yeah, I cook there." I didn't really know what to do with his appraising look. "Are you new to the area? I change the specials all the time—you should come by again."

"This is just my third week here. And I'll be back for sure. Your food is something special."

"You said something about a boot?" Curtis spoke up. If I didn't know better, I'd say he was jealous of the doctor complimenting me, but that was ridiculous. Curtis didn't do jealous, and it wasn't like the doctor had been flirting. He just liked my food.

"I'll send Veronica back in with one in a second and a prescription for a few days of stronger painkillers before you switch to over-the-counter meds." He turned right as he was about to walk out of the room, eyes still on me. "It was nice meeting you guys."

"I bet," Curtis said under his breath.

"Behave." I shook my head. Medicine was obviously making him punchier than usual. "And before you start in on me, I'm taking you back to my place. You shouldn't be alone tonight."

"I don't feel up to a scene." Curtis looked away.

"Yeah, Curtis, that's what I wanted. You with a sprained ankle totally gets me in the mood." I rolled my eyes at him. "No, you're going to lay on my couch, and we're going to watch a movie, and you're going to let me feed you so you don't have the painkillers on an empty stomach."

"Why would you want that?"

"Someone has to help your grumpy ass." I kept my

voice light even as jumbled thoughts piled up in my head. Why indeed? Because I liked him. Because I worried about him. Because he needed it. Because I liked helping. But mainly because I cared. Way more than I wanted to. And for whatever reason, I seemed powerless to stop it. And while chances were high that he wouldn't be the only one hurting before this night was through, I still wanted to take care of him.

FOURTEEN

Curtis

The kid seemed bound and determined to drive me nuts, driving me to his place even over my protests. I was a bit woozy from the painkillers so my objections weren't as strong as they might otherwise be, but I really didn't want to be a burden on him. The injury had been so stupid. I'd been unloading some wood, thinking about my upcoming date with Logan, and next thing I knew I'd been on my ass. That was what anticipation got me. Nothing good could come from starting to look forward to my time with him.

"You sure I'm the one you want to be taking home?" I asked as he helped me get the crutches out of his car. "That doctor seemed awfully happy that we weren't a couple."

"Him? Interested in me?" Logan blushed, much as I'd expected. "I don't think so."

"You're blind. And fishing for compliments from me." I wasn't going to feed his ego, but he did look damn good, goatee filling out, brown work shirt making his hair seem darker than usual, heavy boots and thick belt finishing off the uber-badass effect. "But yeah, he was totally looking like he'd let you fuck him."

I should encourage this—a doctor close to Logan's own age was exactly what he needed, especially if they got to talking and discovered any mutual kinks. Doctor didn't *look* kinky, but I'd been wrong on that front enough to stop making assumptions. But the thought of them together made my teeth grind. And I didn't like the sigh of relief that coursed through me when Logan shook his head.

"I doubt I'm his type. And besides, I've got a lumber-jack fetish going lately." He winked at me.

"Well, by all means. We better satisfy that." *Sorry, Doc. This one's mine for right now.* I used the crutches to follow him into the house. And because I was still feeling salty about the doctor's compliments, I didn't give him too hard of a time when he set to fussing over me, getting me arranged on the couch, foot on a pillow on a footstool with some ice packs, blanket for the rest of me.

"This is the controller for the TV system." He handed me what looked more like a wireless game controller than a remote. "There's games and movies both on the streaming app. Pick anything you want, and I'll make us some dinner."

"Don't go to any trouble—"

He cut me off with a laugh. "Haven't you figured out by now that I love cooking for people? You're not trouble—you're my willing victim. And I'm trying a new recipe for pan-grilled portobello mushrooms over mashed Yukon-gold potatoes. I think you'll like it."

Warmth spread out across my chest. He'd remembered my offhand comment about liking mushrooms. "Doesn't sound too bad."

"I'll take that as a compliment." He leaned down and kissed the top of my head before going to the kitchen. This was even more domestic than our dinner on Sunday, me all settled on the couch listening to him clank around in the kitchen.

It took me awhile to figure out his fiddly controller, but finally I scrolled around the dizzying array of choices. I knew from the posters in every room that he liked older movies, so I called out to him, "You want a new release or want me to pick a classic?"

"Whatever you prefer. Seriously. I'm easy." He popped his head into the room. "Movies are kind of like cooking for me. Escapism that I got into in my teens. I love the classics because my mom was really strict about ratings with me and I ran out of things I was allowed to watch, but I'll watch any genre now."

"Okay." I watched a few trailers before settling on a recent release that promised a lot of explosions. Troy had always liked thinky sci-fi, but I liked some firepower. Shortly after I got it selected, Logan emerged with two plates of food. They looked like something out of one of the food magazines back at the clinic. Snowy potatoes topped with seared mushrooms in some sort of sauce and steamed broccoli dressed with flecks of pepper and garlic. Everything was arranged and garnished just so.

"Wow." I failed in my bid to not let on how impressed I was. I dug in even before he settled himself next to me. "You're making me need to figure out how to grow mushrooms. And I do potatoes all the time, but not like this."

"The secret is whipping them with seasoning, coconut milk, and vegan butter." Logan beamed under my praise, which made me want to dish it out more often. "And I used some of the coconut milk in the dessert."

"There's dessert?" I seriously could not go getting used to this luxury.

"Apple scones. Mason does most of the baking and desserts at the tavern, but his vegan offerings are too crumbly. I wanted to play around on my own, see if I could solve the texture issue."

"I guess I can be the guinea pig. I'm here and all." I tried not to sound too eager and failed miserably. I could go back to my boiled potatoes and beans soon enough.

We watched the movie while we ate, and I congratulated myself on my restraint in not licking the plate. Around the time when the good guys were finishing an epic car chase, Logan cleared our plates and returned with something that smelled the way I figured heaven must—cinnamon, apples, sugar. And the taste and texture lived up to the smell, warm and delicate and pillowy.

"No offense to Mason, but you take whatever he's got on the menu off, and you offer these instead. Maybe do some sort of coconut whip cream or ice cream for those who like things over the top."

"I'll do that." Leaning over, Logan gave me a quick kiss. "Thanks for taste-testing. I've got some left for breakfast tomorrow."

"Breakfast? I'm not sleeping over."

"Sure you are. Do you even have a TV at your place?

You can take the day off, watch movies here while I'm at work, and we'll see if you're up to going back after I get home. The weather's supposed to be horrible again tomorrow, so not like you'd be missing a ton of customers."

"If Nash gets wind of this…"

"If Nash hears that you're all alone with a bum leg, he'll have you over on his and Mason's sofa before you finish complaining. That really what you want? Pretty sure their TV has parental controls. But I'll leave you instructions on how to stream porn."

"Well, you do have *other* benefits over Nash." I gave him a pointed look. "And you're just devious enough to mention this to Mason if I make you take me home."

"Oh, I'm more than devious enough." He gave me another kiss, this one lingering. He tasted sweet, like the scone, and I couldn't help chasing the flavor, licking at his lips, welcoming his tongue. I'd figured the painkillers would ax any interest my body had in sex for the night, but the kiss quickly proved me wrong.

This was different from our usual encounters and twice as dangerous without the confines of a scene. This was just two guys on a couch, ignoring a movie in favor of making out. Nothing kinky. No lesson to hide behind. Just endless kisses, the kind where I wasn't sure whether we'd been at it five minutes or an hour. I'd told myself I'd never again need something like this, but Logan's eager mouth was proving me a liar.

"You're…distracting…" I gasped as he abandoned my mouth in favor of my ears and neck.

"Just showing off the fringe benefits of staying here." He grinned at me before tugging on my collar and licking the spot where my shoulder and neck met. I had on a flannel shirt over a T-shirt, and he worked my buttons while teasing me with more kisses and bites. Whether it was the painkillers or the drugging power of his kisses, I didn't protest when he pushed my shirts off.

Once he had me shirtless, he continued his trail of kisses over my collarbones, down my pecs. He licked at my nipples, flicking with his tongue.

"Bite me," I whispered. It was more request than order, but our dynamic still felt flipped from the usual. And instead of reminding me who was in charge, he complied with a growl, biting and sucking until my head fell back and I was panting, cock throbbing with each breath.

"I'm investing in nipple clamps," he said with a laugh before licking down the center of my chest. I had a feeling where he was headed, and I sure as hell wasn't going to be the one to stop him. It had been a damn long time since I'd had this, and same as with his kisses and good food, I was powerless to deny myself what he offered.

Sure enough, he undid my belt and got my cock out, all while still licking and kissing my chest and abs. As he'd done with my nipples, he started by teasing—little flutters and flicks that drove me straight out of my head. Right when I was about to tell him to get on with it, he swallowed me down to the root, sucking hard. The abrupt change had me moaning.

"Fuck. You're good at that."

"Thanks." He flashed a smile at me before rear-ranging himself so that he was on his knees in front of the couch. I still had my bum foot propped up, so I couldn't move much, had to just take his attentions. Not that it was a hardship when he set a slow, deep tempo. I could have floated for hours on his sucking and touching, but then he started fiddling with my already-sensitive nipples while speeding up, and I couldn't help the groans that escaped my throat.

"Fuck. Logan. You're gonna get me off." I let my hand rest on his head. I had a strong feeling he wasn't as into hair pulling as me, so I just gently sifted the silky strands of his hair.

"That would be the idea." He resumed his efforts, swallowing hard when he had me deep, pinching and pulling my nipples, the perfect blend of soft pleasure and rough touches. The climax sneaked up on me, a gradual tightening in my balls, tension in my muscles increasing until I was panting and rocking my hips up to meet his mouth best as I could.

He hummed, a happy noise like he couldn't get enough of this, and that set me off, a slow burn that crackled through my nerve endings, orgasm building until there was no holding it back.

"Fuck. Fuck. Coming."

He sucked me through it, swallowing it all down before pulling back. "Mmm. Staying now?"

"Fucker." I had to laugh. "You know I can't move after that. You play dirty."

"Guilty." His eyes sparkled as he returned to the couch next to me. Tugging him close, I indulged myself in a long, lazy kiss. I loved the hint of my taste on his lips.

"What do you need?" I asked, hands stroking his torso.

"You to let me get you to bed."

"I meant—"

"So did I." He stood, holding out his hands to help me up. And I was just sleepy enough after coming that I let him. He shut off the TV while I grabbed my crutches. We made our way to his bed, where he resumed fussy mode, helping me out of my pants, getting a pillow for my foot. Why did him taking care of me have to feel so damn good? Why did he have to make it so easy to stay? I didn't know, and that bugged me even as I sank into the welcoming softness of his bed. Sane or not, I wasn't going anywhere, not any time soon.

Logan

Knowing Curtis was back at my place was the best kind of secret all day. I mean, I was sorry he was hurt, but I wasn't sorry for the night we'd spent together, him appreciating my latest recipes, us not watching the movie, and whether it was the medicine or the lingering effects of the blowjob, he'd been almost cuddly in bed, kissing and touching and getting me off with his hand before we fell asleep. For all that I loved kink, I loved that we could be vanilla sometimes, too, enjoy each other's company that way.

We closed the kitchen around nine, and I was very discreet about boxing up some leftovers to bring Curtis. And honestly, I was a little relieved to find him still on my couch when I got home. I totally wouldn't have put hiking back to his place in the rain on crutches past him.

"How's the foot?" I called as I entered the house

through the kitchen door. It was kinda nice, coming in to a warm house, TV going.

"Better. Still hurts, but I'm making do." He used the crutches to meet me in the kitchen. The fact that he was admitting to pain at all probably meant it was killing him. "I could go back to my place now."

"Did you eat dinner?" I asked him, ignoring the part about taking him home. "I brought us a vegan pizza to share—we had some dough and vegetables that needed using. Ditto the last batch of sweet-potato fries. Horatio got overzealous with the fryer."

I set out the food I'd brought, making us plates of salad, pizza, and still-warm fries.

"I kinda lived on those scones you left," he admitted.

"I told you to help yourself to anything in the fridge or freezer." I lightly boxed his arm.

"I know. Scones were that good." His mouth wrinkled, like the compliment made him grumpy.

"I'm glad." I loved preparing food he liked, loved getting past his prickly defenses. "Now eat some real food."

I carried the plates to the living room so that he could prop his foot back up.

"Want me to turn off the show?" He was watching some sort of documentary or reality TV show about fishermen in what looked to be a freezing sea.

"Nah. I'm so bushed after today that I'm not sure I can pay attention to anything anyway. Glad you found something you like to binge."

"It'll do." He shrugged. "Went a bit stir crazy, to be honest. Wish I'd brought some whittling with me."

"Aw. Poor baby. I'll take you back in the morning.

That way you can whittle with your foot up and see if you get any customers. But no charging around with the chainsaw. You can afford a few days off."

"I shouldn't stay here again—"

"I'm tired." I made an exaggerated pleading face at him. "Please. I'll run you back first thing, I promise."

"You work too hard," said the man who should know. He surprised me by putting his plate aside and rubbing my shoulders. "These long hours aren't good for you."

"Nature of the industry." I relaxed into his touch. "Eventually we'll have more kitchen help, and I'll be able to work more sane hours."

"My work comes more in waves—feast or famine."

"And this is a slow time?" Seemed like everyone in town was suffering from the winter blahs with tourism down to almost nothing.

"Actually not usually—there's a big competition up on the Washington coast that I do every year. I'll sell good there and pick up some commissions to float me through to spring when business starts picking up here again. But now..." He made a pained face as he shrugged. "Not sure I can drive eight hours on this foot next week and still be able to carve when I get there. Fuck. I hate this."

"The festival is next weekend?" I thought fast. "I can't miss Valentine's Day the following week, but I bet if I offer Mason two weekends in a row off, he might switch with me. I could go with you, do the driving."

"You ever drive a truck?"

That wasn't a no, so I smiled. "I worked for a catering company for a while. Drove the truck and the van both, and my parents' SUV isn't exactly tiny, either."

"You'd probably be bored—it's a weekend of wood carvers doing their thing. There's local food in Ocean Shores and other places on the North Coast and—"

"Sold. I can scope what other places are doing. Get ideas. And I happen to like watching you do your thing. Also, you were just telling me I need to work less. Other than two days at Christmas, I haven't taken much of a break since the tavern opened."

"Well, I suppose it *might* work out."

"It will." I slipped him a fast kiss. "It'll be fun. You'll see."

"Maybe we could take a few toys with us. A good scene might help me carve better." He winked at me.

"Anything to help." I meant it. I wanted to make sure he didn't lose a big chunk of income, but I also wanted to help *him*, wanted to share this with him, wanted to see him in action. And I knew those feelings were risky as fuck. Where I saw deepening friendship, Curtis inevitably saw a favor to be repaid. This trip could easily be a disaster, but I couldn't stop my pulse from speeding up at the idea of spending that much time together. *You're in over your head.* Maybe I was. But I'd learned to thrive on risks—learning aikido, confronting my bullies, doing culinary school, moving to Rainbow Cove to open the tavern with my friends—and so I was sprinting headlong into this one, and it felt glorious, far better than hanging back and doing what everyone else expected of me.

FIFTEEN

Curtis

"Exactly why are you taking Logan with you to Burning Bears?" Nash had stopped by Monday, looking all official in the police Jeep. I was sitting out in front of my place, whittling, trying to rest my foot even though it killed me to not be more mobile. "And what's this I hear about you having a hurt leg?"

"It's healing." I stuck my foot out so he could see the walking boot. "Just a bad sprain. But if I want to fit into regular boots for this thing this weekend, I probably don't want to be driving eight hours myself. Invited the kid along. Nothing for you to get all worked up over."

"So you and Logan are friends now?" Nash looked as skeptical as I'd known he would.

I shrugged. "He needed a few vegan recipes tested. He's come around some. Like I said, nothing serious. He's grown. Doesn't need you screening his friends."

"He's around Mason's age, but he's always seemed more...vulnerable to me." Nash leaned against the pillar for the awning. "I know Mason would hate to see him hurt."

So would I. Hurting the kid was the last thing I wanted to do. He had so much goodness in him that it was hard not to bottle him up, keep him all for myself, protect him from the world. But Nash was wrong. Logan wasn't vulnerable. He had a steel backbone and was far tougher than anyone around him gave him credit for, and I didn't just mean the Dom stuff. He worked long, hard hours, something I'd seen while I'd stayed with him, and he did it without complaint, putting everything he had into the tavern.

"I'm not going to hurt him." *I hope.* My chest clenched. "But weren't you the one who was all up on me a few weeks back to get out more, make friends?"

"If anyone deserves happiness, it's you." Nash's voice was gentler now. "And if that's what this is —"

"Mason's turned you into a romantic," I groaned. "This is just a friendship. A casual thing. And he knows that. We're cool." I really hoped I wasn't lying. Logan wanted to be friends. He'd said as much several times. So letting us slip from the lessons thing to something more like friends-with-benefits wasn't terrible, right? I sure hoped not because I'd been powerless to prevent our evolution over the last week or so.

"Besides," I added. "He'll get bored. Move on. I wouldn't be surprised if he heads back to Portland eventually."

"Better not tell Ringer and Mason that." Nash gave me a stern look. "And better not send the kid running back there, either. I know you."

"What's that supposed to mean?"

"I mean you always shove people away. Only Troy was bullheaded enough to stay put. And since he's been gone, you've gotten worse."

"I handle myself," I said in a warning tone. I did not want to discuss my shortcomings, not when I was already worried about hurting Logan, about when he'd leave. Nash was wrong. Logan wouldn't leave because I shoved him away. It would be him coming to his senses. Moving on in the natural progression of things. And it would be me left behind, clinging to a few memories, so Nash needed to step off.

Even after Nash left, I continued to stew. I didn't want to hurt Logan. I supposed the kind thing would be to cool this off before we burnt it out, but I couldn't seem to make myself do it. Instead, I found myself anticipating the weekend. I'd been going to this carving competition the better part of a decade now. Troy used to go with me, and last year had been particularly awful with everyone who didn't know asking after him and everyone who did asking after me. Taking someone along would be a buffer against that. Yeah, people might read us as a couple, but I gave zero fucks about that, and at least they wouldn't be asking me how I was coping.

At leasst I didn't have to make the drive on my own. Thursday, I had the truck all loaded by the time Logan finished the last of his prep at the tavern—he'd been putting in even longer hours, making sure Mason and Horatio could cover easily.

"Everything all diced and chopped?" I asked as he emerged from his house with a backpack in one hand.

"And copious instructions. Mason's doing pizza specials because those are easy on him, so we made a huge batch of dough." He inspected the truck bed which was loaded with my carving tools, plus a number of sculptures for sale. I'd be carving cedar they had at the event, but it never hurt to bring some stock with me. "Are you sure you should have done all this with your ankle?"

"I took breaks," I assured him. "And it's doing far better. Swelling's almost completely down. It'll be good to wear regular work boots tomorrow and Saturday."

"You still need to pace yourself."

"Yeah, yeah." I slid into the passenger seat, and that felt damn weird. Hadn't been over on this side of the truck since Troy, which I really didn't want to think about. There would be enough ghosts and memories this weekend.

Logan did something fiddly with my stereo and a wire and his phone. "There we go. Now we can have music the whole way up."

"If you leave me in charge of the music, you might not like it." I grinned at him. Funny how easy my smiles came these days.

"I am fully prepared for a rotation of Bon Jovi and Lynyrd Skynyrd." He laughed as he backed out of his driveway.

"Hey, ask nice and I might add some Mellencamp or Springsteen."

We were taking 101—we could have taken the interstate, but by the time we drove east to catch it, we'd only save maybe a half hour, and Logan was sold on the tourist route, going straight up the coast where we'd get decent views before night came. I'd done 101 both in the truck and on the motorcycle so many times that I didn't have much preference myself, but his eagerness was all kinds of cute.

Troy would have liked him. I'd had the fleeting thought before, but this time it really hit me. Troy would have found his foodie ways amusing and would have given him a list of day trips to try out. He'd have had him on a motorcycle before too long. He would have called him a Baby Dom and had a good laugh about that and about me giving lessons, but he would have liked what he and Mason and Adam were trying to do with the town. He would have ordered the steak and made sure all our friends came out and supported the place, too.

Suddenly my chest was three sizes too small. God, I missed that man. I'd never carve again if it meant bringing him back. But he was gone, and we were here, and I no longer knew how to make any sense out of that. Time was moving on. *I* was moving on, and I wasn't sure whether I liked it one bit.

Logan

Curtis was weirdly quiet the first part of the drive, playing around with the playlists on my phone, but otherwise lost in thought. The sun was out, an early February rarity, and the further north we went, the more scenery there was to distract me. I'd driven stretches of 101 before, but doing the whole trek like this was new, and I loved how each half hour brought something completely different. Since Curtis wasn't objecting, I stopped at several different overlooks to take pictures.

"Your groupies gonna like that one?" Curtis managed

to crack a grin as I quickly uploaded a selfie of me with the ocean and bluffs behind me. I'd made the mistake of telling him about my Instagram, where I had a fair number of followers, mainly fellow foodies who came for the meal pictures, but Mason and I both used our social media to try to promote the business.

"They'd like it more if you'd let me take one of you," I countered as I pulled back onto the highway.

"Take all you want tomorrow when I'm carving and can't stop you. But be sure to save battery life or whatever for the burn Saturday night."

I was really looking forward to that. The carvers would collectively create a huge twelve-foot bear sculpture, and then Saturday night it would be set ablaze in a big bonfire. I was also looking forward to the food—I'd bookmarked places all the way up the coast where we could find vegan food for Curtis and interesting local cuisine for me.

"Do you know what you'll carve or will you wait for inspiration to strike you?"

"This is gonna sound weird…" Curtis's cheeks went pink and he seemed uncharacteristically uncertain. "But the wood will tell me. I mean, I know what sells. Bears at this thing especially. Birds. When I do the carving championships back east, unusual is best—people, pets, trolls, and so on. But as to what exactly comes out, the wood decides. I might be thinking bear and the wood tells me it's a cub playing peek-a-boo or a big head. Just never know."

"That's awesome. I can't wait to see what you come up with." I really couldn't. It felt like a huge deal that he'd invited me along even if he was playing it off like it was just a favor I was doing him. I could tell from the way he kept going quiet that something was on his mind, and I had a feeling about what it was. I wasn't stupid. He'd been coming to this competition for years and years. Of course he'd brought Troy. And I was far from Troy. I knew that. And if it made me sad, knowing Curtis's heart was already taken, I tried to console myself with the friendship we were building. That was something.

Curtis offered to drive after we stopped for food, but I laughed him off. "I'm here as your chauffeur. Let me work. Rest the foot."

However, by the time we reached the Washington coast, I was exhausted. Darkness blanketed the rural landscape when we pulled into the small, old-fashioned motel where Curtis had a reservation. It was near where the carving festival would take place, and the lawn and office were decorated with large carvings.

"I did that one." Curtis pointed to a bear riding a surfboard.

"Oh, man. I love it." I had to inspect it and take a picture while he got us a key. It was one of those places where we parked in front of the room, door facing the road. Inside, it was a simple space with a blue and white color scheme with two beds with flowered bedspreads, older TV in the corner, and small bathroom beyond that. I collapsed on the closest bed.

"I might not move till morning," I groaned. I kind of expected Curtis to go to the other bed, but he landed next to me, further surprising me by grabbing one of my aching hands and rubbing it.

"I'll take that to mean that fucking me through the

bed will have to wait till tomorrow night." He laughed and pressed a kiss to my cheek.

Whatever had been troubling him earlier seemed to have lessened, replaced by the side of him I really liked, the part of him that soaked up my presence, looking for touches and cuddles. I knew he'd scoff at me if I pointed it out to him, so I kept my smiles to myself. We fumbled out of our clothes and snuggled under the covers. It was the first time we'd slept together without orgasms first, and it was nice that we could be this comfortable around each other. And as much as I loved dominating him, I also enjoyed being his body pillow, relishing the way he wrapped his bigger body around me.

He'd set the alarm, but I woke up before it went off. Curtis was kissing my stomach, beard tickling my navel, the only warning I got before he swallowed me down.

"Oh, this is *nice*," I groaned.

"Yeah?" His eyes twinkled in the early morning light. Grabbing my hand, he put it on his head. I loved knowing exactly what he wanted, and I buried my fingers in his hair, tugging lightly as I thrust up into the wet heat of his mouth. His arm wiggled against my leg with a telltale rhythm, and knowing he was jerking off got me painfully close in record time.

"Fuck. I'm close."

He moaned around my cock, eager noises that made my balls tighten.

"That's it. Suck me. And fuck your hand." I turned my head so I could watch him stroking himself. He was matching my thrusts with his hand, a tight grip, and watching his cock move was mesmerizing. It made my orgasm sneak up on me. The pleasure built higher the more he writhed and moaned, hard sucks revealing how into it he was. Finally, I couldn't hold back and my hips bucked and I came in big heaves, his name on my lips. He pulled back with a low groan, body bowing upward as he came, too.

"Oh, fuck. I want to start every day like that." I laughed, but it was true. I liked *him,* not just our ability to share orgasms. I wanted him around, didn't want this thing between us to end. "And I totally owe you tonight."

"Looking forward to it." His eyes gleamed with wicked intent. "Now you want to go back to sleep or you want to explore while I get set up?"

"Explore." I could sleep in some other time. "And help you. You don't want to stress the foot before you even get started."

"Oh, I suppose I could let you carry a few things." He was in a good mood, one that kept up through break-fast at a little diner where he had coffee and oatmeal and toast and I had an omelet. Several people recognized him at breakfast, and he greeted them all like old friends. He introduced me by name, which I supposed was a step up from "kid," but didn't otherwise explain my presence. Not that I'd expected him to. Even if we had been anything other than tentative friends who had a lot of kinky sex, I didn't think Curtis was the type to go trot-ting out the boyfriend label.

I tried not to let that bug me as we got unloaded over at the place where the carvers would work. It was a cold, windy day, but Curtis and the other carvers didn't seem to care. He looked like an ad for Pendleton blankets — total lumberjack porn in a red and gray plaid flannel jacket, gray knit cap, heavy work boots, bulging biceps, groomed beard, and a fierce smile for everyone who came up to him.

I'd taken my own wardrobe cues from him — a heavy work shirt over a hoodie, my thickest belt, and the boots that were starting to feel like a part of me. I didn't care what people close to me thought — I loved my new look. I felt more myself than I had in years. And I fit with the rougher, more rural crowd at the event more than I would have in my old preppy clothes. There were a lot of cowboy hats, camo pants, and denim jackets.

There were around fifteen carvers, each of whom had brought people with them. Lots of families and multi-generational groups and everyone seemed to know everyone else from the carving circuit and other festivals. As the morning drew on, tourists started arriving, many on motorcycles, and, like the carving entourages, a lot of them seemed to be regulars at the event.

"Curtis. You son of a bitch. Been too long." An older, burly man in a motorcycle jacket and leather pants approached Curtis as he was taking a break between carving the pieces. He was accompanied by a woman with long blond hair and a fringed leather jacket.

"Burt. Betty." Curtis did the whole back-slapping thing with the big guy and a gentler hug for the woman.

"We didn't make it last year. Betty had a nasty flu. Troy around? Our oldest just got his CDL. Wanted to pick his brain about where he should think about driving."

The bottom of my stomach wobbled precariously. This was far worse than the people who'd been looking me over with thinly veiled curiosity. I waited to see how Curtis would handle it, but he was silent a long moment.

"Burt. You fucker." The carver nearest to us spoke up. "Didn't you hear? Troy passed on. Two years ago in January."

"Oh, fuck. Man, I'm sorry. That's rough." Burt clapped Curtis on the shoulder. "Know you two went way back. You need anything? Wish we'd known. Betty and me would have come down. Been too long since we headed south."

"Thanks." Curtis nodded sharply. It occurred to me for the first time that I didn't know exactly how out Curtis was with his carving community. Knowing him and his zero-fucks attitude, he'd simply brought Troy around and let people draw their own conclusions. The crowd was welcoming to newcomers, but definitely rough around the edges.

"And who's this?" Betty motioned at me.

"This here's Curtis's new friend. Logan, right?" The other carver seemed happy enough to do Curtis's talking for him.

"Yeah," I said and shook their hands. "Pleased to meet you."

"Whatcha carving today?" Burt inspected the large stump Curtis was working on. "Reckon we might be in the market for another of yours. Betty was wondering if you could do a monkey."

"Monkey? Haven't done one of those." Curtis managed a weak smile for Betty. "But I'll see what I get to later today. This is gonna be two bear cubs wrestling. And I better get back to it."

With that, he put on his safety goggles and ear muffs and resumed attacking the piece with a new vengeance. I knew him well enough to see that he was channeling any discomfort over Burt and Betty's questions into his creations.

"Man. Always such a kick to see Curtis work," Betty shouted to me over the din of the chainsaw, leaning closer so I could hear her.

"Yup," I agreed. "He's something else."

"Did you know Troy?" she asked.

"Nope." I shook my head. "I'm new to the area."

"Ah. Well, he was one of a kind. They don't make them much better than him. Those are some mighty big boots you're looking to fill." Her smile was kind, but her eyes were knowing, like she'd already taken my measure and found me lacking.

"Just here to have fun," I lied. And yeah, I knew that I wasn't Troy. Wasn't ever going to be Troy. But I didn't need the reminder. And I really hadn't needed to see the way Curtis's face had fallen at the mention of Troy. He wasn't over that hurt, probably never would be, and I was kidding myself if I thought this was anything other than a distraction for him.

And I hated myself a little for caring so much, for wanting people to see *me,* not the ghost of the man whose shoes I never could fill. No, scratch that. I couldn't give a fuck about others. I wanted *Curtis* to see me, see what I had to offer. And because of that want, I knew I'd stick it out longer, even though I probably shouldn't.

SIXTEEN

Curtis

I found my zone about mid-morning on Friday. It was kind of like being in sub space — details like people around me and the weather and even my aching ankle became white noise. It was only me and the saw and the joy of creating something from nothing. At a certain point, Logan seemed to have declared himself my business manager, handling the sales for me and freeing me to carve without stopping to worry about counting out change. He left around lunch to get us food, and I immediately missed how he'd been dealing with the people who now wanted to talk and shit.

I'd thought having Logan along would deter people from asking after Troy, but all it had done was raise a different set of questions, ones I really didn't want to deal with.

"That's a young one you brought with you," Walter Wiggins observed. He'd been carving next to me all day. He was an old-timer who'd been in the business a good twenty years before I ever picked up a saw. And few could run off at the mouth like him.

"Older than he looks." God, I was glad Logan had let the goatee grow in. He looked early twenties at least now, and not the nineteen he had before, but he still didn't seem as old as he was.

"Oh, he's a nice kid. Doing good business for you, that's for sure. I'm just sayin' when my Estelle passed on, God rest her soul, I knew I'd never have another...*friend* so good."

Fuck. Was I really supposed to take a vow of celibacy just because Troy was gone? Is that what people expected? I shrugged.

"He's just someone to help with the driving," I said, hating myself for the lie. But really, it wasn't any of Walter's business.

"Here's lunch." Logan came jogging over. "I found this great little sandwich shop in Ocean Shores. She made you a wrap with hummus and vegetables, and I got her special fried-oyster sandwich for me."

If he'd heard what I said to Walter, he didn't show it, beaming at me as he handed over the food. It was a cold, windy day, and his smile warmed me through. And fuck Walter, I couldn't help but smile back.

"Thanks." Left to my own devices, I would have had peanut butter on sourdough and kept right on carving, so this was a treat indeed. "You get a picture of the food place?"

"Yup. I've been taking a ton in between doing business for you."

"I appreciate it. I'm gonna get back to it after I eat. I need to make sure I'll have something worth auctioning tomorrow. And I gotta do my part on the group carving for the burn."

"You boys going to come eat after we wrap for the night?" Walter asked. "My daughter and her friend are coming down from Bellingham this afternoon, so they'll join us."

Walter's school-teacher daughter had brought the same friend the last few years, Gloria, a tall, leather-wearing computer programmer who rode an older model Harley. I expected it wouldn't be much longer before Walter would be telling me about wedding bells and babies.

"This one will put pictures of the food online." I jerked my thumb in Logan's direction, making sure he seemed on board. He gave me a fast nod. "But sure, count us in."

On my own last year, I'd skipped the socializing, but I did like talking shop with the guys I only saw a few times a year, if that. Not everyone in the carving community chose to hang around me, but I didn't sweat it. I had no fucks to give small-minded fuckers who weren't worth the chisel of hate they wielded. There were enough like Walter who made sure I'd been welcome. 'Course some of that had been Troy—he'd been easy to like, got along well with all the good ol' boys and bikers, spoke fluent redneck while being whip-smart and funny. He'd been more popular at some of my events than me. And his large build hadn't hurt anything either—he'd known how to intimidate when needed.

I'd worried more about Logan, but he was holding his own, taking pictures of people's work, making sales for me. When Walter's daughter and Gloria showed up,

Logan admired their new matching ink and the bike and made himself two friends for life. By the time a bunch of us headed to Ocean Shores for food after a fast break for showers and non-sawdust covered clothes, he'd collected names and numbers and had Gloria chatting to me about websites she could build me.

"I don't need a website," I protested. We'd ended up at the same pizza joint we went to every year. They owned more than one piece from Walter and me and others in the group, displayed along with various carved and painted fish and license plates and vintage photos in the large dining room. Walter's daughter was lactose intolerant, so she split the no-cheese, all-the-veggies pizza with me. Logan, of course, had to sample various pies including mine.

"Walter's business doubled last year after I got his up and running. Flat out doubled. I can optimize it so that you and him show up whenever people look for chainsaw carving. You'll see."

I glared at both her and Logan. "This is just a ploy to get me to buy a new laptop, isn't it?"

"Yup." Logan wasn't apologetic as he popped a black olive in his mouth. "Gotta join this century. I'm coming for your phone next."

"Oh, hush. It works."

"I like this one." Gloria waved a slice of pizza in Logan's direction. "Keep bringing him around."

Huh. There was an idea. I let myself imagine that world, one where Logan didn't move on, didn't find his ideal sub, didn't get his big dreams...

Nope. Much as I liked that picture for me, liked the idea of bringing him east to the big carving championships and returning next year here with him, I wanted him happy even more. My strongest wish was for him to get everything he wanted. Needed. Deserved. And that wasn't me. It would be like trying to shove the sun into a cardboard box—he deserved so much more than what I could offer. So I just smiled at Gloria and didn't say anything.

Conversation moved on to who was going to the Oregon Championship in June in Reedsport and then the nationals in Wisconsin in August. I'd be going to both, most likely. Would Logan still be around in June? August?

He asked all sorts of questions about both events, and that image of taking him with me got stronger. Fuck. I didn't eat much after that.

"You okay?" Logan asked on our way back to the truck.

"I can drive." I held my hand out for my keys.

"Like hell. You're limping pretty bad. I'm going to get you ice from the machine when we get back to the room."

"I don't need taking care of." I slid into the passenger seat simply because I didn't need a parking lot argument. I wasn't feeling very civil.

"I think you have whatever the carving equivalent of sub drop is." Logan took the road that led back to the motel. "You rode endorphins all day. Now they're fading and you're cranky and in pain."

He wasn't wrong, so I snorted. And it was easier to let him think that was the entire issue than to tell him I was tangled up in wanting things I had no business lusting after.

"I've never had sub drop," I lied.

"Ha." Logan's laugh made it clear he didn't believe me. "Luckily, I've had all day to come up with a plan for you."

"Oh?" In spite of everything, I was curious as hell.

"You still want to mess around? I'd understand if you're too tired." His grin said he knew I wasn't turning him down.

"I could get interested."

"Good."

When we got back to the motel, he didn't waste any time in going into Dom mode. "Strip. And then on the bed, on your back. I'll return in a minute. No touching your cock." He slid out of the room after his order.

Leaving me alone to stew was a new trick, and my stomach trembled as I undressed. Following his orders, I sent the covers fluttering to the floor and sprawled on the sheets. The prospect of whatever he had planned and his commanding tone had my cock hard and aching with a steady thrum that countered the twinges in my ankle. He returned with a bucket of ice. As he used it to fill a large zipper-top plastic bag, he looked me over like I was the last slice of that pizza from dinner.

"You knock this off, and I'm going to be very disappointed. Don't disappoint me." He pushed a pillow under my foot and arranged the ice on it. He set the half-full bucket on the nightstand next to me.

"Ah. Fuck. That's cold."

"Oh, you haven't seen anything yet." His smile was pure mischief. Rummaging in his bag, he came up with the quick-release cuffs. "I need to make sure you're not going to wiggle around."

There was a question in his eyes, so I nodded. I liked how he could control a scene but still give me significant choice. Sitting on the bed next to me, he bound both of my hands to the flimsy headboard. I expected him to whip out one of the floggers next, so I was totally unprepared for his kiss.

This was still new for us, and it was the first time he'd kissed me during a scene. Being restrained while he owned my mouth made my pulse hum. His tongue delved deep as his hand tangled in my hair. His commanding mouth promised all manner of dirty things and had me moaning in no time flat. I was breathing hard by the time he pulled back.

"Close your eyes," he ordered. There was a rustling sound and then something soft covered my eyes. He moved slowly enough that I had ample time to say no, but even though blindfolds weren't a huge kink of mine, I didn't object. I wanted to discover what he had planned. "Remember, keep your foot still, no matter what. Keep that ice pack on."

"Okay." My throat felt thick, and the need to please him coursed through me. Again I expected the bite of pain any second, so an icy rush down my shoulder had me gasping. "Fuck. Cold. Fuck."

"We're just getting started." He followed the cold sting with his hot lips. Ice. Kiss. Repeating all down my collarbone. My nipples tingled, thinking they were next, but the ice hit my bicep instead. He licked and sucked his way down my inner arm, an area I'd never once thought of as a turn-on, but it made my cock twitch. I wasn't usually one to get self-conscious, but I was still glad I'd taken that shower before dinner.

After my arms, my good leg was his new target, ice tracing patterns on my thigh before his mouth followed. Maddeningly, he didn't go near my cock, instead attacking my abs. I tried to pay attention to what he was drawing with the ice—felt like words or maybe loopy hearts, but I was drifting too much to put together the clues. His mouth was more aggressive now, and I knew I'd have marks on my belly and chest from his love bites. He alternatively soothed and tormented with the ice. He finally reached my nipples, but he was a devil, icing one while he pinched and sucked the other before switching sides.

"Thought…you'd…flog me," I managed to pant.

"This is more fun." He resumed his torture of my nipples, making my hips rock before I remembered the ice pack on my foot. My cock was in agony, so much that when the ice touched it at last, I moaned with relief. But it was short-lived, as he only did the briefest of teases before moving to my balls.

"Oh, fuck no. No. Go back to my chest."

"Who's in charge?" he asked right before mouthing my balls. The ice was evil, almost too much, but then his mouth redeemed him, flicking and dancing over the sensitive flesh. The ice found my inner thighs next, cold tingles racing up my spine before his mouth soothed. His goatee tickled, adding to the sensation overload. He urged my good leg up and back, opening me to a new assault, this one along my ass. This time I figured correctly where he was headed, and I moaned even before he reached my rim.

I hadn't had this in years, and my cock leaked against my stomach as his agile tongue fluttered over me. I had a feeling this was a novelty for him, too, but he was damn good at it for a newbie, tracing circles with his tongue before finding all the spots that made me groan while he sucked. I heard the snick of a bottle open seconds before a slick finger joined his tongue.

"Yeah. Fuck me."

"Oh, not yet." His breath was hot against my chilled skin. "You're going to beg me for it."

He worked a finger in, aiming right for my gland. And as if that wasn't enough, his free hand found an ice cube and held it to my nipple while he lined up a second finger.

"Fuck. Please. Need it."

"That's it." He rearranged himself so that he could suck my cold nipple while his fingers went deep. Felt like he might have three in now. He knew how to work my gland, too, hitting it with each thrust, varying the pressure until it was hard to breathe.

"Logan. Come on. I'm ready."

"So demanding. You gonna stay still for me?"

I'd totally forgotten I even owned an ankle, let alone that it hurt. "Uh-huh. *Please.*"

He withdrew his fingers, and rustling sounds were sweet relief as I could guess he was undressing. Finally. I groaned my need. Not being able to see him was torture. There was a telltale ripping sound. Condom. Good. *Soon.*

"Please. Fuck me. Now."

He pushed my bent leg further back, hooking it over his elbow before his cock nudged my hole. I was plenty slick and ready, but the first thrust still had me hissing.

"That's it. Let me in." His voice was gentle but firm, just like this whole experience. I'd had all manner of pain play over the years, but nothing that had undone me like Logan and a few ice cubes. He'd taken care of me, sent me soaring, surprised and delighted and tortured. I'd never known anything like it.

His cock slipped deeper, and we both groaned. Fuck. I needed this so bad. Needed things I hadn't let myself realize until he came along.

"Fuck me." *Take me. Don't leave me. Stay.* All sorts of words bubbled up in my throat, but I managed to hold them back.

"You want it hard?"

"Yes. Do it. Give it to me." Ragged moans filled the air as he sped up, slamming deeper. Any hesitation or nervousness he'd had the first time we'd fucked was gone now, and this was a master, one who calculated every angle, every thrust. He owned me. Mouth. Flesh. Ass. Everything I had to give was his for the taking.

"Touch my cock," I begged, pulling on the cuffs.

"Fuck. I need to see you." He pushed my blindfold up, and I blinked against the sudden light. But when my vision cleared, what a sight he made. His pupils were blown, face slack with pleasure as he slid deep over and over. And his eyes never left mine, staring so intently I wondered what he was seeing.

Trust. Tenderness. Appreciation. Lust. They were all there, hanging between us, each look laced with more and more emotion until I couldn't stop myself from moaning. "Need you. Logan. Need you."

"I've got you." His hand gripped my cock, and he started a slick slide that matched his thrusts. "You gonna come for me?"

"Fuck, yes." My body was sprinting toward orgasm,

senses on overload. Felt like it might char me through, but I still wanted it, welcomed the heat and burn and promise of enough pleasure to fry my already-sizzling nerves. He was going to be the end of me, and I wanted it.

"Come for me. Now." His hand tightened, but it was the command that sent me over. I could deny this man nothing at all.

"*Logan.*" My body bucked, and my forgotten ice pack hit the floor with a smacking noise.

"God, I'm coming." He thrust hard and fast, face clenching, neck taut with pleasure. His eyes were screwed shut, but at the last second, they fluttered open and the depth of emotion there hit me like a punch. He *cared*. It was there in every touch, every look, every thrust. And damn it, so did I. I wanted good things for him, wanted his pleasure more than my own. I looked away first. I didn't want this, hadn't asked for it, yet here we were. And fuck if I knew what to do with it.

He pulled out, undid my cuffs, and for the first time I utterly craved his caretaking, the way he rubbed my wrists, got my icepack back in place, cleaned me up, and then cuddled me close. His whispered praise was the best drug on the planet. I let myself revel in the warmth of his affection. He was everything I hadn't let myself acknowledge missing, let alone needing, but I did. Tightly locked, hidden places inside my soul soaked in his attention, barren soil that had stopped even waiting for rain. I might not know what to do with the emotions rolling around in my chest, but all I knew was that I was no longer strong enough to shove Logan away.

SEVENTEEN

Logan

Even after we switched to the other bed, Curtis stayed close to me all night. It was everything I'd ever wanted and nothing I'd expected. The sex had been a revelation, kinky and loving at the same time, an emotional power trip as he'd submitted to me. And he felt it, too. I could tell by his eyes, by the way he went pliant in my arms. Things were changing between us, encounter by encounter, moment by moment, and while it scared me, I also reveled in it.

I would have happily spent all Saturday in bed, losing myself in him and these feelings, but there was a second day of carving to see to. Being a weekend day with slightly warmer weather, there was more tourist traffic. That meant more customers for me to try to win over while Curtis carved. And the carving itself was becoming serious, with grim-faced carvers racing to get pieces done before the afternoon auction for charity.

Curtis himself was in some sort of robotic trance,

churning out small pieces that sold as fast as he got them done and moving between several big pieces at the same time. He was absolutely a performance artist, larger than life, and I couldn't believe that this was the same guy who'd been in my arms hours earlier begging me for relief. Power and muscle and charisma—and it was all mine. It wasn't that far from being able to harness lightning, and I was about that awestruck at my luck.

His charity piece was a moose head on a pedestal decorated with fish and river stones.

"You going to have it done by four?" I asked when I made him take a quick break for food.

"Yup." He shook his fist at the wood, like it personally had offended him. "It's coming. That and Betty's monkey."

The monkey was adorable in a whimsical pose, holding a platter that could be used for a beverage or plant. Betty and Burt forked over a nice-sized check for the privilege of figuring out how to get it home.

"Man, it is so nice to see Curtis carving happy again." Gloria came by after lunch. I liked her and Walter's daughter a lot. I envied them their motorcycles and matching tattoos and strong, close bond. She patted the top of the monkey. "Last year was all angry birds who looked ready to peck us all to death."

"He's grieving," I said loyally. "It's a process."

A process I really hoped I was helping, not hindering. And I hoped all the lighter carvings were a good sign for us.

"Well, you keep at it. Troy was something else, but I think there's something there for you guys, too."

Grrr. I didn't need the reminder that even if what we

had was special that I'd never live up to the sainted Troy. All weekend I'd heard snippets of Troy stories, and the guy seemed like a cross between Santa and a Harley ad. I heard the swirling gossip, too. Everyone loved him. Everyone missed him. Everyone was skeptical that Curtis could ever move on. Including me. Oh, well. All I could do was smile and nod.

By four, I was about tired of smiling, but then Curtis needed my help moving the moose sculpture, and my smile got easy again. I couldn't help it. The piece was easily the best thing anyone had produced all weekend. And Gloria was right—it was definitely a happy moose, surrounded by dancing fish. *I did that. I made him happy, even if only for a night.* I felt strange pride carting the thing over to the display area with him. And it was no surprise when he netted the most bids, raising a hefty sum for the charity and getting himself several custom orders from the losing bidders.

"Curtis." Another carver, a small man with a pinched face who hadn't been at dinner last night, came over. His carving of a shark had earned about a third of what Curtis's moose had.

"Otis." Curtis didn't look too happy to converse with him.

"See you have a new boy with you." Otis's tone made it clear this was *not* a good thing. He looked me up and down. "Troy that easy to replace?"

Otis was damn lucky that Curtis was between me and him because I had some aikido moves I was dying to test out on his tiny head.

"He's just a friend." Curtis kept his tone even and cool even as each word made my heart pinch. I supposed

I should be glad we'd moved as far as friends, but I didn't want to be his *friend*. Or his "just" anything. Just a friend. Just a ride. Just a kid. I didn't want any of it.

Otis snorted, but Curtis continued to project his zero-fucks attitude. "You take care now, Otis. I'll see you in June. Reckon I'll be taking home the championship again. I'll be sure and show you the trophy."

"Someone's going to take you down a peg this year. I vote me or my brother Earl. We're each twice the carver you are." Otis puffed himself up like one of those desert lizards.

"Trouble?" Walter came ambling over. "They're about to start the burn."

"Nah. No trouble here." Curtis gave Otis a measured look before heading to where the twelve-foot sculpture of three bears was about to be lit up. I followed him.

"He was…unpleasant."

"Eh." Curtis shrugged. "Maybe. There's all kinds of nasty folks. I don't pay them any mind. Just go out and carve. Otis doesn't have to like it. Sorry if he hurt your feelings."

No, you did. I imitated his shrug. "Nah. I'm used to the kid comments."

"You're not looking much like one these days." Curtis's look held more heat than the kindling at the base of the sculpture bonfire. And, okay, that went a ways to making me forget about the friend's comment.

We hung back on the edge of the crowd as the bears took flame, a giant bonfire whose heat could be felt even where we stood. The wood popped and crackled, and the scent of burning cedar was heavy in the air. People milled about in clumps, some with drinks, many who seemed to be old friends. Someone had a guitar and a country melody wove its way through the night.

"Man, that's something," I said, admiring the fire.

"Yeah, it is," Curtis said, looking right at me. My skin heated in a way that had nothing to do with the fire. Maybe he was simply thinking ahead to sex back in the hotel room, but I couldn't help but feel Curtis was really seeing me for the first time.

The shadows lengthened, full darkness descending, and Curtis made no move to go find Walter or a friendly group.

"Cold?" he asked, stepping closer. "We can go whenever you want."

"No. I want to see it a little longer. It's…magical." And it really was. The bonfire. This weekend. This man.

"We'll stay, then." Curtis shocked the stuffing right out of me when he laced our hands together. It was dark and no one was paying us any mind, but it still felt… radical somehow. Like Curtis was flipping off Otis and anyone else who didn't care for him. And I'd had him naked, marked his body, done kinky sex, waited weeks for that first kiss, and still this simple act of holding hands threatened to top all of that.

This. This is when our story really begins. My heart leapt and danced just like the flames licking up the sides of the wooden sculpture. The future was uncertain, and all the doubts about whether I could compete with a ghost weren't going away, but there was a certain rightness about this moment that couldn't be denied. It would be easy to hold back, pretend that I wasn't falling for this man, but then he squeezed my hand, and I knew it was futile. He was probably going to break my heart, and I was still a goner for him. And I was greedy. I wanted a thousand more moments just like this one, us standing together against the cold, rest of the world be damned.

Curtis

Something about the fire made me need Logan in the worst way. Maybe it was the big blaze. Maybe it was my record-breaking sales haul for the day or the high of finishing the pieces. Maybe it was being pissed as fuck at Otis and anyone else who wanted to have an opinion on my personal business. And maybe it was Logan himself. The way he looked at the fire with his eyes all wide and soft. The way he squeezed my hand. The joy on his face, at least part of which I knew I was responsible for. He really did have the most expressive face, and I wanted to see more, revel in the emotions I could cause.

I was good, keeping my hands to myself while we loaded up and he drove to the motel, but the second the door shut behind me, it was *on*. I pushed him back against the door, claiming his mouth in a hard kiss. His gasp of surprise was fuel to my fire, and I shoved a hand under all his shirts to pull him closer. His phone jingled in his pocket and his hand flopped around between us.

I grabbed his wrist. "Don't even think about it."

"It could be—"

"And it'll still be just as important in twenty minutes."

"Oh, is that all?" He laughed and leaned in for another kiss. He didn't pull his hand away, and I used it to tug him toward the bed. Banging him against the door had its appeal, but my knees were exhausted after the long day, even as the rest of my body was raring to go.

In between kisses, I pushed his clothes off and fumbled out of mine. Lord, but I hadn't had kisses like this in years and years. Deep ones. Drugging ones. Soft and gentle ones. Hard and demanding. Tongue fucking. Biting. Growling. And I wasn't sure which of us was leading. Wasn't sure it even mattered. We ended up in a heap on the bed, me on top, but he wasn't complaining any, yanking me down for another kiss. This wasn't a scene. Wasn't a pre-arranged sex date. Wasn't a playful morning wakeup. No, this was need, flat-out and all-consuming. Raw. Powerful. His fingers dug into my shoulders in a way that made my cock throb, but I wasn't in search of the rush of pain—what I wanted was more of this.

I couldn't remember the last time I'd rubbed off with someone, but my body knew what to do, surging against his, hard cocks dragging across each other. He wrapped his legs around me, holding me tighter as we continued to kiss.

"Close," he panted. "Please…"

Oh, that was new, him being the one begging. And I liked it. "Tell me what you need," I ordered.

Even like this, my whole body lived to serve him, wanted to turn him on, make him happy. He could have asked for anything right then, and I would have tried to make it happen. Harness the moon. Carry the flames. Run the ocean.

"Want to come," he moaned. "Need you to touch me."

Shifting my weight, I got a hand between us, gripped both our cocks together. "Like this?"

"Fuck, yeah." He reached for the lube on the night-stand and drizzled some in his palm. Joining my hand with his, we made a slick channel for our dicks to slide through. It reminded me of holding hands at the fire — there was a promise here, something new blossoming between us as we shared this connection. It wasn't just me. Wasn't just him. It was both of us, together.

Even though the angle was awkward, I kissed him again, needing his mouth even more than I needed the orgasm that was building.

"Fuck. Fuck. Close." His hips bucked against mine, cock thrusting up faster and harder. The pressure and friction against mine was so good.

"That's it, baby. Come for me." I nipped at his lips. "Gonna get me there, too."

"Fuck. Curtis. Need you."

"You've got me." And he did. He had everything I had to offer, meager though it might be. Nothing I wouldn't give him.

"Coming," he whimpered seconds before hot fluid coated both our fists. The added slipperiness allowed me to go faster, and it didn't take much before I was groaning and joining him. It wasn't the deep, lingering orgasm of a fucking or a long, drawn-out one from a scene, but the crackle and sizzle through my nerve endings charred me, a forest fire springing up from a single match. Didn't matter how we came together, but he took my breath away, consumed me, changed me.

"Fuck. Something tells me that twenty minutes was a vast overestimation." He laughed as he held me close.

"Give me another twenty and a shower, and I'll go

again. Make it up to you." I pressed a clumsy kiss against his face.

"Hell, if it gets any better than that, I might not survive." Rolling away, he retrieved his pants and pulled out his phone.

"Oh, fuck me." He flopped backward onto the bed.

"Didn't think that was on the table," I drawled, still in a good mood and slightly stupid from the orgasm. "But it could be arranged."

"No one's getting fucked next week," he groaned. "My parents are driving down for this coming weekend. They want to support the Valentine's special on Saturday night and talk more about investing. And they can get their sculpture then, too."

"I thought you were close to them. Don't want to see them?"

"I don't really want to hear again how I look like a mugshot. And if they don't invest, I don't know what Mason's going to do. What we're all going to do."

"You look damn good to me." I sat up and kissed his shoulder. "And I think they love you. They'll get over their snit about a little face fuzz. And you know they'll invest."

"I guess." He sat up next to me. "It's just more stress that I don't need this week. I'm worried enough about the Valentine's dinner."

"It'll be good." I squeezed his arm. "I have a feeling Nash is going to drag me out since Mason's working the event, and the man thinks it's his new mission to get you more business."

"You guys are cool, then?" He gave me a sheepish look. "He lectured me earlier in the week about staying

ANNABETH ALBERT

away from you, but I didn't want to piss you off by telling you before we left."

"He stopped by," I admitted. "Gave me the same lecture. But we go way back. Nothing for you to get worried about."

"Yeah. I was thinking, though… If people are going to know…"

"Oh, no." I knew exactly what he was thinking. "Nash figuring things out is one thing. You don't need to go telling your parents anything about this."

"Why not? They might stop bugging me so much about moving back if they know I've got something here." His smile didn't reach his eyes as he got off the bed. "And besides, they want me to be happy, like you said."

"I didn't mean *that*." I scrambled off the bed, ignoring the lingering ache in my ankle, heading in the direction of the bathroom. "Listen. We've got a good thing going, but I've told you, I'm not a meet-the-parents kind of guy. Don't go borrowing trouble when you need them for the business."

"But you're both important to me. I want them to like you."

I snorted. "Parents don't like me. Ever. Trust me, it's easier if they don't know." I hated how his face fell, so I held out a hand. "Come shower with me."

"Fine." Logan's tone said he wasn't done with this, not by a long shot. He was such an optimist and undoubtedly had a rosy vision of his parents and me getting along and breaking bread instead of them wanting to break my head for messing with their sweet baby.

And I was making things worse by not simply ending this now, telling him without waffling that there was nothing here. But I couldn't stomp on him like that. Not now. Not when even after the bone-melting sex, my body still needed more. I'd said over and over that I didn't do addictions, didn't do luxuries, and he was both. But I wanted to ride this high a little longer. There'd be time enough for us to untangle eventually, time enough for me to regret my own stupidity, but I just wanted to store up a few more memories first.

EIGHTEEN

Logan

"Your hair hasn't grown any." My mom clucked over me as soon as they were in my house Thursday night.

"I like it." Truthfully, it hadn't grown any because Curtis had touched it up last night before a quick lesson in goatee shaping. And all that had been foreplay for a blistering scene where I'd flogged him before we'd fucked, clinging together afterward like it might be the last time. Which it damn well better not be.

"Connie. Let him have his hair." My dad sounded tired after their long drive. "If he wants to look like a domestic-terrorist suspect, that's his doing. It's a phase."

"I'm not fifteen," I reminded him as I carried Mom's suitcase into the spare room. "And I don't look like a criminal. Plenty of people around here have a similar look."

Dad grunted as he set his suitcase next to Mom's at the foot of the bed. "Well, you'll stick out at the country club next time you visit. But I suppose you don't care about that…"

I really didn't, as the country club with our parents had always been far more Seth's scene than mine, but I didn't want to start the weekend by hurting their feelings. "I'm sure I can still clean up nicely. I wouldn't want to embarrass you in front of your friends, but honestly, I'm not sure they'd care about a haircut and a few tats."

"Tattoos?" My mom gasped. "Tell me you didn't."

"Not yet. But probably soon." I'd been quizzing Curtis about his tattoo-artist friend over in Eugene. I'd been so jealous of Gloria and Walter's daughter's tats that it felt like it was time for me to take the step. "It's not like I'm thinking of one on my forehead."

"Oh, Logan, I really don't know what to make of this rebellion." Mom let out a soft sigh as she sat on the edge of the bed.

"It's not a rebellion." I matched her sigh with one of my own. I was twenty-seven, not fifteen, and I was so ready for them to realize that. "This is just me discovering myself."

And it really was. I'd loved feeling like I'd fit in at the carving festival, loved looking in the mirror and seeing this guy looking back, didn't miss my preppy shirts and pants. I liked my thicker, hardier clothes and boots.

"This isn't you. I know you." She shook her head, and I had to question if she really did. Maybe all they knew was the ideal I'd invariably struggled to live up to.

"We can talk more in the morning." Dad patted her shoulder. "Everyone's tired tonight."

I'd always liked how protective he was of her, how he always seemed to know what she was feeling, but right then it felt very dismissive of me, and I gritted my teeth. "Fine."

In the morning, I had to go into the tavern, so they worked from my place until after lunch. When I got home, they were getting ready to pick up the sculpture from Curtis. And apparently, Curtis wasn't the only masochist in town, because I'd volunteered to come along and help Dad load it up before I had to be back for the dinner rush.

Seeing Curtis without being able to let on what we were to each other was going to suck.

But not seeing him might suck worse, having to wonder how things went with my folks when they picked up the sculpture. And so I found myself driving Dad's car to Curtis's shortly after two. They'd brought the SUV, so there would be plenty of room in the back for the sculpture.

"Wow," I exclaimed after we arrived at his place. He had the piece ready to go under the awning, and I couldn't help my wonder at seeing it completed. The oil finish he'd added gleamed, and each painstaking detail really stood out—the troll's impish grin, the tilt of his little hat, the bend in his knees, even his long fingers were defined. "This is one of your best."

"Thanks." Curtis had an uneasy smile, as if he were afraid that I might throw myself into his arms. Which, come on, I had more restraint than that. He needed to trust me.

My dad wrote a check to pay for the balance he owed, scowling even though I'd seen him drop that amount on a really nice dinner before.

Worried about Dad's back, I made sure I was the one

to help Curtis wrestle the heavy sculpture into the rear of the SUV.

"F—man this is heavy." I narrowly avoided cursing. "Maybe this isn't going to fit after all."

"Oh, it'll fit. I've loaded into far tighter spaces."

I couldn't tell if Curtis was intentionally being dirty, but I snorted like a seventh grader anyway.

"Behave," he growled.

"Ah—*ow*." My hand got squashed between the troll and the floor of the SUV.

Curtis finished shoving the sculpture in and stepped closer. "Here. Let me look. Did it break the skin?"

"No." I let him take my hand because his touch was too damn nice to pull away from. "Just pinched. Nothing's broken."

"Good. I like you in one piece." He gave me a meaningful look, and for a second I forgot my parents' presence and smiled up at him, close to leaning in and—

"Logan, are you hurt?" My mom came over and Curtis abruptly dropped my hand.

"I'm fine," I said, offering her a much more forced smile than the one I'd given Curtis. "You ready to leave or you find more to buy?"

"We can go," Dad spoke for her. He was frowning at Curtis as if there was a lot he wanted to say and wasn't. *Fuck.* This was not how I wanted this meeting to unfold. I wanted them to like Curtis, to see him like I did, but they were both glaring at him as if he'd personally injured my hand. *Time to go.*

"I'll drive you guys back to my place and head in on the bike for the evening shift." I tried to tell Curtis with my eyes that I'd call later, but he either wasn't paying attention or didn't care because he walked away before we were even done loading up, no trace of the guy who'd kissed me so desperately only the day before yesterday.

Mom waited until we were headed back to my house to speak. "What is going on with you?"

"What do you mean?" I wasn't trying to play dumb — there was just so much churning in my head that trying to read her mind was beyond me.

"You and the wood carver. There's something going on there." Her voice was higher-pitched than usual.

"We're friends —"

"Don't lie to me. I saw your Instagram all weekend — you went away together. That sounds like way more than friendly to me."

"Since when is it okay to social-media stalk me?" I groaned. I hadn't thought about them seeing my pictures from the weekend. I'd been having so much fun taking pictures of the carving and the festival that I hadn't paid attention to little details like how many pictures were of Curtis and what conclusions people might draw.

"You're my child. Of course I want to keep up with you."

"Yeah, I went to a carving competition with him. It was fun."

"He's a little old for you to be having fun with," Dad said sharply. "He's got...what? Twenty years on you?"

"Fifteen," I mumbled. Why did he have to make something that didn't bug me sound so dirty and wrong? When Curtis and I were together and alone, I honestly didn't think about the age difference anymore. Sure, he had more experience than me, but that was rapidly coming to mean less and less. What we shared together was what really mattered.

"Still. He's taking advantage of your…friendship," Mom pressed as I pulled into my driveway.

I flashed back to Wednesday again—Curtis tied to my bed, red marks over his back from the flogging, him begging to be fucked. If anyone was taking advantage, it was me, goading him into the lessons, keeping this going even after the pretext of the lessons went away. I was getting far more out of this arrangement than Curtis, but I couldn't tell my parents any of that.

"He's not. He's a good guy. And it's just a casual friendship," I lied, trying to keep my promise to Curtis to not tell them everything. I got out of the car and followed them into the house through the kitchen door.

"You deserve far more than a casual friendship," she insisted, seeing straight through my protests. "Don't you think so? Don't you think you deserve a real partnership? A relationship you can tell your family about?"

Well, now she was hitting at both my deepest wants and strongest fears. I did crave a real partnership with Curtis, one where we could be open about our relationship, one where I could tell my parents exactly how happy he made me. But he didn't want that, and so instead I was stuck with this awkward conversation.

"I want that," I admitted softly, leaning against a kitchen cabinet.

"With someone your own age," she added quickly, and I groaned. I could practically see the "give Seth another chance" lecture brewing.

"And you'd have better luck doing that back in the Portland area." My dad's voice was firm, and his face was stern. He took a seat at the table where he'd set up his laptop and paperwork earlier.

"I told you. I want to make it here. I love working with my friends. They're counting on me." My voice came out far thicker than I liked.

"I've reviewed all the financial information Mason sent over—I'm just not sure there's a viable business model here." He gestured at a stack of papers. "All the wanting in the world isn't going to print money for you guys."

My chest throbbed like it had been smacked. "It's a great idea for a business. And it'll pick up when the resort reopens. Tourist season will help, too. It's just been a rough few months."

"I'm not sure you can count on that."

"Are you saying no to investing?" My voice was hoarse. "Because you're upset about who I'm friends with?"

"It's not about that." My father waved my concerns away. "It's about good business sense. And your future. I don't want to watch you squander that away—either personally or professionally."

"I'm not." My phone buzzed with a reminder alarm. Time to head to the tavern, to ensure the future my parents weren't so certain about. "Look, I've got to get back to work now. We can talk more about this later, but *please* don't choose not to invest just because you're frustrated with me."

"I'm not ruling anything out." His voice was gentler now, but his mouth was still a harsh line. This wasn't over, not by a long shot.

"I'll see you guys later. And be sure and come by for

dinner." I grabbed my helmet and biking jacket and headed for my bike in the garage. I wanted to make things right with them and hated being mad at them. And being mad at Curtis sucked, too. Why did he have to be so damn stubborn? Things didn't have to be tense with my parents. Us acting like a normal couple, not like we were ashamed or hiding something would have gone a long way. I wasn't down for being his dirty secret, and I had enough to handle with my parents acting all ashamed of what I was becoming—I didn't need it from him, too. I deserved better.

Curtis

I hated seeing Logan leave with his parents. I felt like I'd let him down somehow, and I worried that his hand was hurt worse than he was letting on. I knew he wanted me to get along with his parents, but I'd lived a good many years. I could tell when people took an active dislike to me, and those two radiated disdain.

I was considering whether or not to text Logan, see how his hand was doing, when my phone rang. Janice's number flashed on the screen, and my stomach flopped, same way it always did when Troy's mother called. It was usually some small favor, one I was happy to do, but fresh grief always sprang forth at her greeting despite my best efforts to contain it.

"Janice! What can I do for you?" I kept my voice easy. She didn't need any of my bad mood or frustrations.

"Oh, Curtis, I hate bothering you, but it's Chopper. I

don't know what to do. He's been throwing up, and he's all sluggish now."

I started putting away my tools even before I answered her. "I'm on my way. You hang tight. Call the vet—see if she can get us in before she closes."

"I can do that." Janice's voice trembled.

Hurrying through clean-up, I flipped my sign to closed and headed to her place where she greeted me at the driveway.

"He doesn't want to move."

"Did you call the vet?" I followed her in, cold sweat running down my back. I didn't know what Janice would do without Chopper, and while he was getting up there in years, I'd hoped we'd have a while before any sort of painful decisions had to be made. Whenever I saw him, I'd see the puppy Troy had carried under his jacket, so sure he was what his mother had needed in her life after her old poodle had passed on.

"Yes. She said to bring him right in." She showed me to the base of the stairs where Chopper lay breathing hard.

"Hey, buddy, not doing so good, huh?" I stroked his flank. "I'll carry him to the truck."

"I…got my shoes on. I'll…get my pocketbook." Janice had gone distinctly gray around her lips, shoulders sagging as well.

"It's okay." I paused before lifting the dog to pat her shoulder. "You want me to take him on in? I can give you a call as soon as we're there."

"Would you?" Her eyes were large blue pools of emotion. "I mean, I should…"

"I'd be happy to help. And you're not gonna do Chop

any good if you go making yourself sick." I led her to her chair. "Let me do this for you."

"All right." She gave me a quavering smile. "You'll call?"

"As soon as I have news. I promise." Scooping up Chopper, I carried him to the truck, got him settled on the passenger side floor.

The vet was an older woman around Janice's age with a long braid down her back, Dr. Locklear, and she was the sister to one of Nash's officers.

"Oh, Chopper, what did you do to yourself?" She stroked his muzzle as I got him settled on the exam table. To me, she said, "No Janice?"

"She wasn't feeling up to the trip out. She's mighty nervous, though, so I'll be calling her with updates."

"All right, we can bill—"

"I'll handle that," I said firmly. I had a feeling this might get pricey, and no way did I want that burden for Janice.

"That's fine." She felt Chopper's stomach. "I don't think we're dealing with a blockage, but I'd like to get some diagnostic tests and blood work to give us a better picture of what we're up against. We'll also get him some fluids as he seems very dehydrated."

I called Janice with an update as the doctor took Chopper back for the tests. I hated feeling this helpless. And I hated too how this made me think about Troy—all the memories of him helping Janice train Chopper. Hell, even his name was Troy's doing. If we lost Chopper, it would be like losing another piece of Troy, and I just wasn't ready for that.

It was a long wait, and I kinda wished I had Logan's

phone with that silly fishing game instead of the stacks of pet and decorating magazines. Finally, the vet emerged.

"Good news! No blockage." She led me back to the exam room. "My best guess from the blood work is that he ate something he wasn't supposed to. But the fluids helped enormously, as you can see."

On that note, one of the vet techs led Chopper into the room—he was walking and wagged his tail when he saw me. Relief coursed through me, and my eyes felt suddenly heavy and liquid.

"I'd like to see him soon for follow-up blood work, but he seems so markedly improved that I'm not sure we need to keep him overnight. Bland food only—I'll give you a sample of some special chow that may work."

"Janice will be relieved to have him back, I'm sure." I petted his head. We handled the special chow and the not-insignificant bill, and then I drove back to Janice's with a much more energetic Chopper sitting on the seat next to me.

"Oh, I'm so glad he's okay." Janice's eyes were bright with unshed tears as she greeted Chopper and me in the driveway. "Thank you. So much. Don't know what I would have done if you hadn't answered the phone."

"Any time. Anything for you," I said and meant it.

"I thought you might be too busy. What with all that's going on with you." Her voice was a bit sharper as she led Chopper to his bed in the living room. She had the room much too warm again, and sweat beaded up along my collar.

"What do you mean?" I asked. Janice wasn't usually one to trot out sarcasm, but she'd had quite the scare, so I was inclined to forgive her tone.

"Del Hawkins delivered my groceries while you were gone. He saw fit to tell me he's worried about you, keeping company with some young kid." Frowning, she shook her head.

Fuck. I'd figured my business was getting around town, but I hadn't thought about Janice maybe finding out.

"I'm not seeing anyone, least not anything serious." My chest pinched with the denial. I could almost picture Logan's hurt expression. "And in any event, he's twenty-seven."

"That's *young*," she clucked. "Too young for you. You're...a certain age now. Not one of those young fellas anymore."

"I'm not that old," I protested, although her words made me feel every one of the years separating me and Logan.

"You know, after my Roger passed on, I never once looked around. Didn't even occur to me." Her words reminded me of Walter's quiet judgment. Why did everyone seem to expect me to pack away my sex drive in mothballs, give up the chance of companionship? Was that really the best path forward?

But I didn't know how to even mention the word sex to Janice, so I just shrugged.

"You have to wonder, what would Troy think of this?"

The thought I'd had the previous weekend came back. He'd have been amused by Logan. Maybe they wouldn't have been tight friends, but I didn't see him as outright hostile to the notion. "Never know. He might like Logan. He's a great—"

221

"No." Janice recoiled like she'd been slapped. "He'd never approve. Don't you think his memory deserves more?"

Well, fuck. That hit me in the most soft, raw part of my heart, the place that had never healed. Never would. Hell if I even knew what Troy deserved. What he would have wanted for me. In the first awful days after Troy's accident, only two things had stopped me from joining him—knowing that Janice would be all alone with no one to look after her and the deep conviction that Troy would hate me for even considering it. And maybe my views on the afterlife were murky, but I'd known I couldn't let him down like that.

"He'd want me to live," I said quietly. "Not sure of much beyond that—"

"Well, I am. He made *vows* to you. That counts for something."

"It does." Most people in town didn't know about that. We'd never exchanged rings or thrown a big party. But when it had become legal here in Oregon, Troy had insisted on going to the courthouse, making it official. He'd been worried about my work—if I injured myself and the hospital wouldn't let him make decisions—and he'd wanted to make sure the house was in both our names. Practical shit like that. Little did either of us know he'd go first, and I still felt immense guilt that I'd inherited, not Janice. It wasn't right. And she'd stead-fastly refused any efforts by me to gift her any of it.

"Well, act like it." She huffed her way over to her chair. "Now Curtis, I love you like you were my own, but we both know this is foolishness."

"We're friends," I said weakly, each word slicing me

open. And her saying she loved me made it that much worse. We weren't affectionate, her and me, but I knew she cared. Knew she meant well. And knew there might some truth to her words.

"Well, I guess I can't stop you from having *friends*, but just think about what you're doing."

"I will." My throat burned, raw feeling keeping up even once I was back in my truck. I knew what I needed to do, much as I hated it. I was about to pull out when the phone rang. Nash. I almost didn't answer it, but my spine tingled.

"What's wrong?" My fears asked for me.

"Logan was in an accident. On his bike. He was—"

"Is he okay?" Oh no. No. This could not be happening. This shit day could not be getting this much worse.

"He's alive. It was a low-speed collision, thank God. No visible broken bones that we could see at the accident site, but they're taking him into Coos Bay for a full evaluation, especially for a concussion. Can't be too safe about a possible head injury."

"You tell his parents?"

"Yup. They're on their way. Thought you'd probably want to know."

"Yeah." I swallowed hard. Fuck. I could not deal with this. I was not prepared. Not again. Not ever. My truck pointed its way north, even without my permission.

I made my way to the hospital in a daze, not sure how I managed to avoid getting pulled over by the highway patrol. The hospital was a large complex that served the whole southern coast, but I knew my way to the ER well enough. Bile rose in my throat on the walk from the parking lot, memories flooding me, one after

ANNABETH ALBERT

another. My folks. Troy's father. Troy. Nothing good ever came from this place.

I spotted his parents right away in the ER waiting room. His mother's face was tear streaked. Fuck. They should be with him. Unless...

My boots carried me over toward them when the rest of me would have put down roots on the entry mat.

"What are you doing here?" his father growled at me before I could even get my question out.

"Ed. He's Logan's friend." Logan's mother patted him on the arm.

"You know as well as I do they've got no business being friends. This is the wrong place for Logan. Wrong business and wrong direction for his life." His tone suggested that I was the reason Logan had moved here, like I was the thing keeping him here, neither of which were true. I'd say that his condemnation stung, but after the day I'd had, one more hurt barely registered. So they didn't want the two of us involved? Join the fucking club. My conversation with Janice loomed large, full of harsh realizations I couldn't escape any longer.

"How is he?" I kept my voice even.

"Conscious. They took him back for an MRI right away, though. Barely let us see him." She bit her knuckles.

"Drivers around here have no sense. They don't respect cyclists." Logan's father glared at me like I was responsible for the driving habits of Rainbow Cove.

"He never should have come here. He doesn't belong in this place," his mother added before I could respond about the bad drivers.

I didn't know what to say in the face of their anger

224

and sadness and frustration. I knew deep down that they were right that he didn't belong here. Logan was meant for better things. Greater things. Meant for so much more than me. Meant to have his big dreams. And those weren't going to happen with me or the area tying him down.

"I'm not going to hold him back," I said at last. "Not gonna keep him here. I just want to make sure he's all right. That's all."

And with that I walked to the far corner of the room, slumped in a chair next to a pile of outdated magazines for the second time that day, and prepared for another long wait and more uncertain news. Whatever the outcome, I knew nothing was ever going to be the same again.

NINETEEN

Logan

"Lay still." The MRI tech repeated the same order I'd heard over and over the last few hours. I still wasn't sure exactly what had happened. One moment I'd been biking to the tavern, about to turn onto the street that led to the town square, and the next I'd been in a ditch, cold and blinking against a killer headache. Apparently a passing driver had spotted me—whomever had side-swiped me hadn't been so kind—and the ambulance people weren't sure how long I'd been out, which was why everyone was all concerned about a head injury.

Other than the headache and some nasty road rash, nothing seemed broken even though everything hurt. The whir of the MRI machine didn't help my head, and it took forever. I'd briefly seen my parents before the orderly had whisked me back to imaging, and I hated how worried they'd looked. I was still frustrated with them about Curtis and about their reluctance to invest in the tavern, but I loved them and didn't want them scared.

"And you made it." The tech, who had a beard to rival Curtis's, grinned down at me as he helped me transfer back to the gurney. "It's going to take a while for the neurologist to read the images, so you get to hang out downstairs. Be sure and tell the nursing staff if you experience anything out of the ordinary—vision shifts, vomiting, feeling weak. The neurologist on duty will probably come down and examine you herself before they let you think about leaving."

He released me to the same orderly who had delivered me to imaging, and she took me back to a cubicle in the ER.

"Can you tell my parents I'm out of the MRI?" I asked her. "I know they're worried."

"I'll tell them they can come back," she promised.

It didn't take too long before they came bustling in, holding hands and looking haggard.

"Oh, Logan. Your face." My mom teared up.

"It's just scrapes," I tried reassure her but she was too far away to pat. "I'm fine."

"I hate this." She pulled a chair close so she could squeeze my hand. The three of us watched a bad cooking show on TV, and she didn't let go of my hand until the neurologist came in two episodes later. The doctor was a tall woman with hipster glasses, and her manner seemed to encourage both my parents to dial down the anxiety.

She looked at my eyes and ears and had me do some basic math and memory questions before testing my balance.

"The MRI was clean. No brain bleed or skull fracture. I think you have a mild to moderate concussion, though, and we should probably keep you overnight for observation."

"No way. I *have* to work tomorrow night. We're doing our Valentine's meal. I'm the chef. I can't miss that."

The doctor gave me a sympathetic smile. "How about this? I'll come back to see you first thing in the morning, and if everything's still looking good, we'll talk about sending you home. I'm not sure you'll feel up to work later in the day, but we can try."

"Logan, listen to the doctor," my mom insisted. "Better safe than sorry."

"Exactly." The doctor nodded. "I'm going to put in the request to transfer you to a room upstairs. And you tell the nursing staff if you start having any new symptoms, okay? No playing hero."

"I'll let them know," I promised, hoping my mom would loosen her grip on my hand. The doctor left, but still my mom clung. I was seriously starting to need a break. And more circulation to my fingers. "Do you guys need food? Coffee? I'm sure they can tell you where they move me to."

"I guess I might be hungry." My father stood. *Thank God.* Now for him to take Mom with him so that I could breathe. "And I suppose someone should tell that friend of yours out there that they're keeping you overnight."

My mouth fell open, which made my head hurt worse. "Curtis? Curtis is here, and you didn't tell me anything the whole time we were watching the stupid TV?"

"Most emergency rooms have a family-only visiting policy," my dad blustered.

"And we were worried about upsetting you," Mom added.

"Well, consider me upset." I glared at both of them. "I can't believe you did this. I want to see him."

Dad rubbed the bridge of his nose. "Maybe—"

"No 'maybe.' I want to see him. As soon as I'm in the room, if they won't let him come back here."

"We'll consider—"

"Make. It. Happen." I used a tone of voice that I'd never used on them before, the one that came from the same place as my Dom voice.

"Okay, okay. I think your headache is making you cranky." My dad shook his head at me like I was a misbehaving toddler he was indulging. "I'll go talk to him."

"Thank you." I gritted out the words. Still shaking their heads, they both left the cubicle. My phone had been smashed in the crash or I'd have texted Curtis myself. The orderly returned before my parents, taking me up to a room with two empty beds. I'd volunteered to walk but she'd just laughed and wheeled me through the halls and helped me into the bed like I was eighty.

"You rest," she said before leaving me alone.

I didn't, of course, instead gnashing my teeth over worries about Curtis and the tavern. The TV wasn't a good distraction. I heard my mom's heels before she entered the room, and I braced myself for another argument.

"Here's your friend." My mom's voice was fake nice, as if I were supposed to forget that they'd kept me from him. But Curtis was there, standing behind both of my parents, and that was all that really mattered. And he didn't look any too happy, either.

"Can you give us a minute?" I asked. No way did I want to talk to Curtis with them hovering, especially not with Curtis glaring at their backs. "Did you get food?"

"I suppose we can walk. Maybe get some snacks." A muscle worked in my dad's jaw.

"I'm *fine*," I assured them. "Staying here tonight is just a precaution. You could head back to my place for some sleep."

"We'll walk." Mom ignored my suggestion, much as I'd expected. They left the room, shooting Curtis a warning look.

God, save me from overprotective parents. "I'd give a pinky finger for siblings right now," I joked once they were gone. "Preferably really demanding triplets. I'm sorry they were so awful to you. They didn't tell me you were waiting."

"Figured." Curtis stepped closer to the bed. "How are you? Really, no bull."

"I'm banged up," I admitted. "Everything hurts. My head especially, but they said it's just a mild concussion. And I'm going to live. I was lucky."

"Yeah, you were." Curtis looked so distraught, paler than usual with his mouth a thin line. I motioned him closer, patting the side of the bed.

"Come here," I ordered.

"That voice doesn't work when you're hurt." Curtis managed a shaky laugh as he complied and perched on the edge of the bed.

"I *know*. Didn't work on my parents, either." I reached for his hand, squeezed. "I really am okay. I'm sorry for scaring you."

"Not your fault." Curtis didn't meet my eyes. His voice was more exhausted than I'd ever heard it. "I'm glad you're okay now."

"What's wrong?" I could tell something was off, more than simply me being hurt.

"Nothing. Just a long day, that's all. We can talk once you're back on your feet."

Oh, I did not like the sound of this. "We can talk now."

"No. You need rest. And your parents—"

"Can damn well wait."

"They mean well. They love you." His eyes were heavy and sad.

"They told you to stay away from me, didn't they?"

"They're right," he whispered. "I should. But we can talk—"

"Right now. Curtis, are you seriously breaking up with me just because I got hurt and that scared you?"

He took forever to answer. "I'm not sure there's really anything to break up."

And with that, my heart shattered, and I dropped his hand. He had another think coming if he thought I was letting him get away with this.

Curtis

I was killing the kid. His poor scraped and bruised face scowled at me with big, pained eyes. And I really did want to wait on this conversation. Tonight needed to be about him resting quietly, letting his folks take care of him. It was entirely selfish of me to even be here, but I just hadn't been able to resist the chance to see for myself that he was going to be okay. But as always, he was too perceptive, and he'd probed and prodded until here we were, having the last conversation I wanted to be having.

"What do you mean? Of course there's something here. You *know* there is." He gestured wildly and then winced. "Last weekend? That meant nothing? You know as well as I do that this has moved far beyond lessons, beyond friendship, even."

"But it shouldn't have." I knew that now. And it wasn't just Janice's lecture or his parents' warning. I'd known all along this was where we were headed. "I'm too old for you, and—"

"Bullshit." He glared at me. "You know I don't care about that."

"You should." I gently brushed his bruised cheek. "You've got so many big dreams—houses, gardens, your career—you deserve someone who can share all that with you."

"It could be you." His chin tilted, stubborn as the rest of him.

"No, it can't." I kept my voice soft, but the sadness still came out. "My time for dreaming is over. I'm sorry."

"You're wrong." Logan's eyes bored into me, steely spikes. "You're here. You're alive. You're not the one who died."

"I *know* that," I growled.

"Do you? Really? You have to stop punishing your-self for being the one who lived, Curtis. He wouldn't want—"

"You don't know a damn thing about what he'd want.

232

Who he was." Each word was an **angry** lash, and he recoiled against the pillow.

But he wasn't completely cowed. "You're right. I don't. But I know he loved you. And if he loved you, he'd want you to live again. Dream again. Love again."

"You're wrong." My ears still **rang** with Janice's angry accusations. "He deserves more from me than me taking up with some kid—"

"Is that all I am to you?" His mouth wrinkled up.

No. The heart I'd assumed long dead was shattering anew, but I also understood on a bone deep level that I was doing the right thing here. Right for Janice. Right for Troy's memory. Right for me. And especially the right thing for Logan. "You're a good person—"

"And so are you. But you're being a coward here. You got scared when I got hurt. I get that. And then my parents—"

"Are right," I said firmly. "You can do far better than me. And you're right, too—you got lucky here. You need to make the most of your second chance. Follow your dreams."

"And if my dream is you?"

"It's not." Of that I was convinced. His big dreams had no place for a broken-down woodcarver who'd lost his heart a long time ago and who would only hold him back.

"You're as bad as my parents and everyone else, thinking you know what's best for me. Well, you're wrong." His eyes spit sparks at me. "And you're a coward. You don't want to try. That's what this boils down to."

"Believe that if it helps."

"You want to leave? Want to end this? Go on. Leave. But don't lie to me and tell me you don't care. Don't lie to me and say we're not suited. You want out? There's the door. But you don't get to lie to me—or yourself. You care. I care. We match. This is fear, plain and simple."

"No, this is me wanting better for you. And if I have to end this to make that happen, then I will. And you can call it fear if you want. But I call it doing the right thing." Heart hammering hard, I stood up. I had to leave before I broke down, before I let him talk me into staying. He wasn't wrong about fear, not that I could admit that to him. I wasn't afraid of much in this life. But I was scared of holding him back, of clipping his beautiful wings. I was scared of losing Janice, who'd been a rock in my life for twenty-odd years now. I was scared of losing what was left of Troy, of severing that bond even more than death already had. And mainly, I was scared of losing Logan, of letting myself love again only to lose again. I wouldn't survive it, of that I was certain.

And if that made me a coward, so be it. I'd be a coward who was doing the right thing, setting this gorgeous spirit free. I wasn't worth him losing his relationship with his parents over. Wasn't worth him fighting this hard for, that was for sure.

"Goodbye," I said at the door, leaving whatever was left of my heart there next to him, bloody and raw. It wasn't enough to offer him, but it was his nonetheless. He said nothing, eyes grim, mouth moving like he couldn't quite think of the right curse for me. That was okay. I couldn't, either.

Lord knew I certainly tried out enough of them on the drive home, cursing myself with every name I could think of. I'd let this go too far. We never should have hooked up. But I'd been drawn to him, had been from first glimpse. Something about his optimism, his confidence, his enthusiasm had called to all the cold and lonely places inside me that craved some sunshine. But I should have known better, should have known I'd only hurt him. I'd been selfish, wanting some warmth and sun to carry me through this endless gray winter, when I knew good and well that I didn't deserve luxuries. Coming to crave things that weren't meant for me always lead to heartache. Always.

I counted oncoming headlights to keep my eyes from blurring, keep my attention on the road. But my brain kept seeing Logan's wounded eyes. I'd hurt him—I'd seen it in his eyes, heard it in his voice, even through the angry words. All I'd ever wanted to do was build him up, make it easier for him to meet his dreams. Find his perfect sub, perfect life. I wasn't supposed to ever get to this place where I wished it could be me, where I wished I'd met him…

To make sure he got his dreams, I'd have to let ago of my secret ones, and that was just the way it had to be.

TWENTY

Logan

I flopped back against the bed as Curtis left, an action that made my head swim and my sore bones hurt. But it didn't hurt as much as him leaving. Curtis was a coward. Before, I'd seen him as so damn brave, going on when life had handed him one shitty turn after another. His parents. Troy's dad. Troy. And I'd seen him take intense amounts of physical pain, transform it into something beautiful, use it to fuel his pleasure. He was magic and strength and courage.

But then he'd left. Said he was doing the right thing. Fuck that.

I punched the mattress. He wasn't doing the right thing. He had some damn misguided notions of nobility, but in reality he was scared. His hands had been shaking as my parents had left, and he'd been so pale. And I'd caused that, caused him worry, probably caused him to flashback to bad events in his past. I'd wanted to hold him, promise him I'd never scare him again, promise him

I wasn't going anywhere. But those were empty promises, and he would know that better than anyone. I shouldn't be surprised that he'd given in to the fear, pulled back, hidden behind this stupid idea that he was wrong for me. And the stupider one that Troy wouldn't have wanted him to be happy.

I'd never met the man, and it was damn cold in his shadow, but from all accounts, he'd loved Curtis fiercely. And if I'd loved someone like that, I knew I'd want them to be happy more than anything else. I would want to be remembered, but I'd want them to find happiness where they could. I didn't see why Curtis couldn't believe that Troy would want that for him. I wasn't trying to replace him or erase him from the book of Curtis's life. I only wanted the chance to write a few new chapters together. I'd figured maybe there was a piece of Curtis's heart left to be won, but I'd figured wrong.

There wasn't. There was only a man too scared to fight for us.

Fuck. I hated this. Him leaving. Being stuck in this bed. The headache that meant running after him wasn't going to happen. Most of all I hated him giving up on us before we ever had a chance.

My parents came back far too soon, and I'd lost any amount of patience for their coddling.

"Did your friend upset you? You look terrible." My mother hurried to my side as they entered the room.

"I'm fine. Just tired. Very, very tired—"

"Should we talk to the nurse? Is it sudden exhaustion?" Even my father was prone to overreaction.

"No. It's been a long day. I think I'll feel better if I rest."

ANNABETH ALBERT

"Oh, of course you should rest, sweetie." Mom brushed my hair with her fingers.

"Alone." It pained me to have to spell it out, but I knew if I didn't they'd camp out in the visitor chairs all night. As it was, their expressions went from concerned to kicked, and the grim set to my father's jaw said I was going to have a fight on my hands.

"Someone should be with you." His tone was no-arguments, but I wasn't deterred.

"The nurse call button is right here. And they're checking on me, too. You can trust the hospital."

"I'm not sure that's such a good idea."

"*Please.* We can talk in the morning. You can get a room here in Coos Bay if you don't want to drive back to Rainbow Cove, but I can't rest if I'm worried about you guys, too."

There were another few rounds of "are you sure" and "we're worried about leaving" before my father threw up his hands. "Fine. We'll get a hotel room close to the hospital. First thing in the morning, we'll be here when the doctor comes through. I want to talk to her about this anger, see if maybe it's a side effect."

"It's not the concussion," I groaned. "It's just that I'm twenty-seven. I need my space."

"We'll talk in the morning." Mom patted my hand like she hadn't heard a word I'd said. But finally they left, and I was alone to replay my conversation with Curtis over and over until I dropped into a fitful sleep, woken up at regular intervals by the nursing staff.

I wanted to make things right with him, convince him to give us a chance, but I didn't know where to start. And I still didn't have any answers by morning when, true to her word, the doctor came through early, even before breakfast.

My parents' doctor radar must have been strong because they hurried in right after her, clutching giant coffees.

"We're here," Mom said breathlessly.

"You're lucky to have such...involved family." A smile tugged at the doctor's mouth, and I had a feeling she'd say something different if they weren't right there. She put me through the same battery of tests she'd done the night before, asking questions and looking in my eyes before having me stand and checking my balance.

"Well, you're no worse," she proclaimed. "I feel pretty confident now that you have a mild concussion. We can probably release you, follow up in the office in a few days, see if you're still having symptoms."

"Thank you." It was bad enough that I'd missed Friday night at the tavern. Nash had updated Mason and Adam, and I'd spoken to Mason on the hospital room's phone last night. He'd been understanding and worried, but I couldn't miss tonight, too.

"I'm going to prescribe no driving until we know more about what lasting symptoms you're having, and I'd like you to rest as much as possible, even though I can tell that you're stubborn and you're going to try to work."

"I'll rest after work," I promised. "And I'll take it easy, ask others for help in the kitchen. As long as I'm there. That's what matters."

As long I'm there. Was that what I needed to convince Curtis of? That I was there, that I wasn't going to leave, that his worst fears weren't going to come true.

"Chances are high you're going to keep having the headache. No pushing it, okay?" The doctor gave me a stern look.

"He won't," my mom promised for me. Both my parents thanked the doctor profusely, and then we waited for the nurse to bring my discharge papers.

It wasn't until we were in their SUV, me in the backseat like I was fourteen again, that they dropped the hammer.

"We want you to come home with us. Recuperate there," my mom said. "This place isn't good for you."

"What? No way. I can't miss work."

"You heard the doctor—you could keep having headaches and concussion symptoms for a while. Rest is the best thing for you," said the man who hadn't taken a sick day in a decade.

"A five-hour car trip is hardly that restorative," I pointed out.

"You could sleep most of the drive." Mom waved away my concern. "We'd feel better if you were back with us."

"I can't leave the business indefinitely. I can't leave them in the lurch like that."

"You wouldn't be." Dad spoke up. "We want to invest—"

"Thank you." That was a relief. A bright spot in an otherwise awful twenty-four hours.

"—but only if you agree to move back home, look for work in the Portland area after you're recovered. We'll invest in your friends, and you can come visit whenever you want, but this place is no good for you."

"What do you mean? This accident was a freak thing.

Could have happened in Portland easily. Cyclists get injured everywhere."

"It's not just the accident. This just isn't the right place for you. Not the right business. Or the right friends. You're better off back home around more people like you. Where you have your dojo and your old friends and *safe* spaces."

"Mom. You can't roll me in bubble wrap. And I'm stronger than you assume. Why don't you think I can make it here?"

"Oh, Logan…" She sighed, hands moving restlessly. "You've always been…different. Fragile in some ways. And it's our job to keep you safe. This place is only going to hurt you—the business woes, your choice in friends, the dangers."

"I'm not fragile." My head pounded, but I kept my tone firm. "I'm a strong person. An adult. And I wish you guys could see—could see who I've become instead of the bullied kid I once was. I look out for myself now. I'm the one keeping me safe now. "

"And how's that working out?" My dad's tone was much more frustrated than Mom's more plaintive one. "You're hurt. Your friend the woodcarver clearly parted on less-than-great terms with you last night, and your business is failing. Come on, Logan, be reasonable here."

"Leave Curtis out of this. He didn't do anything wrong." I really believed that, even as much as my heart was aching. He was wounded, battle-scarred by a life that hadn't always been kind to him. He was scared, and I wasn't sure I could blame him. He hadn't meant to hurt me this much, of that I was sure. He cared. He just wouldn't let himself have this for whatever reason. "I l—like him. A lot."

"I'm not sure you're the best judge of character. Remember your so-called friends?"

"*Dad.* That was junior high. It's been fifteen years. It's time we all moved beyond that. Are you really going to withhold the investment if I won't return to Portland?"

"I'm not sure we have much choice," he said as he pulled into my driveway. "If you won't see reason—"

"I'm not leaving. I'm building something here. Something I'm proud of. And I'm sorry you can't see that, but I can't let this go."

Can't let go. Exactly. I couldn't let Curtis go. I had to figure out how to stay and fight for us, not run away because my parents wanted it.

"Why don't we go inside and you can rest?" Mom's voice was pitched to be soothing, but I felt anything but calm.

"Why don't you leave?" I couldn't believe that the words actually flew out, but as soon as they were out, I meant them. "If you can't support me, then I think you should go. We could all use some time apart. You want me to think, but you need to think as well."

"Logan, honey, you're sick. You shouldn't be alone."

"I'll call Mason or Adam. My friends. The ones I'm not going to let down."

"I don't think you mean this, son." My dad's voice was so damn patronizing that I literally growled.

"I want you guys to leave. When you're ready to treat me like an adult and not make ultimatums, then we can talk."

With that, I stormed into the house, went straight to

my room, and closed the door. I could hear them talking, debating my sanity and my seriousness, but at last I heard them gathering their stuff, heard the door slam and the car start and pull away.

Fuck. My. Life. No Curtis. No parents. No investment for the business. Only a splitting headache for all my troubles. I had to fix this, but I had no idea how to start. I couldn't give Curtis courage. Couldn't make my parents see me as an adult. Couldn't manufacture money out of thin air. Couldn't live with the fact that maybe my best wasn't good enough.

I buried my head in the pillow. All I could do was hope that a plan would come to me soon.

TWENTY-ONE

Curtis

I woke Saturday with what felt like an entire beach's worth of grit in my eyes and the sort of bleary, empty feeling that I hadn't had in a long time. Something was missing, and it only took a few floundering seconds before I remembered.

Logan.

I'd left him there. Walked away. Done the right thing, but never had that felt so damn awful. I checked my phone. No new messages. Which had to be good, right? Surely Nash would have let me know if Logan had taken a bad turn. But I'd kind of expected a message from Logan himself, some sort of plea to reconsider. Maybe his phone was lost or broken. Or maybe he simply cared less than I'd thought. Maybe he was relieved to not have to be the one to walk away. Perhaps I'd made things easier for him.

But that thought was cold comfort and just made me angry at the universe for bringing him to me. I hadn't wanted this glimpse of what life could be like with someone like him, each encounter giving me a whole new set of things to miss. I'd come to crave his smile, his good food, his caretaking, *him.* And now I got to deal with the loss. And it sucked.

A large part of me wanted to stay in bed, not face the world. But there was security in my routine, something I could cling to, even as it failed to soothe me. Checking in on the plants did nothing. Ditto setting up for a Saturday's worth of carving. It was decent weather, so maybe I'd get a tourist or two before it was time to go to Janice's and get Chopper for his follow-up blood work at the vet's office.

I tried to lose myself in carving, but the zone was maddeningly out of reach. I had to take a break before I trashed a perfectly good piece of cedar simply because the bird I was carving wouldn't cooperate. I was pouring myself a much-needed cup of coffee when my phone rang. *Logan.* I almost re-sprained my ankle dashing for the phone where I'd left it on the counter. But it wasn't Logan or anyone calling about him. It was Mason's friend Brock.

"Yeah?" I barked.

"Hello to you, too." Brock had an easy laugh. "And I'm calling with good news. The resort committee has decided to commission your carvings for the lobby. Our team was impressed with your sketches and your feel for what makes the area special."

"Oh…uh…" I couldn't feel anything. I'd wanted this for weeks and weeks. My biggest commission ever, and now it felt awfully hollow. Or worse, like something I hadn't earned. I'd hurt Logan. Surely I didn't deserve good news like this? I didn't need my mood lifted. I needed to wallow in my hurt.

"You'll do it, right?" Brock sounded impatient.

"Yeah, of course." The words came out on autopilot.

"Good. I'll send over a contract for you to look over, and then we'll be in touch about materials and exact specifications. We'll want to take you on-site so you can get a feel for the space."

"That works." Somehow I said what Brock needed to hear, and we ended the call with him promising to call again on Monday morning. I stood there with my phone in my hand, staring down at it for a long moment.

Logan.

This was the best news of my professional life, and all I wanted to do was call Logan and tell him. Not Nash. Not any other friend. Not Janice. Logan. I wanted to call him and him alone. And I couldn't. Wouldn't.

Fuck it. I'd been given what I most needed and nothing that I wanted. Before I realized what I was doing, I'd hurled the phone all the way across the room to land against the linoleum floor by the coffee pot. It shattered, battery coming loose, plastic cracking.

"What did you do?" I yelled at myself. Troy had given me that phone. And I had no need of a new phone. This one had worked just fine. No complaints. It wasn't the phone's fault that I wanted Logan and couldn't have him.

I tried to put the battery back, press the broken case back together, but it was hopeless. Fuck it. I couldn't even keep a phone safe. Couldn't be trusted around anything nice. Not quite knowing where I was headed, I strode outside, picked up my saw. Letting anger and frustration and hurt and longing fuel me, I attacked the nearest piece of wood, a wide chunk of cedar that I'd been figuring would make a decent owl or maybe a pair of jumping fish. But as usual, the wood spoke. This time I wasn't even listening, and it still spoke, still drove my carving. This was the zone, but it was all fucked up, a terrible, awful place where my hopes drowned, where I buried my sorrows in the carving.

And when I was done, sweat dripped from me, every muscle screaming, chest heaving with exertion, I stepped back to look at what had emerged.

A sun. A gorgeous, beaming sun, every ray curving with an almost hopeless optimism.

It was everything that was missing from my life. Everything that Logan had brought. Fuck. What had I done? What had I let go of?

You could never hope to keep the sun under a pile of sawdust. It's better this way. Now he's free to shine. But I didn't believe my own lecture, and when I wrapped up work to go to Janice's to collect Chopper, the sun seemed to mock me from its new perch on a stump near my other finished works. Two tourists had asked me about buying it, and I'd all but growled at them that it wasn't for sale.

Things between Janice and me were still awkward, but she was happy enough to let me take Chopper.

"I had a mind to bake some cookies while you're gone." She offered me a tentative smile. "Think you could eat a few?"

"Guess I could." Swallowing saddle soap sounded more appetizing, but she was trying, and I really did love her. So I took Chopper to the vet, got a clean bill of health that his liver and kidneys were working okay now, and then took the long way back to Janice's. Guess I was dreading the cookies. Or maybe I was feeling guilty. Or just lost. Whatever reason, I found myself not far from Janice's place, in front of a small gray house with a partial view of the cliffs. The narrow lawn was well kept. One would never guess that this house had sat empty the better part of two years now, only sporadic visits like this connecting it to its former life.

Or maybe that should be reversed. It was only visits like this that connected me to it, that tied me to *my* former life where this had been a happy home. Chopper at my heels, I unlocked the door, went inside for the first time since I'd made sure everything was all set for the winter rainy season.

I kept it clean and well-maintained. It wouldn't be falling apart on my watch, but I couldn't be inside more than a few minutes before it started feeling like tomb. Or a ten ton weight around my neck. It wasn't supposed to be *mine*—it was Troy's dream, something that had been ours, our one symbol of coupledom. No rings. No matching tats. No special anniversary. But we'd bought this place together. Sweated together here. Made it into something we were both proud of. I would have lived in a cardboard box for that man, but he'd wanted this, so here we'd landed.

And there by the front window was Troy's favorite recliner. If I squinted, I could almost see him there napping. Here by the entryway was the tile we'd laid together. There in the kitchen were the maple cabinets he'd picked out and I'd hung while he hovered like a new parent. There was the table where we'd shared so many meals. Good, simple food. Lord knew Troy wasn't a chef like Logan, but he'd kept us fed. And I wasn't picky. I'd been happy just to be there with him. Across from the fireplace was the couch. Was that the last place we'd kissed? I thought so, but my memories were more dusty than the floorboards.

I hated that I couldn't remember the last spot I'd seen him here two years ago. Was it the kitchen that morning? The bathroom? There had been a last time, and it hadn't registered until it was too late. I remembered all the firsts—first night here, first meal, first holiday season —why couldn't I remember the lasts? But that wasn't how memory worked.

How long could I keep this place as a bulwark against the ravages of time? How long until all the "firsts" were fuzzy, too? I wasn't a museum curator. This wasn't some noble mission of mine, either. I was just a man who owned a house he could no longer bear to live in. Parting with it had seemed unthinkable for the past two years, but now…

I took a deep, musty breath. Despite my best efforts, the place was stagnant. Just like me. I stopped trying to picture Troy here and tried to picture things ten years from now. I'd be over fifty, still living at the gas station. Tending things here, but it would be getting more and more rundown from disuse. Chopper, he'd be long gone. House might be too much for Janice by that point, and she might well be gone, too. We'd be alone, this house and me. Other houses in the neighborhood would move on, just like people did, renovations coming and going, tourists and new residents alike.

Houses aren't meant to stay empty. Troy's voice echoed across the years, a snippet of memory from when we'd first seen this place. It had been an old vacation-rental then, in piss-poor shape, but he'd seen the potential. I tried to see the place, not as a collection of my own memories, but rather as potential again. Someone else would see this tile and know they had a rug to match. They might see the kitchen and picture enchiladas and cold beer on Tuesday nights.

Maybe I couldn't free my own potential, free myself from the clutches of grief, but I could free this house.

"Come on, boy," I called to Chopper. "It's time to go."

And on the short drive to Janice's, I felt lighter than I had in a long time. In fact, the only other thing that made me feel as good as this decision was...

Logan. And there I was again, thinking about things I couldn't have. I needed to move on, in every sense of the word, and yet all paths seemed to lead right back to him.

Janice met us at the door with some cookies and coffee for me and many pats for Chopper. I waited until he was dragging a toy to his bed to speak my mind. I was never very good at preamble, so I just went for it.

"I'm going to put the house on the market. Find a young family who wants to live there year-round maybe. It's been empty too long." *And so have I.*

She went pale and clutched the edge of the table. "Troy loved that house."

"He did. And he'd want someone else to love it. I plan to be picky, not sell to investors or people looking to tear down, but it's time it was lived in again, and it just can't be me. I wish it could. Wish I was wired different-ly." I turned the coffee mug round and round in my hands.

"This about that young fella, isn't it? The one you said was nothing serious?"

"No. This is about what that house deserves, which is some love and attention." Even as I said it, an echo sounded deep in my brain. *You deserve that too.* "You said yesterday you were worried about Troy's memory. I don't want a crumbling house to be his legacy. Let me sell it, and then I want to give you the money. Put it aside for if you need—"

"I don't need anything." Her voice was sharp. "He married *you*. That's your money. Not mine. I won't take a cent. This place is mine, free and clear, and that's all I need."

"Janice." I started to reach for her hand but stopped at the last second. "We've known each other, what, twenty-five years now? Troy and Hank, too, they'd want you to be happy. Maybe get a little place for you and Chopper with other seniors nearby—"

"Just because you're moving on doesn't mean I plan to."

"They wouldn't want this for you," I persisted. "It would break Troy's heart to know you gave up photography, shut yourself up here—"

"I think you should leave now, Curtis Hunt. You leave and take these foolish notions with you. I know what Hank and Troy deserve, which is more than I can say for you." She pulled herself to stand and pointed at the door with a shaking finger.

"Janice. Please." I held up a hand even as I walked toward the door. "Don't do this. We've got too many years between us. We're all each other has—"

"No, we're not." She shook her head, eyes glassy and

bright. "You want more. The good Lord took everything from us and left us here to endure together, but you're wanting more than that."

"Is it so wrong?" My voice broke. I hated that she was right. "Is that such a bad thing? To want to love again? Be loved? Share that with someone?"

"No." She sighed heavily. "Human nature, I suppose. But we had once-in-a-lifetime loves, Curtis. You don't get that twice."

Except maybe some people do. It had been so long since I'd felt anything resembling hope that I didn't recognize the trembling in my gut at first. What if people did get a second chance and I was about to miss mine? I didn't answer her, only swallowed hard.

"You go on now, and you think on that." She pointed at the door again. "You can't catch lightning twice."

But I did. I thought hard as I walked slowly to the truck. No. Not lightning. Sunbeams. I'd held two suns between my hands, the first fiery and giant and awe-inspiring, almost too much to hold onto, the second bright and cheerful and warm, exactly what I'd needed in this dreary winter of my life. And in my grief, I'd forgotten one vital detail—spring always follows winter. New growth. New chances. And Logan had the potential to be my life's spring, if only I'd let him.

TWENTY-TWO

Logan

"Dude. The second we close, you're going home to bed." Horatio paused from prepping salads to shake a finger at me. "I can't believe you've lasted this long."

"Balls of titanium," Mason agreed, coming in to collect orders that were up. "But I'm with Horatio—you need to be home resting. Don't make me take you to the ER so the doctor can yell at you some more."

"I'm okay." I didn't even try to claim good, but I was hanging in there, throbbing head, aching body, bruised heart, and all. Everything hurt. I didn't have any new symptoms that would warrant real concern, but I felt like I'd been smacked around in the surf for a few hours. The lights in the kitchen made my headache ten times worse, but sunglasses would make it hard to tell ingredients apart. I'd be happy when we were done. "But, man, what a night, right?"

"This is incredible," Horatio enthused. "We've never been this busy."

I hadn't been out to the dining room, but judging by the orders coming back, we were hopping. Mason had reported visitors from Eugene and Coos Bay with a few tourists from even farther. Adam said his mother's B&B was full up with people who'd booked the dinner-and-room package.

Mason came back several orders later with a puzzled expression on his face. "Okay. This is getting strange."

"What is?" I was plating ravioli, but I'd long mastered the art of garnishing and conversing at the same time.

"Just had Curtis pay for a fourth couple's dinner. The first two were clearly friends of his from Eugene, but these last ones, I'm not even sure they know him."

"Curtis is here?" I narrowly avoided dropping the ravioli. "And sober?" Curtis had to be one of the thriftiest guys I'd ever met.

"Yeah. He came in with Nash, but not only did he pay for the two of them, he keeps getting the check for others. It's like he…invited them or something? Did he say anything to you about helping us get business?"

"Nope." My heart hammered. If he was here, if he was doing this, he had to care, right? Maybe all hope wasn't lost. I'd been planning on dragging myself to his place after work and telling him why I refused to let him walk away from us, but I hadn't been sure whether it would make any difference. Was he here as an apology? To help our business? To send me a message? To prove something to himself? There were a lot of possibilities, but they all told me that maybe I had a chance and put a bit more bounce into my step as I finished the plates.

"Strange." Mason shrugged before grabbing the

plates. "Anyway, just another half hour. Traffic's slowed a lot. Can you make it?"

"I've got it."

Horatio and I handled the last few orders and desserts before starting the cleanup. I hadn't even gotten to the grill when Mason came in. "Go. Your guy is still here. He told Adam he can give you a ride. You look ready to fall over."

"He's not my guy," I said, tone more mournful than I'd intended.

"Well, go remedy that." Mason chased me from the kitchen with a dish towel. I found Curtis sitting at Nash's usual table by the door.

"I hear you're playing Cupid." I studied him carefully. He looked good. Dressier than I'd ever seen him in a white, western-style fancy shirt and new-ish jeans. "And you dressed up for dinner."

"Yeah, well, Nash deserved a nice date." Eyes wary, he offered me a sheepish grin.

"And the you-paying-for-people thing?"

"I might have made some calls." He looked away. "Given some folks a little incentive to make the drive."

"Why? I thought you hated this holiday."

"Well, yeah. But I don't hate *you*. And you guys needed a good night. Just doing my part for the town."

"Charitable." My head throbbed, and I wasn't sure how much more careful banter I had in me.

"You look like dog puke," Curtis said bluntly. "Let's get you home."

I was far too exhausted to argue with him, and I let him escort me to his truck. I didn't even turn down his steadying hand. He headed in the direction of my

255

place, but I dozed off before he'd cleared the town square.

"Can you wake up?" Curtis sounded concerned as he shook my shoulder. We were parked in my driveway, and I struggled to blink my eyes open.

"Yeah, yeah. Just tired." I exited the truck, stumbling toward the porch. "Feels like I could sleep a week."

"You should."

"I need to shower first," I groaned. "I can't stand to sleep when I'm reeking like the fryer."

"Okay, but you're going to let me come with you. I'm seriously worried about you falling over."

"You can supervise." I made a dismissive gesture as I lurched toward the bathroom. I started stripping off my clothes under his watchful gaze. "Why are you here, anyway?"

"We can talk later. Right now, let's get you clean and into bed. I'm here now. Not going anywhere, okay? We'll talk after I'm convinced that we're not headed back to the ER."

"You sound like Mason," I complained. "He even told me to take tomorrow off."

"Good. You should listen to him." Still clothed, Curtis turned the water on for me and helped me step into the tub. "Fuck. Logan. Is there anywhere that's not bruised?"

I glanced down. I did look a bit like a garish Christmas tree, decorated in angry bruises and scrapes. "Dunno. It all hurts."

"I bet." Curtis's face was strangely pained as he held the curtain while I quickly soaped up and rinsed. "You really shouldn't have worked."

"Lecture later." I let him towel me off and then stumbled to my bed where I landed face down.

"Can I put some of your lotion on you? Would that help?" Curtis sat next to me, stroked down my back.

"Too sore." I couldn't believe I was turning down his hands on me, but right then, I just wanted to rest without distractions.

"Okay. You sleep." He pulled the covers up around me. "I'll be here."

"Why?" I mumbled into the pillow.

"Because I want to be." He dropped a kiss on my head. I wanted to explore that thought more, wanted to know what had caused his apparent about-face, but I was already drifting, sleep more powerful than even his considerable hold over me.

Curtis

Taking care of Logan felt better than anything had in days. I was still beyond worried for him, but just being with him settled me. I straightened up his place. I'd heard through Nash that Logan's parents had lit out in a hurry. There was a story there, but Logan needed rest, not a quiz game to satisfy my curiosity.

Satisfied with my picking up, I took off my clothes and carefully lay down next to him, not close enough to disturb him, but close enough to know if he needed anything in the night. He mumbled something as I settled down.

"Sleep," I whispered.

"Don't want you to leave." His hand floundered

around. I captured it in mine.

"Not going anywhere."

"Too far away." He scooted closer.

"I don't want to hurt you." I tried to move away, but he trapped me, throwing a leg over my thighs and landing with his head on my chest.

"You did." His tone had the earnest quality of the really drunk or really tired. "You totally did. But you're here now. And I'm not letting you go."

"Not trying to escape." My throat felt thick. Was it going to be possible to undo all the pain I'd caused him? Sure, he was happy enough to see me tonight, but he was also dead tired and emotionally wrung out. Tomorrow he might feel up to handing me my ass.

And thoughts of him rejecting my apology kept me awake far after he fell back to sleep on my chest. Despite the pleasure of holding him as we both slept, I woke up early and, after stewing in my own thoughts for a few hours, I edged out from under him. He looked like he might sleep a full twelve hours or more, completely sacked out. I called Nash on the landline to tell Mason that Logan wouldn't be in and was following orders to rest today.

Finally around the twelve-hour mark, I went to rummage in his kitchen. I wasn't the chef, so I felt a bit silly making him breakfast. A peace offering might make him less likely to kick me out. Besides, taking care of him felt so damn good that I actually whistled while I made some basic pancakes with applesauce in place of eggs and plated them with some blueberries and coffee and juice on the side. I put everything on a tray I found in the cupboard and carried it into the bedroom.

I called to him as I sat on the side of the bed with the tray. "Hey, Rip Van Winkle, you need to wake up, eat something, and then you can rest more."

"Hey." He stretched and blinked. "You're still here."

"Said I would be." I couldn't tell from his tone whether my being here was a good thing or not.

"And you made me food?" A small smile crept across his face. "Breakfast in bed?"

"Yup. Figured you needed to eat." I settled the tray on his lap as he sat up. I grabbed my own plate off the tray along with the second fork.

He took a bite. "These are terrific."

"You ask for the recipe, I'm going to know you're still suffering a head injury," I joked.

"I really like them. They're especially good because I didn't have to leave the bed to make them. Not that I would have minded cooking for you."

"I know you would have cooked. But you're not the only one who likes doing the whole caretaking thing. Sometimes it's nice to spoil you."

"Since when?" His face hardened, and I didn't like his wounded tone. "What changed? You didn't seem much interested in taking care of anything Friday, sounded like all this was too much for you."

"I fucked up," I admitted. "I said a lot of things I probably shouldn't have—"

"Yeah, you should have, especially if you meant them. If you think I'm just a kid that you're cheating on Troy's memory with, then I'm not sure I want you here. If you're scared to have this be more than casual hookups, then I'm not sure I can do this. I can't be jerked around again, Curtis. I deserve more."

"I know you do." I reached out and stroked his fuzzy jaw. "You deserve a lot more than me, that's for sure."

He made a frustrated noise. "You keep saying that. But what if I deserve *you*? What if we deserve each other? What if *you* deserve to be happy with me? Would that be so hard to believe?"

"It is," I admitted. "But I'm working on it. I'm not sure what I did to earn you, earn this."

"Maybe it's just a gift from the universe?"

"Universe has never been that kind to me. Ever."

"But maybe it's time. Perhaps you were overdue some good luck."

I made a scoffing noise. "I'd say I don't believe in luck, but I can't think of another explanation for how I feel about meeting you. I'm so lucky to know you."

"And yet you were willing to throw that away." He scowled at me.

"I was afraid."

"Duh. That was really obvious. But I'm more hurt that you didn't want to work those fears out with me. I'm so damn sorry for scaring you. But it was a freak accident."

"I never said it was something you did on purpose." I threw my hands up. "Fear's not exactly logical. And I never, ever wanted to care so much about you, never wanted to feel that way about someone again, like my heart would literally stop if anything bad happened to you, like my soul might crumble if you were taken from me. I hated feeling like that."

"Oh, Curtis." His eyes softened, and he reached for my hand. "I care about you like that also. Does that help, knowing that you're not alone in this thing? I care. I worry about you, too. Every time you start up the chain-saw, my heart skitters, thinking about you getting hurt."

"I didn't want that for either of us. I don't want the power to hurt you."

"Well, too bad. You've got it. And you did."

"I know. I'm sorry. But I'm here now, and I want to try. Screw my fears. Screw whether or not I deserve you. We're both here, and maybe we owe it to the universe you seem to put so much stock in to give this a real try."

"What made you change your mind? You were pretty damn emphatic that you'd be bad for me. And that you weren't interested in moving on from Troy."

Clearly, he wasn't in a rush to forgive me, and I sighed. "I do think I'm too old for you. Too bitter. Not fancy enough. Your parents hate me, with good reason. You could do better."

"But I want you. You're one of the best people I know."

"I wasn't really ready to hear those things before. And you're right about moving on. Right about him wanting me to be happy again. It wasn't until I really thought about going through life without you, where I'd be in ten years if I pushed you away, that I realized how much I need someone like you in my life."

"You do?" he whispered. "Really? You need me? Or you just don't want to be alone, which is okay—"

"You're fishing again." Unable to resist any longer, I brushed a kiss across his mouth. "You. Specifically you. I need you. Need your optimism. Your sweetness. The way you take care of me. The way you dominate me. Your kinky side. Your food. I need it all."

"I need you, too." He leaned in for another, more

lingering kiss. "But I can't deal with you on a guilt trip, beating yourself up for wanting this, for needing me. This should be something *good* for both of us. Something worth celebrating."

"I'm going to work on that," I promised. "You're right. It is good. And we are lucky to have found each other. I can't promise to erase the guilt overnight, but I am working on it. I want to be worthy of you."

"You are." The next kiss of his was the sweetest of all. "I wish you could see yourself the way I see you. You're the strongest person I know. And when you carve, you're a force of nature. I'm lucky to have *you*."

"Speaking of carving, I have to show you what I rage-carved yesterday. I think it's for you."

"Rage-carved? That sounds awesome. I can't wait."

"And I also have to go phone shopping. I might have accidentally on purpose smashed mine when I realized I couldn't call you."

"You can *always* call me. Even when we're mad at each other. I would have answered." Another long kiss, this one full of promise and potential. "And I'm all for a new phone for you, but can shopping wait? I need a new one, too, but I want to finish eating and then devour you for a few hours."

"Hours, huh?" I liked the sound of that.

"Count on it." He winked before taking another bite of pancake. My throat tightened again. I was so damn lucky to have him. He made me want to try. Made me want to be brave. Made me want to shine like him. We still had a ways to go, but I was bound and determined to do right by him.

TWENTY-THREE

Logan

Part of me wanted to push Curtis back on the bed and send the dishes clattering to the floor, but I really was starving after two days with minimal food. And then I had to use the bathroom while Curtis put the dishes in the kitchen. Sane, adult actions. But the second he was back in in the bedroom, I patted the bed next to me.

"Take off your clothes and come here." I used the Dom voice simply because I enjoyed seeing his eyes heat up. "I meant what I said. I want to spend the rest of the day in bed together."

"You should rest," he said even as he peeled off his jeans.

"I am. We can have very lazy, loving sex, but I need you right now. Don't make me wait. Not after the last few days."

"No. I won't do that." He stretched out next to me. "Need you, too."

His kiss was tentative, almost as if he were still

bracing for me to change my mind, kick him out. That wasn't happening. Yeah, I'd made him work for his apology a little, but there had never been any doubt in my brain that I'd take him back. He'd been scared, not deliberately cruel. I could forgive that, although I knew we had a long road to walk together.

But we could tackle his trust issues later. Right then, all I really wanted was more kisses. I pushed on his shoulder, and he went willingly to his back, dragging me on top of him. My head was clear for the first time in forty-eight hours, and I fully intended to make the most of it.

I licked at his lips until he let me in, mouth parting on a gasp. He tasted sweet, and not just from the pancakes. This, being together again when I wasn't sure we'd get the chance, was sweet. Him clinging to me like I was a life buoy was even sweeter. I loved how he let me control the kiss, own his mouth with deep strokes of my tongue. He gasped again, little moans escaping.

His hands rubbed my back. I kept kissing him as he explored my muscles. This was the best buzz ever, better than mimosas with brunch or New Year's champagne. Being drunk on Curtis was the best feeling in the whole world. His head fell back, and I mouthed his neck, teasing the line of his beard, biting lightly at his Adam's apple, dipping lower to the sensitive spot where his shoulder and neck met, the one that always made him moan.

"Fuck. I love this. Love kissing you." He sounded as drunk as I felt.

I love you. Period. Full stop. But it was too soon to voice that, so I simply kissed him again, harder and deeper.

With my lips and tongue, I tried to tell him the truths my voice couldn't. *I'm falling for you. Have been falling from the very start. I need you. I'm never giving you up.* He kissed me back with a ferocity that made me think maybe he was hearing what I couldn't say.

His hands gripped my ass, pulling me closer so that our cocks ground together. His long fingers swept up and down my crack. He wasn't aggressive about it, his touch light and more exploratory, so I relaxed into the sensation, not tensing up when he delved deeper, circled my rim.

I moaned, almost without realizing what I was doing.

"Like that?" he whispered. "Love driving you crazy. Can I…"

"Yeah." *I trust you.* More words that I couldn't vocalize, but as I passed him the lube from the nightstand, I knew it was true His warm, callused fingers fired up nerve endings that I tended to ignore unless I was exploring on my own. But having Curtis touch me was like quenching a thirst I didn't know I had. And unlike encounters with others, I had a deep trust in Curtis. He let me have control whenever I wanted it. Whenever we both needed it. A single filthy suggestion from me could flip this whole dynamic, and I loved knowing that every bit as much as I liked the touches from his talented fingers.

He worked a single slick finger in as we continued to kiss, lips more needy and demanding now, both of us moaning. Even from the awkward angle, he managed to tease with shallow thrusts, playing with the resistance instead of barreling through.

"More," I groaned.

"Yes, sir." He grinned wickedly up at me. He was joking, but that reminder that I was in control made my pulse speed up. His finger went deeper, found the spot that made the intrusion more than worth it.

"Oh, God." My hips bucked, increasing the friction of our cocks rubbing, but it wasn't enough. I was both close to the edge and maddeningly far away. Frustration tinged my voice. "Wanna ride you. Need more."

"Yeah?" His eyebrows went up, but blessedly he didn't ask if I was sure. I could tell from his heated gaze that it wasn't an unwelcome suggestion.

I fumbled for the condom box and scooted back so I could roll one onto his cock. I liked being the one to make him ready, and I took time to tease him while putting on the condom and getting him slick.

"Fuck. Don't make me wait." It was less order and more begging, which I loved. "Please."

"Mmm." I slid forward again, holding his cock steady with one hand. Pushing back, I rocked my hips in short bursts. It burned, which I'd expected, but the stretch also felt strangely good, like muscle fatigue after a long bike ride, and that I hadn't expected. Hadn't anticipated liking this part, but I did, pleasure unfurling warm and intense in my gut as I teased myself much as he had, little thrusts and retreats, making the resistance into something almost fun.

"That's it. Whatever you need. Just take it." His head fell back, eyes shut, muscles straining like he was being tortured, low moans saying he was loving it.

I slid further onto him, gasping when his cockhead grazed that spot inside. Tilting my hips, I repeated the motion, more deliberately now. The sensation was almost too intense. "Fuck. Fuck."

Acting without my permission, my hips rocked faster. Harder. Deeper. And then…holy fuck, he was all the way in, my ass resting on his thighs and it went from almost-too-much to way-too-full in a heartbeat. I struggled to catch my breath, breathe through sensations that were as much about the emotional intensity as the physical.

"Hey." Curtis held my gaze, eyes soft and concerned. Not looking away, he grabbed my hand and brought it slowly down his chest to rest on his neck.

"What…" This was significant, but I was having a hard time processing the gesture. "You don't like…"

"I trust you." His eyes never left mine, and in them, I saw entire galaxies worth of feelings. "Completely. I trust you."

"I trust you, too." Just saying the words eased the pressure in my chest. Hand still on mine, he pressed down.

"I'm yours. Always. Even like this. Especially like this. Yours."

"Mine." I swept my thumb up and down his wind-pipe, not pressing, more simply exploring previously off-limits territory. The amount of trust he was showing in me was staggering. He was pushing his limits for me, trusting me even when things had gone sideways with others. I could do the same for him.

I started rocking again, shallow movements at first, then longer slides up and back.

"Mine," I said again, leaning forward to bite his neck.

"Yes. I'm yours. Your sub. Your man." Curtis's eyes

finally fluttered shut, but not before I saw the emotion shining there.

My man. It felt like I'd waited forever for him to see himself that way. I wanted that so badly, wanted to believe that he was mine, really mine. My heart. My soul. My man.

I rode him slowly, but even that pace was enough to have us both groaning. Leaning forward, I kissed him again. I'd remember the taste of him as long as I lived, a craving I wasn't ever going to be rid of. I matched the thrust of my tongue to the rhythm of my hips.

"Fuck. Fuck. Logan. Tell me what you need," he gasped against my mouth. "Tell me how to get you off."

"Want you to come," I moaned. "Want to make you as crazy as you make me."

"Oh, that's happening." He laughed darkly. "But not before you."

Holding my gaze again, he slowly gripped my cock, a question in his eyes.

"Yeah," I said, giving him permission. "Touch me."

His hand was slick, as if I'd missed him getting some lube, and it felt amazing on my aching cock. Working together, we found a sort of synergy—kiss, hand, ass, all moving together, all straining for the same goal.

"Tell me. Tell when I can come." He stretched his free hand over his head to touch the headboard, the picture of supplication, totally giving himself over to my whims. Fuck, but I loved this man.

"Not yet. Close," I panted.

"Fuck, yeah." He seemed to take that as a personal challenge, adding a twist to the strokes from his hand, hips raising up to meet my ass. The muscles in my back tightened one by one, and my thighs burned. I was so damn close. Then Curtis pressed my hand to his neck again. "Yours. All yours."

His trust, more than any of the incredible sensations, set me off. God, I felt so much for this man. Everything. He was my everything, and I choked out a "mine" as I spurted all over his chest and stomach. Getting marked with my cum seemed to shatter his control, and he fucked up into me, quick, deep strokes that had him joining me as I panted and shuddered.

"Fuck. Fuck." Curtis gathered me close after I'd pulled off and taken care of the condom.

We were both a mess, but I didn't care. We'd get to the shower eventually. Holding him was all I needed. All I'd ever need. In that moment, nothing else mattered. Not the long road we still had to walk together. Not the business or my parents or anything else outside this room and this man. He was all I needed, everything I wanted in one confounding, complicated, irreplaceable package.

Curtis

Logan dozed off again after we showered, which I'd kind of expected. The poor guy was still recovering from his ordeal, and his body needed sleep to heal. While he napped, I ran back to my place to grab the new sculpture and a change of clothes. It felt weird to take a Sunday completely off, but the weather was dreary and gray again. I wouldn't be missing too many tourists. And besides, Logan was more than worth any lost business.

As I loaded the sculpture into the truck, my gaze

ANNABETH ALBERT

drifted to the tarp by the back of my place. My bike. For the first time in two years, I missed it. Missed the wind on my face. The speed. The power. Zipping around obstacles. Riding with the group. Spontaneous road trips. All the good times. And when I thought about the life Troy would want for me, me riding my motorcycle was high on the list. I'd bought my first bike at seventeen. Twenty-five years I'd ridden, most of them right alongside Troy. He wouldn't want me alone. Wouldn't want the house sitting empty. Wouldn't want to see me give up riding out of fear and guilt and grief.

Remembering when Logan had asked about going for a ride, I smiled. Maybe not today, but I was going to make that happen for him. He shared so much of himself with me. I could share this missing part of me, reclaim it for him. For us. Because it was past time I stopped letting my fears rule my life. Logan made me want to get back to the business of living.

By the time I got back, Logan was in the kitchen, because of course the man couldn't go that many hours without cooking something.

"I'm hoping you'll eat split-pea soup," he said after greeting me with a kiss.

"That you cooked? I'm sure it's good. But before we eat, can I show you something? I kind of carved you a sculpture."

"The rage carving? Now I'm curious." Still in just socks, he followed me to the truck.

I hefted the sun down, carried it to his porch. "Here. I don't think I want to sell it, but if you don't want it, you can give it —"

"Give it away? Hell no." Logan's eyebrows rose like I was about to torch the thing. "I love it. But why a sun?"

I looked away and rubbed my beard. "It's how I see you. See, before you came around, my life was shades of gray and brown. Like winter on the coast. Then you come into my life, and you're like the sun I didn't know I was missing. Or something like that."

"You're a damn poet." He leaned in and kissed me again. "And I love it. I want to put it in the living room. Rage carving and all. I don't think I've ever been a sun for anyone other than my parents, but parent-and-kid stuff is different than this."

"Speaking of them, what happened there?" I carried the carving into the living room, propped it up a good distance from the wood stove.

"They made an ultimatum. Move back or they wouldn't invest in the business. So I sent them packing." Logan did a sheepish half-smile as he headed into the kitchen. "I'm tired of them acting like I'm a kid in need of rescuing."

"You are most definitely not a kid." I pulled him in for another kiss by the stove.

"Says the guy who kept calling me that." He gave me a pointed stare.

"That was more about self-preservation," I admitted. "A way to keep my distance. And I'm sorry. I won't do it anymore."

"Thanks. But now I'm not sure what to do. I don't want to tell Mason and Adam that we're not going to get the funds. I could empty the rest of my savings account, but I'm not sure that would buy us enough time. We need another investor."

271

"I'll do it." The words were out before I really thought them through, but as soon as I said them, I knew it was the right call.

"What? You? You don't have that kind of cash. You can't empty your savings, either. I mean, the playing cupid thing last night was great, but we need a big infusion. I can't let you do that."

"Actually, I do have it." I took a breath as I prepared to tell him something that not even Nash knew all of. "Troy had a very large life insurance policy. I was the sole beneficiary, and his mother refuses to take a cent from me. Then his partners in the trucking company bought out our stake, so I've got that money, too. I'm not hurting, and I've been looking for something to do with the money."

"Wow. It's good that he left you so well taken care of, but I'm not sure I can let you spend it on us. I don't want you doing it because you feel guilty, either."

"It's not guilt." My voice was sharp before I softened it again. "He'd believe in what you guys are doing for the town. He loved this town, hated seeing it falling on harder and harder times. Things are slowly turning around, and you guys are a big part of why."

"Really?" Logan's eyebrows went up. "I had no idea you were that supportive. Mason said you weren't exactly...enthusiastic at Chamber of Commerce meetings."

Feeling my skin heat, I shrugged. "I might have given him a hard time. You can ask Nash. I don't exactly handle change well. And I've been somewhat...cranky. But you're influencing some of that."

"I am?" Looking away, he blushed as he stirred the soup.

"You are. You make me want to be a better person. More like you. You always see the good in things." That was kind of sappy, so I quickly added, "And the way I see it, my guy at the bank keeps harping at me about investing some of it. So I'll invest in you guys. Once the resort opens, you'll be in the black, I'm sure."

"So you'd buy in? Not just a gift or a loan? I can't let you just give us the funds."

"I'll buy in. I mean, don't expect me at any meetings, but yeah, we can do this up proper with paperwork and such. Figure Mason's gonna insist on that. And I'll leave the running to him and you guys. Only thing I'm gonna ask for is that you keep the veggie burgers stocked." I grinned at him.

"We can do that." Logan nodded earnestly. "But what if… If you and I go south, I don't want to do that to the guys, have you pull out of the business just because you're mad at me or whatever."

"First, you and I aren't gonna break up." I pulled him to me, pressed a kiss on his neck. "But if you're worried, we can add something to the paperwork that makes it clear the investment is its own thing. Even if you decided to move on from me, go your own way, I'd want to do this for you guys. *With* you guys. I'm not going to stop being your friend, Logan, even if you decide I'm not the one for you."

"You are." He turned so we were face to face. "You are the one. And I don't want to break up either. I just…" He sucked in a deep breath. "What if this is just a rebound thing for you?"

"A rebound?" I had to laugh at that notion. "At the risk of being crude, I fucked around some after Troy's death. Had a Dom-with-benefits friend in Eugene. And I did plenty with Troy, too. I'm pretty sure I'm fresh out of wild oats to sow or points to prove. You're it for me."

A rosy blush spread up his neck to his cheeks. "You're it for me, too. And I don't…uh…I'm not really one to fuck around. Or share. Is that going to be an issue?"

"Not really." I shrugged. Honestly, him possessive was pretty cute, but I didn't want to be the one holding him back. "You're young. If you told me you wanted to scene with others to practice your Dom skills, I'd work on being okay with that. And if you were into…sharing, I'd manage that, too. But like I said, I've done a damn lot in my life. You want to be monogamous, then that's what we'll be. You change your mind on that? That's fine, too. I plan to stick around a good long while regardless."

He let out a low growl. "The only one I want to practice my Dom skills with is you. I'm not saying I don't want to do more workshops or stuff like that, but you're the only one I want to fuck. Besides, I'm greedy. I kinda want to know what going bare feels like."

"That's a good goal." I laughed and brushed a kiss across his mouth. "I want to get to that point, too. And I'm all about being here for your practice."

"You better watch it or I'm going to skip the soup and practice right now." He winked at me.

"Eat first. You need to build your strength back up. How's the head?"

"No headache. My body still aches but not as bad as yesterday. I'll survive. Maybe when we go phone shopping I can also bike shop. My frame got too bent to fix. And I know you're going to say to give up the biking—"

"Nope." I looked him in the eyes so he could tell I wasn't being flip. "It's important to you. It's a part of you, just like your karate. I'm not going to ask you to change for me."

"But it scared you. And I hate that. I hate that I made you worry."

"I'd cover you in bubble wrap if I thought it would help. But it wouldn't. Life is dangerous. And it sucks sometimes how it all comes down to luck. You could give up biking and get a bad burn at the grill. I know all about shitty luck. But you know what you've shown me?"

"What?" His teeth dug into his lower lip.

"I have pretty damn good luck mixed in with the bad. I met the neighbor who taught me how to carve when I needed something, anything in my life. Met Troy right as shit went south with my parents. Had his dad in my life when I needed that role model. Had Nash to keep me steady, too. Life has had a way of bringing me the people I needed when I most needed them. And now it brought me you. And the way I see it, I'd be stupid to let fear keep us apart." Somehow I strung together a coherent summary of my last few days of thinking. And because that was a damn lot of words, I looked away, afraid I'd said too much.

"I'm glad it brought me you, too." Logan turned my face so that I had to look at him. "I'm sorry for all the shitty luck, but I'm not sorry to be here with you. I mean, I know Troy will always have your heart, and I—"

"A piece," I corrected. "A piece of my heart. He'll

always have a piece of my heart. But I think there's still some left. And I want to share it with you."

"You do?" His eyes went big and liquid.

"Yep."

He didn't even let me get the whole syllable out before he launched himself at me, kissing me deeply. In his kiss was all the potential I'd almost tossed away out of fear—the joy and hope and laughter and love that could be mine if I took the leap, opened myself up to the possibility. I'd meant every word, too—life had brought him to me, the first good luck I'd had in a long while, and I'd be stupid to throw him away. I kissed him back with everything I had, trying to tell him that I wasn't going to let this chance pass me by.

TWENTY-FOUR

Logan

"I still can't believe that Crazy Curtis is loaded." Adam flashed a bemused smile as he polished the bar. It was shortly after lunch on a sleepy Wednesday and we were empty, so there was little point in me hanging out in the kitchen.

"Call him that again and you'll be shining your thick skull instead of wood." I glared at him. On second thought, returning to the kitchen would spare me Adam's idea of funny.

"I know. I know. No joking." He rolled his eyes at me. "Because love has robbed you of your sense of humor."

Mason had been immediately on board with Curtis joining us as an investor, but Adam had taken somewhat longer to warm up to the idea.

"You just wait." I shook a finger at him. "You're going to find someone, and you're going to be a total fool over them. And I'm going to laugh myself silly."

"Nope. Not happening." But his eyes went soft and sad and made me regret the dig. "Isn't he supposed to be here by now?"

"Soon." I glanced at the door. Curtis was picking up paperwork from the lawyer and bringing the papers for us to sign and a check for Mason to deposit. And then he and I were going to enjoy my first night off in two weeks. After I'd recovered from my bike accident, I'd worked straight through without my usual days off to try to make it up to Mason. I felt bad for how much he'd had to cover for me. But finally, he'd insisted that I take a night off.

My phone rang, and I fished it out, heart speeding up. I hoped it wasn't Curtis saying that he'd run into a delay. He'd bought a new phone and was slowly figuring out all its features. But to my surprise, it wasn't Curtis's number flashing on the screen, but my dad's. I almost didn't answer, but my brain shifted from worry about Curtis to concern for my parents. What if something was wrong? I stepped away from Adam and the bar and pressed Talk.

"Yeah?" Just because I was worried didn't mean I was leaping at the chance to talk to them. I hadn't wanted to be the one to reach out first, the one to apologize and smooth things over. I'd had enough years of doing that. I needed them to make the first move.

"Logan. So glad you picked up." My dad sounded like he was forcing his voice to be casual.

"Is everything okay?" My curiosity and fears got the better of me.

"I guess. Your mother is very sad and down that you haven't called, though. I'm worried about her. And you. We miss you, son."

"I miss you. too," I admitted as I paced to the far side of the room, away from Adam's prying ears. "But she could call me. It's not all on me to make things okay. You guys were out of line."

"Yes, we were. And I'm sorry about that. We weren't treating you like an adult. And we shouldn't have made an ultimatum. But we both love you so much. Don't you think we can try again?"

"I love you, too. But I'm not moving home. I love it down here. Far more than I ever did living in Portland. I love the weather and the beach and the people and the business we're building."

"I'm going to work harder on respecting that choice. But can you blame us for missing you?"

"No. And as long as you're not trying to talk me out of living here or the friends I have, you're welcome to visit as often as you want."

"I take it by friends you mean your woodcarver pal?" His voice was cautious.

"His name is Curtis, and we're a couple now. And if I have anything to say about it, he's going to be a part of my life for a long time to come."

"Okay. I mean, we still think he's too old for you and—"

"No 'and.' He's not too old or too anything else for me. He's what I want. He's who I love." I hadn't said the "L"-word to *him* yet, but I meant it. I loved him, and I wanted to keep him around forever.

"All right. I can try to respect that. I'm sure your mom will, too. We just want you to be happy, Logan. Maybe we can meet him next time we come down. Really meet him. Sit down for a meal or something."

"Thanks. That might work." I kept the eagerness out of my voice. Dad was trying, and that meant a lot, but it didn't mean that everything was going to be all rosy overnight.

"And we want to talk about the investment. We were hasty and upset, and we'd like to try again there, too."

"No. We've got it handled. I think we should keep our relationship separate from business for a while. I want you and Mom in my life, but it's probably best if we let the tavern be my thing."

"Okay." Dad sighed, and he sounded genuinely disappointed.

"I mean, I'm not saying never, but we're good for now." I gentled my tone.

"I'm glad. I love you, Logan. We really do." His voice was soft, and I wished I could reach through the phone, give him a hug. "And we're sorry. For everything."

The front door tinkled and Curtis came in, looking badass in a black leather motorcycle jacket in place of his usual flannel.

"I love you, too. I need to go now, but we're going to work this out." For the first time, I really did believe that. We'd work out a way forward. They loved me. I loved them. Things might be tense and complicated, and that love could be exhausting at times, but I still wanted them in my life.

I hung up with Dad, pocketed my phone, and made my way over to Curtis. "Hey, you. I was getting worried."

"Sorry about." A sheepish look crossed his face. "But I was working on a surprise for you. I think you'll like it. Maybe."

"I'm sure I will." I liked him taking care of me, surprising me, doing nice gestures, every bit as much as I liked taking care of him. Things felt more balanced now —he let me in, let me show him how much I cared, and he did the same for me in both little and big ways.

"But first, paperwork." He held out a folder. I fetched Mason from the back, and all four of us signed the agreement before Curtis wrote a check with an alarming number of zeroes, one that would let Mason book a lot more advertising and keep us afloat until tourist season started back up again.

"Are you sure you're okay working dinner?" I asked Mason when we were done with the paperwork. "I can—"

"You guys have a date. Go." Mason made a shooing motion. "I'm doing a beer cheese soup and roast beef panini special. It'll be fine. And fun. Stop feeling so guilty for needing time away."

"He's right." Curtis steered me toward the door. "Besides, I gotta show you the surprise before I lose my nerve."

"Oh, now I'm curious." I followed him to the parking lot. Curtis's truck was nowhere in sight, and he led me over to a shiny motorcycle. My eyes opened so wide the edges of my vision blurred. "This is yours, right? The one that was under the tarp?"

"Yeah." He rubbed his beard. "You asked for a ride. And I figured it was time. Don't need it turning into a pile of rusty parts. Spent the last few days cleaning it up for us to go for a spin before our other plans. If you want to, that is."

"I want to." I grabbed his hand, squeezed it hard.

"But this is a big deal for you. You don't have to ride again for me. I'm totally fine if you never do anything with motorcycles again."

"I want to ride again for *me*. I miss it. Miss the feeling of riding. Miss the friends I used to ride with. I'd like you to meet them. I'm tired of holing myself away because I'm too scared to live again. Riding was a huge part of my life, and I need that back. Want to share it with you."

"I want that, too." I licked my lips.

"Good." He handed me a thick leather jacket and a helmet. "Ready to try?"

"Where are we heading?" Our other plans were taking us to Roseburg that night, and I wasn't sure if I was up to that long of a ride the first time.

"Another surprise. But not far. I thought we'd ride some of the back roads around town, and then switch to the truck or your car for tonight."

"Okay." I tried to quiet the hammering of my heart as he fiddled with the helmet, double checking the fit. He talked me through riding, giving me patient instructions about leaning into curves and trusting him.

"This isn't a scene." I laughed. "And I do trust you. Let's do this."

I climbed on behind him, holding him tight. Nerves aside, I was super excited to share this with him. I'd dreamed about motorcycles for years but never had the nerve to try one. He gave me courage I never knew I had. We were good for each other that way—helping each other triumph over fears, taking new risks. True to his word, he drove slow as he left the parking lot, taking side streets and warning me before turns. I held tight to him, unable to stop my grin. This was fabulous, everything I'd imagined. Just like Curtis himself. He was my every secret wish come to life. He was a true gift, one I intended to treasure.

Curtis

I drove Logan all around town—the little side roads—and we looped around Moosehead Lake before heading back. I'd known all along where I was taking him, but I'd wanted to enjoy the ride first. He might not get the significance of what I wanted to show him, and that would suck. Hell, I wasn't sure that *I* understood exactly what I was doing. As I pulled into the drive of the house, my breath caught. I hadn't been by since I signed the contract with the realtor, and it was a little jarring, seeing the big yellow sign in the front yard.

Logan tossed me a questioning look as I hopped off the bike. "I know where we are. This is your house, isn't it?"

"Yeah." I nodded sharply before gesturing at the sign. "But not for much longer."

"You're selling? That's what you wanted me to see." Logan's face fell as he too got off the bike. "Oh, Curtis, I don't want you doing that for me. This is your *home*. It means something to you, and I don't ever want to take that from you."

"I'm not doing it for you. Or even for us. I simply can't live here with all the memories tucked around me. Too much smothering from the past. I wish I could be the type of person able to let the past and present live together, but that's just not me. And it's a good little house. I've told the realtor that I want her to find a family for it, maybe a young couple starting out. It deserves a fresh start. Just like me."

"A fresh start, huh?" Logan studied me carefully. "You sure that's what you want?"

I nodded. "It is. You make me wish for new things. You've got big dreams, and I don't want to tie you to my past. I'd much rather chase after your vision with you. If you'd like me to, I mean."

"Of course I want you." Logan pulled me close. "But I want *all* of you. Past included. If you chose to keep this place, I'd understand. I don't love you in spite of your past—I love you because of it. Because it's part of who you are."

My throat tightened. I really didn't deserve this man. "You love me?"

He blushed and looked away. "I think I could. Didn't really mean to spring it on you like that. But I mean it. You wouldn't be who you are without Troy, and I never want to push him out of your life. I love you, and your past with him is part of the package. I don't ever mean to erase that. I just want the chance to love who you are right now."

"Thank you." I had to almost choke out the words. "And I know that you don't want to trample on my memories. That means a lot to me. And it's because I loved before that I know what it feels like, know what it means to have that in my life. I'm falling for you, too. And I choose a future with you."

"I want that, too," he said softly.

I wasn't sure if I could get the rest out with a steady

voice, but he deserved the effort. "Someday—not too soon, but when we're both ready—I want to make your dreams come true. I'd like to find a little piece of property outside town, go in on it together. Enough room for a big garden. Get Johnny to help us figure out the build. When I say I want a future together, I mean I want it all. Wholeheartedly. I want everything with you."

"Oh, wow." Logan squeezed my hand tight. "I love that idea. So much. And I'm patient. We'll know when the time's right for that."

"Exactly." I exhaled, relieved he wasn't rushing ahead, even more relieved that he hadn't dismissed the idea. We'd grow into that dream together. "And now, we gotta make one of your other dreams come true. If you're still game, that is."

"Are you kidding? This is my first tat. I've been a nervous wreck all day, but I want it. I'm ready."

"Good. I'm getting one, too."

"You are?" His eyebrows went up. "Another surprise. You're just full of them today. Going to tell me what it is?"

"Nope." I grinned at him. "Let's switch to the truck for the drive to Roseburg."

As he clung to me on the ride back to my place, I knew I was making the right choices. Taking the leap with him to have a relationship. Investing in the business. Selling the house. Telling him my secret dream for us. I didn't want to think about a world where he wasn't mine, and for the first time in a very long time, I couldn't wait to see what the future brought.

"How is Troy's mom taking the house sale?" Logan asked on the drive to my tattoo artist in Roseburg.

"She's not happy."

"Because of me?" Logan sighed. "I hate that us being together hurts her. I know she's important to you."

"She is," I admitted. "And she always will be. I think she'll come around somewhat, but she's got her own road to travel. I can't walk it for her." I saw that much more clearly now. "All I can do is keep reaching out to her, hope that eventually she reaches back again."

Like Logan, I hated that she was hurting, but I also couldn't put my grief on her timetable, couldn't put my life on hold. We'd spoken twice in the last two weeks, though, and I had hope that she wasn't going to completely cut me out. She'd told me a funny Chopper story, agreed to think about a side fence come spring. We'd find a way forward.

The place I liked in Roseburg was downtown, in a little strip mall. Not much to look at, but the owner did amazing work, had been doing my ink for years. And like most of the friends I'd told about Logan, she was nothing but happy for me, eager to meet him.

"Virgin skin," she crowed as he took off his shirt on her orders. "This might be your first, but it won't be the last."

"We'll see." Logan was looking a bit green, so I squeezed his hand.

"You don't have to go through with it. You don't have anything to prove to me."

"Yeah, but I want to prove it to myself." His jaw took on a determined set, and he offered up his bicep. As with the other visions for his life, he had very specific ideas for this—a bicep cuff that looked like the edge of a bike gear. It was very him—badass without being cliché like barbed-wire or flames might be. And it was the sort of thing that could be added to and expanded over the years if he wanted more of a full sleeve.

Although he sweated and stayed pale, Logan made it through the tattooing process.

"Not so bad?" I asked as the artist prepared to finish.

"Flogging's worse." He grinned at me, before seeming to remember we weren't alone and blushed.

But the artist just laughed. "I agree. Way worse. And if you want me to tattoo a flogger or a whip next time, you let me know. I've got a secret book for kink-friendly art."

"Oh, cool." Logan blushed worse.

"You guys are adorable. And you're done." She turned to me after helping Logan up from the chair. "Now what are you getting and where?"

"Right here." I pointed to a spot above my ankle and handed her a small sketch I'd done. "A sun."

"You really want a sun?" Logan asked as the artist began to sterilize and clean her tools. "You don't have to—"

"I want to. I want a reminder that life always comes around and that there's always a sun after the storm if you wait." I gazed meaningfully into his eyes, and it was like the whole rest of the shop fell away, and it was only the two of us. "Fresh start, remember?"

"Yeah." He nodded, eyes soft and brimming with emotion.

Then because I needed to lighten the mood before we started making out right there, I added, "But next time we're both looking at the kink book."

"Ha." He grinned at me before dropping his voice

and leaning in. "I think I like you better with *my* marks on you, not some picture of a whip."

"Is that a promise or a threat?" I told him with my eyes that it was gonna be a long two hours until we could be alone again, and that I had high hopes for when that happened.

"Promise. Always a promise," he whispered.

"Good." Then it was my turn in the chair, and I sank into the same place I always went while getting ink. It wasn't quite the zone of carving or the blissful white place of a scene, but it was close. A peaceful place where all the noise in my head faded away. Where I could be sure about my choices and decisions.

I'd taken the right path. Being here with Logan was everything, and I wanted that reminder every morning when I put my socks and boots on. Maybe I didn't know every step of the journey before us, but I knew he was the sun I wanted to follow on the trek. My sun. My second chance. My everything.

TWENTY-FIVE

Logan — Seven months later

"He's coming back." Mason stopped me as I looked out the window for the hundredth time. Curtis was due any time from his days-long drive from the US Chainsaw Championships in Wisconsin. I simply hadn't been able to swing taking twelve days off during our busiest month ever for the drive plus the competition itself. I'd missed time in June to watch Curtis take the crown at the Oregon Championships. And before that, we'd gone to Kink Fest in Portland in April. We'd taken the bike for that, and it had been an amazing trip along outer roads and smaller highways. Traveling with Curtis was the best, and I was super sad to have missed this trip. Maybe next summer we'd have more kitchen help and me leaving wouldn't be such a big deal.

This summer's business had been great. It remained to be seen what another off-season would bring, but things were better than they'd ever been. My menu was full of seasonal favorites, and our dining room full of tourists most evenings. Life was good. Or at least it would be when my boyfriend made it back home.

Ding. My phone chimed with a text, and I rushed to where I'd set it on the bar. *Home.* The single word sent a dozen emotions spiraling through me.

"He's at the house," I reported to Mason. "I'm going to hurry—"

"And get out of here," Mason finished for me with a laugh. "Go home to your man."

"Don't have to ask me twice." I threw the bar towel at him and headed for my bike. It was a new model, an upgrade from my last one, and I took extra care with my helmet before pedaling like my ass was on fire. Curtis was sitting on the porch when I pulled in on the bike and stood as I stowed it.

"You're back." I launched myself at him for a fierce hug. And he squeaked. Like a mouse. Not a Curtis noise at all, and I'd heard him make just about every sound possible from whimpers to begging to loving words and happy sighs. "What the…"

"I kind of have a surprise for you." Curtis stepped away, carefully cradling his arm.

"Are you hurt?" I looked him over through narrowed eyes. Wait. Not an injury. There was something under his arm. The thing that had made the noise. An animal. "Is that a dog?"

He moved so that he was under the porch light and I could see the little furry tan face. It was a puppy of inde-terminate breed, but not a small one judging by the big floppy ears and oversized paws. I thought I saw some beagle in there. Or maybe spaniel. Regardless, he was damn cute.

"Where'd you come from, little guy?" I let him sniff my hand before I pet him.

"Found him in a box near a Dumpster at a truck stop outside Spokane. Their shelters were full up, so he decided to hitch a ride south with me." Curtis gave me a crooked grin. "Mad?"

"Me?" I held out my hands for the furry bundle. "Nope. I love dogs. My parents were always damn picky about pets, so I didn't have one growing up. Is he for me?"

"Well…" Curtis did a very un-Curtis like thing and blushed. "He's for us. Together. If that's what you want, I mean. I figure, I'm here most nights now. I can help you train him, keep him with me while you're at the tavern."

"Does this mean you're moving in?" We'd covered this topic all summer, me wanting him to move more stuff in, him dragging his heels, me trying not to push even as I wanted us together forever. His house had sold at the start of summer to a nice family moving to town from Grants Pass, but he hadn't brought more than clothes into the house I increasingly thought of as ours, storing everything else at his shop. This was where I cooked him dinner and breakfast, where we made love, where we got kinky, where we slept together. The old gas station was where his business and carving stuff resided.

"This guy's gonna be a runner," Curtis said, infuriatingly side-stepping my question. "He's going to need a fenced run, maybe a big property to explore. What would you say to going for a ride this weekend, see if there's any for-sale signs in the woods? Johnny said there might be something close to him that could interest us, but not sure if you want to be that far out. We can explore."

"Exploring sounds amazing." I grinned at him as I stroked the puppy. "You think we're ready for that?"

He shrugged. "There's some places with trailers already on site. I figure we could do that awhile, get a big garden in before spring, decide exactly what we want to build. We can do it in stages. But this guy's going to need more room if we keep him."

"We're keeping him." I leaned in for a kiss. "And I'm keeping *you*."

"This place has always felt more like yours." Curtis scratched his neck. "So, yeah, I think we're ready for something that feels like us. Feels like a start to your dreams."

"You're the start." I pulled him into the house before the whole neighborhood got to watch us make out. Yeah, we needed that rural house and soon. My spine tingled as I thought of all the fun we could get up to with no close neighbors. "You're all I need. I don't need the huge garden or the eco cabin or even the dog. I just need you."

"You gotta admit the dog's pretty cute," Curtis joked, but his eyes were full of tender emotion.

"So are you." Still holding the dog, I kissed him slow and long. "God, I missed you. Next year I'm coming with you. I don't care how many favors I have to pull."

"Missed you, too. But I liked knowing you were back here, waiting for me."

"Always." It was a while before we pulled apart, puppy squirming between us.

"What should we name him?" I asked.

"If I say Ed, do you think your dad will like me more?" Curtis gave me a crooked grin.

"He doesn't hate you." We'd seen my parents in April when we'd gone to Kink Fest, not that my parents knew that was the real reason for the trip. The ice had started thawing, but my parents still weren't exactly huge Curtis fans, although they'd been pleasant to him and my other friends on their visits since then. Baby steps. "And I don't want to be hollering my dad's name all down the beach."

"What about Sunny? I was trying that one out in the truck. He reminds me of you a little, all boundless energy and optimism. I mean, there he was in a box, but he was sure I was a friend come to rescue him, didn't cower one bit."

"I'm going to take that as a compliment. I think." I laughed. "Sunny it is."

As I set him down, my gaze drifted to the picture on the end table by the couch. It was a photo of us in June, at the unveiling of Curtis's sculpture installation for the resort's lobby. I looked about ready to burst with pride over him, and he looked as if all the attention was making him need an escape route. But what I really liked about the picture was that Troy's mother Janice had taken it. She'd surprised us, coming to the unveiling. I'd met her a few times prior, trying to win her over with recipe trading and gifts of scones and other baked goods. She hadn't said much at the unveiling, but then the picture had arrived in the mail about a week later. Curtis had gotten all emotional as I'd rushed to put it in a frame straightaway. Her unspoken approval meant a great deal to him, and I was so glad for him that their rift seemed to be mending.

"You don't mind me springing him on you like this?" Curtis grabbed my hand.

"Of course not. I love your surprises." I kissed his knuckles.

"And I should have told you what I was thinking about us going land shopping, but it wasn't until I saw him in that box that I really wrapped my head around the vision. Him. You. Me. A little cabin with a great big kitchen. I'm ready. But only if you are, too."

"Yes. I love you. I'm beyond ready to share my life with you, make a home together."

"You're young—"

"Which means I'll have plenty of energy for painting and sanding." I shook our joined hands lightly. "I'm not changing my mind. You're the one for me. The one I love. The one I want all my dreams with."

"You're the one I love, too," Curtis whispered. He didn't say the words as often as I did, which made them extra special. I knew he felt it, though, could sense it in every touch and kiss and nice thing he did for me. "You're my dream. The one I want to come home to. I love you, Logan."

"Then let's find ourselves a property to dream big with." I leaned in and kissed him again while the puppy danced at our feet. The last few months hadn't been without their ups and downs, but they'd led us here, to this place where we could start a new chapter in both our lives. We'd had to figure out how to be a couple, how to let each other in, how to trust. It turned out that Curtis hadn't just given me kink lessons—he'd taught me how to love.

And despite any doubts he had, he was extraordinarily easy to love. He might have a prickly exterior, but my wood carver had a heart as strong as oak, roots thirsty for affection. I intended to make sure he always had his fill, that he never doubted how much he was loved and cared for. We were going to build a life together, log by log, bolt by bolt, meal by meal, season by season. And I couldn't wait.

~The End~

Want more Rainbow Cove books? Next in the series is the novella, LUMBER JACKED where Curtis's friend Johnny gets his happy ending. Then Adam gets his book in HOPE ON THE ROCKS. If you enjoyed TENDER WITH A TWIST, I'd be honored if you'd consider leaving a review, as reviews help other readers find books.

Want ficlets, contests, and updates on other favorite characters? Make sure you're in my Facebook fan group, Annabeth's Angels, for all the latest news, contests, and freebies. And newsletter subscribers always get the latest news on releases, freebies, and more!

http://eepurl.com/Nb9yv

Want more books like the Rainbow Cove series? Be sure and check out my other series and single title books!

ACKNOWLEDGMENTS

Rainbow Cove is a fictional town on the southern Oregon coast. Any resemblance to real places, people, or events is entirely coincidental. Many thanks to those who helped with my research in chainsaw wood carving (yes, it really is a thing!), coastal living, and other matters. A special thanks to my editor, Edie Danford, for her tireless work and her help in pushing me to go deeper into Curtis and Logan's journey. My proofreader, Jody Wallace, does amazing work and deserves huge kudos as well. Wendy Qualls, Karen Stivali, and Layla Reyne keep me on track with writing sprints and support. My Facebook group, Annabeth's Angels, has been so supportive of this project, and I treasure all my readers. Thank you to everyone who has reviewed, tweeted, shared, and cheered me on—your support is priceless. My family puts up with my crazy hours, and I love them for their understanding. Writing and publishing is a journey, and I'm so grateful to everyone who has helped me along that journey.

Arctic Sun

Arctic Wild

Arctic Heat

Hotshots series

Burn Zone

High Heat

Feel the Fire

Up in Smoke

Shore Leave series

Sailor Proof (September 2021)

Sink or Swim (February 2022)

Perfect Harmony series

Treble Maker

Love Me Tenor

All Note Long

Portland Heat series

Served Hot

Baked Fresh

Delivered Fast

Knit Tight

Wrapped Together

Danced Close

True Colors series

Conventionally Yours

Out of Character

Single Titles

Better Not Pout

Resilient Heart

Winning Bracket

Save the Date

Level Up

Mr. Right Now

Sergeant Delicious

Cup of Joe

Featherbed

AUTHOR BIO

Annabeth Albert grew up sneaking romance novels under the bed covers. Now, she devours all subgenres of romance out in the open— no flashlights required! When she's not adding to her keeper shelf, she's a multi-published Pacific Northwest romance writer.

Emotionally complex, sexy, and funny stories are her favorites both to read and to write. Fans of quirky, Oregon-set books as well as those who enjoy heroes in uniform will want to check out her many fan-favorite and critically acclaimed series. Many titles are also in audio! Her fan group Annabeth's Angels on Facebook is the best place for bonus content and more! Website: www.annabethalbert.com

Contact & Media Info:

facebook.com/annabethalbert

twitter.com/AnnabethAlbert

instagram.com/annabeth_albert

amazon.com/Annabeth/e/B00LYFFAZK

bookbub.com/authors/annabeth-albert

Made in United States
Troutdale, OR
01/26/2024

17202469R00192